GREATER
THAN HIS
NATURE

twenty tales of mad science

edited by Eirik Gumeny

ATOMIC CARNIVAL
BOOKS

GREATER THAN HIS NATURE

Atomic Carnival Books
Albuquerque, N.M.

First Edition

Cover and book design by Eirik Gumeny
Cover illustration by Frank R. Paul, 1926, public domain

This book is a work of fiction. Names, characters, places, brands, and events are either the product of the author's imagination or used fictitiously. Any resemblance to actual persons, places, incidents, monsters, or apocalypses, living, dead, or otherwise, is entirely coincidental.

*How dangerous is the acquirement of knowledge,
and how much happier that man is who believes his native
town to be the world, than he who aspires to become
greater than his nature will allow.*

Frankenstein, Mary Shelley

To a new world of gods and monsters!

Bride of Frankenstein,
William Hurlbut and James Whale

Table of Contents

Editor's Note
We Belong Dead

MAD SCIENCE HAS NEVER BEEN KIND TO ITS CREATIONS.

From the moment Mary Shelley's "hideously deformed" Creature first lumbered into the written world, bleeding-edge scientists and their experimental offspring have found themselves in the long and lonesome shadow of Victor Frankenstein and his stitched-together giant. A country clouded by clear-cut notions of good and evil, of right and wrong, opinions orbiting around antiquated interpretations of God's law. In the centuries since, literature—and the greater sphere of pop culture—have done little to excise themselves from this darkness.

From Nathaniel Hawthorne's "Rappaccini's Daughter" in 1844 to David Cronenberg's body-horror reimagining of *The Fly*, all the way through to this year's *Guardians of the Galaxy, Vol. 3*, there is a single, common thread running throughout the subgenre: a primal disdain for science and her achievements. Every one of these stories, and countless others, argue that scientific advancements should only be approached with hesitancy, that the natural order is infallible, and anyone or anything who dares broach these limits is a degenerative monster, prone to violence and deserving of death.

Now, there are, admittedly, various levels of sympathy interwoven into these stories. *Frankenstein* certainly gives the Creature more depth than the doctor, while Hawthorne paints Beatrice Rappaccini's death as an unforgiveable tragedy. And James Gunn makes it explicit that Rocket Raccoon and his family of cybernetically-enhanced animals are the victims of torture, that they are blameless and therefore worthy of pity and love.

But, touches of mercy aside, all of these stories still end the same way.

The doctor and his inhuman creations must die.

In Robert Louis Stevenson's *Strange Case of Dr. Jekyll and Mr. Hyde*, Hyde is so unrepentantly evil and full of vice that Jekyll commits suicide to keep him from existing. 1960's *The Amazing Transparent Man*, 1962's *The Brain That Wouldn't Die*, and scores of their B-movie siblings not only kill the mad scientist and his creations, but burn down his laboratory, too, just in case. Michael Crichton's *Jurassic Park* ends with the island being bombed into oblivion. That the dinosaurs were just being dinosaurs is no matter. Cloning them was an affront to the way things were, and these innocent animals must pay in blood and fire. Even Rocket needs to die, just a little, before he can escape his past. (It's probably worth noting, too, that the animals he saves at the end of the movie are all un-experimented on, and thusly allowed to live.)

But this sentiment is perhaps best epitomized by the climax of James Whale's *Bride of Frankenstein*. The Monster, having narrowly escaped death, spends the movie wandering around, helping people and just trying to exist. He is, naturally, shot at and chased away for his troubles—and because he's a godless freak lumbering through the Hays Code-heavy year of 1935, he also kills plenty of innocent people, too, in case the audience was tempted to feel sorry for him.

Eventually, the Monster stumbles upon Doctor Pretorius and the two hatch a scheme to strongarm Henry Frankenstein into creating a mate for the monster. Against his better judgement, Henry does, and, amidst flashing lightning and walls of sci-fi machinery, the Bride of Frankenstein is born.

The Bride, built specifically for the Monster (which is its own can of misogynistic worms) screams upon seeing his stitched-up visage. She refuses to hold his hand. The Monster is once again rejected, this time by the one being that should have understood his plight—the one soul(less corpse-person) that should have understood *him*.

Depressed and dejected, broken-down by a world that refuses to make space for him—that refuses to see him as anything other than an atrocity—the Monster declares "we belong dead" and pulls a lever to instigate a *very* dramatic murder/suicide, killing himself, the Bride, and Doctor Pretorius. Henry Frankenstein, however, having seen the error of his ways, gets to escape to his happily ever after.

Because even when the monster isn't an actual monster, he must still pay.

Because there is a natural order to life: only what is and what should never be.

Because playing God—because *science*—is immoral and abhorrent.

So what does that say about those of us who *are* experiments?

***

This is not a disabled anthology.

Certainly, I am disabled and chronically ill—and with a towering height, a bum knee, a veritable allergy to the sun, and a dead man's lungs inside of me, I do share more than a few attributes with Frankenstein's Monster—and numerous authors included within the pages of this anthology are disabled and chronically ill. And, yes, several stories touch on disability and illness directly, others indirectly, and, when submissions were open, I made an effort to include disabled and chronically-ill voices.

But this is not a disabled anthology.

Most conspicuously, not *every* writer included in the pages of *Greater Than His Nature* identifies as disabled. Some might even go so far as to believe themselves to be able-bodied. This was an intentional act on my part, for reasons that, conveniently, I will now explain.

First and foremost, disability is not a monolith. There are over forty million disabled people in America alone, dealing with at least ten thousand diseases. And all those different people will handle all those different diseases, well, *differently*. Some disabilities are more readily apparent; some illnesses are invisible. Some of us have no problem asking for help; some of us refuse to even ask for the salt shaker. (And some of us can't have salt, anyway.) Some folks are reclaiming the word cripple; some folks are adamantly against it; some push back against descriptors of any kind. Some of us crack jokes as a reflex; some of us don't find anything funny about any of this at all. And some of us do all of the above, depending on the day of the week.

Second, disabled folks—and disabled writers, especially—shouldn't need to carve out our own spaces in order to be seen. This isn't to say, of course, that creating common communities is bad, or that there's anything wrong with books featuring disabled writers solely—I, personally, am a huge fan of those anthologies and special issues, and I've been published (or tried to get published) in a few of them—see also: we are not a monolith, above—but simply that the disabled and chronically ill shouldn't be shunted *only* to those communities and books.

There is often an expectation implicit in "disabled fiction" that disability will be prominently featured. That our "struggles" need to be explicit and central to the story. As if entire swaths of our day aren't spent the same way as *healthies*—those temporarily non-disabled who walk among us—watching television and playing video games and taking care of our dogs and fighting and fucking and working and daydreaming about worlds of reverse mermaids and murder-spiders and bloated flesh-monsters tearing down the Golden Gate Bridge.

It's similarly not uncommon for readers who aren't disabled to come at such a book with preconceived notions sharpened and at the ready. Some shade of pity, usually, or fascination, or disgust, or maybe just puffed-up self-posturing about how advanced and accepting they are. I've read reviews where a reader docked a book a star because the characters weren't explicitly disabled enough. They came here for the disabled *experience*, damn it, and how dare those cripples live their lives like they actually live their lives.

Because, to them, if we're not fighting and struggling and nobly suffering—it's always fucking noble, isn't it?—then what are we even doing here?

Because, to them, we need to *earn* our right to exist.

While you and I may know the myriad intricacies of chronic illness—the ups and downs, the good days and the bad days and the ones lost entirely to pain—tack the word "disabled" onto an anthology, and suddenly the stories therein are subsumed. Readers can't seem to see the forest for the trees, the soul beneath the stitches.

So, no, this is not a disabled anthology. Not today, anyway. And not because those readers and reviewers are in any way *right*, but specifically for the reasons they're wrong.

We are not the limitations placed on us by the healthies out there.

We are not only our disabilities.

We should get to live alongside the rest of the world.

✳✳✳

"We belong dead."

These words are not uttered in *Frankenstein,* the 1818 novel, but they may as well have been. Like his later Hollywood counterpart—and every monster and medical marvel after and in between—Shelley's Creature searches for happiness and companionship, for a home, and comes to the realization that he deserves no such thing. The world goes out of its way to make clear that the only place for a freak like him—like us—is alone on an ice floe, or burned alive, or buried beneath the rubble of a tower laboratory.

Whichever version of *Frankenstein* you choose, the Creature's death is a tragedy, either a cold-blooded murder or an act of pitiable self-destruction from a soul unable to face the sneering scowls of society. A sad event, certainly, but, as is so common in the pantheon of sci-fi and horror fiction, a misfit of science must always be defeated by the able-bodied and the *normal*.

Greater Than His Nature is, I hope, an antidote to that outdated way of thinking. I'm not going to promise you that every experiment meets a happy ending, that every lab-cradled creature is good at heart, or that every scientist is well-intentioned, but I will tell you that *normal* has very little place here. The shunned do not slink off in surrender, and even the most lonely aren't truly alone. If anyone suffers, it sure as shit isn't noble. The dead come back, organs grow where you least expect them, corporate greed is corrected with calamity, and "healthy" is shown to be a disease all its own, the most damning by a long mile.

The disabled and chronically ill are not a monolith.

We are not the monsters "mad science" makes us out to be.

But that doesn't mean we're going to go quietly.

Eirik Gumeny
September 26, 2023

With Flesh, He Will Create
K.L. Mill

DEREK WAS PUMPED, AND NOT JUST FROM THE COCAINE he'd snorted off the cadaver. It had taken nearly a year, but tonight the stars had aligned with the harvest moon, and he'd been handed a nearly flawless specimen for his ultimate experiment. "John Doe" had arrived at the funeral home with rather cryptic instructions to cremate immediately. *Will do,* thought Derek. *As far as you know.* He had enough cremains saved up in a Ziploc to fill any urn in stock and fool even his tight-ass boss.

As he washed the body, Derek blasted Marilyn Manson's "Don't Chase the Dead," which seemed appropriate, as did the black t-shirt he wore with "It's Pronounced FRONKENSTEEN!" in bold white letters across the chest. The lean, muscular corpse had zero imperfections—well, aside from the bullet hole in his torso. Derek was a little surprised to find the bullet still inside, just below the left scapula, but it was easily removed with tweezers, the remaining blemish hidden by a few stitches.

Mary Shelley wrote of the "spark of being," but Derek knew the secret was really in his chemical cocktail-filled hypodermic, injected directly into the heart. That, and a tricked-out defibrillator that could deliver 2500+ volts, cranked to full power. Derek stared at the syringe, mesmerized for a second by the swirling, murky elixir. Then, gripping it like a dagger, he plunged it into the cadaver's chest, a whimper of euphoria escaping him. He slammed down the paddles, and as voltage surged through the spasming body like the coke in his veins, Derek could feel the chains of humanity shatter and leave him as he ascended to rightful godhood …

The faint tang of ozone hung in the air. The body twitched. A good sign. Derek was leaning in for a second jolt when the corpse inhaled sharply. His eyes fluttered open; they were wild, terrified, confused.

He s fucking alive! Derek instinctively grabbed the man's wrist to feel for a pulse … but couldn't quite process why the skin beneath his fingers was undulating, darkening, sprouting hair. Or where that guttural growl was coming from.

Derek's last thought, before he was completely disemboweled, was that he really wished he hadn't removed that silver bullet.

The Soulless Eyes of a Fish
Jonathan Fortin

THE REVERSE MERMAIDS CHASE US THROUGH THE CORRIDOR, their fish heads flapping left and right atop their slender human legs. It occurs to me, perhaps for the first time, that maybe we should have given them legs that were a bit less athletic. But no, we thought. If we're giving them human legs, they've gotta be *sexy* human legs.

"They're gaining on us!" shouts Tim, our unpaid intern. He's the last one left—the only other person in the lab the reverse mermaids haven't eaten.

"Just keep running," I say. "We've almost reached the bathysphere."

"My legs are gonna give out any second." Tim wipes his sleeve against his glasses, presumably to clean the blood spattered against them, but the blood only smears, blinding him further.

The reverse mermaids—or "revmers," as we affectionately began calling them—are getting closer every second. They run with the grace of gazelles, but their heads still look like beached fish trying to bounce their way back into the water. They're so damn ridiculous that I have to stop myself from laughing, no matter how much blood paints their rainbow-shine scales.

On either side of us are glass walls, windows to the deep blue ocean. More revmers are swimming outside. A hammerhead variant smashes its skull against the glass. It probably won't crack anytime soon, but ...

Suddenly a long, frog-like tongue comes lashing out from

behind us. Its grappling hook tip scratches the glass wall, narrowly missing my face as it retracts back into an open maw. Dozens more tongues spear after us, the air whistling with each precise attack. Tim and I pick up the pace as best we can, but we're both panting heavily, having spent more time in desk chairs than on treadmills.

I know the question in your head: why? Why reverse mermaids? Well, with so many species becoming extinct, my team and I sought to create something that would fill the gaps left in the food chain. It would be amphibious, with both lungs and gills, to survive in any terrain. And it had to be big enough to feed many predators at once, as they were increasingly struggling to find prey.

But why *reverse mermaids*? It's a complicated answer that would go over your head if you're not a geneticist, but basically, after a long and deliberate process, we determined that this was the design that would best suit our needs. We needed a Great Corrector. A species that would help put the planet back on the right track. That's an enormous amount of pressure to put on a new species. So why *not* give it a grappling hook tongue? Why *not* design them to breed like rabbits all year round? Why *not* make badass hammerhead and swordfish variants?

And, yes, I know what you're thinking. Yes, I've watched *Jurassic Park*. In fact, I love *Jurassic Park*. And I love that Ian Malcolm quote that I *know* is in your head right now, about being so busy wondering whether we could that we didn't consider whether we should. I just never thought it would apply to *me*. I always figured our extinction would be caused by climate change, or nuclear Armageddon, or A.I. I wasn't a part of anything like that. I was just making reverse mermaids in an underwater lab. What could possibly go wrong there?

As a hooked tongue embeds itself in Tim's arm, I'm forced to admit: a lot. A *lot* can go wrong.

Tim screams as his blood paints the windows. The hammerhead pummels the glass even harder, its unblinking fish eyes widening with an almost sexual hunger. The revmer that got Tim opens its mouth wider, jaws dislocating, revealing rows of shark teeth. Those were technically Tim's idea, so if he gets ground up in them, it's his own damn fault.

The revmer retracts its tongue, ripping Tim's arm clean off. Flesh tears like paper and bone dislocates from bone. Tim howls, still spraying all over the place, even getting his blood on my lab coat. I wince, drop him like a hot potato, and keep running. He's dead weight, now. Besides, maybe he'll distract the revmers. Maybe they'll be too focused on gobbling him up to notice me reaching the bathysphere. Several do swarm him to lick away more and more of his body, glugging happily all the while, but others run right past him and keep chasing me with those long, sexy legs.

Then the glass wall cracks. The hammerhead revmer is actually breaking through. Any minute now, water will come pouring in.

"Shit!" I scream, whole body electric, but the bathysphere is only ten feet away. All I have to do is get in, and I'll be safe.

There's a deafening crash as water blasts in and begins filling the corridor. It carries the revmers after me—trout, swordfish, and hammerhead variants alike. A wall of water chases me, consuming more and more of the corridor, rife with revmers. Grappling hook tongues scrape the walls and floor as the tidal wave nears. It reeks of salt, both from sea and from all the blood.

I hurtle into the bathysphere and slam the door shut just before the water hits it. This little sphere is cramped enough that I have to hunch over, and the rusty scent makes my nose itch, but I exhale in relief anyway. There's a little circular window that gives me a view of the flooding corridor, and I quickly feel a jolt of weightlessness as the water lifts the bathysphere from the floor.

Soon, the deluge is complete, and the corridor is full of dark blue water. Revmers swim through it, most heading out the broken window, but the dings echoing around me suggest others are attacking the bathysphere. Tim's severed head bounces off the window before drifting away again.

A shape emerges through the crimson cloud of his blood: the hammerhead, swimming straight towards the bathysphere, staring at me with the soulless eyes of a fish. I swallow my panic by cackling. Let it try to smash this window. It won't stop me!

I pull the necessary levers, preparing to launch forwards—but nothing happens. The bathysphere is malfunctioning. Dead in the water.

Just like me.

It had only taken them eight hours to kill our entire crew, save me. Just eight hours. And it won't take long for them to start breeding: doubling, then quadrupling their ranks, until there are millions.

First, they'll take over the sea.

Then they'll come for the land.

The reverse mermaids swim before the window with the grace of dancers, their fins billowing like veils as they kick through the deep blue water. A lump forms in my throat. Ever since they escaped, I've been too busy running to stop and look, *really* look, at the fruits of our labor. Now that I do, I can't help but gape. This … this is beauty. We've created something beautiful. Something most people could never dream of. I stare at the posterior of a revmer as she paddles past me, feel an unexpected flash of arousal, and have to laugh again. We humans really are the fucking worst.

It occurs to me that maybe our mission was successful. Maybe the revmers really will be that Great Corrector, taking care of the worst problem threatening the world. And you know what? Let them. Maybe they'll be better than we were. And if they aren't, then maybe one day they'll make a Great Corrector of their own.

The hammerhead begins slamming its skull against the bathysphere window. I open my arms wide to embrace the coming flush, ready to drown in my life's work.

The Body Farm
Andrew Kozma

WHEN JULES WAS SHORT ON CASH, he'd head over to the Body Farm and get a few nascent organs grafted on. Most of the time they were small. A pea-sized gallbladder or a starter liver, something he'd only nurse for a week or two. Sometimes he'd take on an ear, which wasn't an organ, but the surgeons said grafting on the real thing worked better than trying to reconstruct a ruined ear out of leftover cartilage.

Jules didn't like the ears. Even though there were none of the working parts needed to make an ear hear, he swore he heard more and differently with a baby-sized ear on his bicep or calf. And then there were the people who'd talk into the ears, their voices high-pitched and slow as though talking to a pet.

It's not that Jules was ashamed of his work with the Body Farm. There were plenty of fleshweeds who played at being "gracious hosts" according to the Body Farm's promotional materials, and he saw large numbers of people on the bus and the rail who carried strange lumps under their shirts or on their hips. The homeless were virtually bejeweled with glistening livers and kidneys, the bright marigold-yellow and sky-blue organs spilling out of vents in their clothing, but those grafts were the result of chop shops. Jules had read how those places would put a heart on someone in a hurry and a sloppy technician would forget to hook in the return-vein valves. In a day or so, the poor, desperate host would bleed to death once the arteries adjusted. The police didn't even pretend to care. The harvesting lobbies were just too strong.

So, no, what Jules was doing was nothing to be ashamed of. People needed the organs he brought to fruition. He was making lives better. He was making people whole again.

"Get this damn sausage off of me!" he yelled at Nurse Jaclyn.

She shook her head, more amused by his anger than annoyed, and kept moving at the same steady pace she always moved.

"You're getting paid a lot for that there penis," she reminded him, methodically arranging the surgical tools and spraying down everything with disinfectant.

As if in response, the penis on his bicep stood up. *Are you talking about me?* Jules imagined it asking. *You're talking about me, aren't you?*

Outside of the Body Farm, he'd strapped it down under a baggy shirt. Not because he was embarrassed, no, but because it was obscene. And he was eager to get it off his body, if only because he was now thinking about it as though it were another person, something completely out of his control. Every other organ he'd hosted became a part of him, as much a part of him as any aspect of a job could be.

Local anesthetic. The always different doctor's quick scalpeling. And the penis was gone.

"Hey, doc, I need another organ if you have one handy."

The doctor looked down his long nose at Jules. He hemmed and hawed, sounding like an old air conditioner starting, then failing, then starting again.

"Mr. Juniper, you know we like to give the body a rest between grafts."

Jules laughed conspiratorially. "Oh, yeah, I know. I know. That's what you tell the new fleshweeds, but I've been a regular here, what, two years?"

"Three," the doctor said, looking over Jules' chart.

Jules smiled. He knew how long he'd been coming here, he just wanted the *doctor* to know, too. He could see the knowledge working over the doctor's expression, his eyes narrowing.

"We have a lung," the doctor said, finally. "You've done lungs before?"

"Of course!" Jules said, a little too casually. "Easy-peasy."

And it *was* that easy. Ten minutes later, Jules walked out of the Body Farm with a lung attached below his right armpit. It looked like a decomposing fish hanging onto his skin with its teeth, like those remora he read about in middle school, or maybe he was thinking of a lamprey? Really, the only animals he ever saw around the city were rats that looked like squirrels and squirrels that looked like rats, and that's what the lung looked like, really. A baby rat-squirrel, hairless and desperate.

It must've been his thinking about the squirrels that found Jules heading over to Hermann Park. It was still early in the day, not even past two o'clock, and if he was feeling industrious he'd be checking out the local bars to see if they needed a last-minute barback or door guy. But he'd just gotten a new organ! He should probably take it easy. Relax. Get the organ outdoors where it could get sunlight and fresh air.

Jules lit up a cigarette as he crossed over into the park. Though the Body Farm listed non-smoking as one of the credentials of their gracious hosts, the doctors and nurses smoked all the time, and shared cigarettes with Jules even. Clearly, smoking didn't hurt the baby organs enough to matter.

Still, as he weaved his way through a group of young kids on a kindergarten field trip, he felt guilty. The organ in question was a lung, after all. And already he could feel how its breathing was almost completely in sync with his own—and here he was feeding it the smoke that probably ruined the lung it was destined to replace.

He stubbed the cigarette out on the sole of his shoe and tossed the butt into the grass. A squirrel or a rat ran by to snatch up the butt and disappear into a bush.

Hermann Park was full of people of all different stripes scratching another day off their calendar. Some were joyous, wading through the fountain like lunatic ducks. Others looked like the week had beaten them down, eyes bruised with lack of sleep.

The rest, they didn't care one way or another, their day-to-day life no more exciting than punching numbers into a calculator.

Jules lit another cigarette and inhaled deeply. The baby lung puffed up at his side.

It wasn't until a few days later that Jules felt the changes for real. The lung was a little bigger—lungs were longer-term projects, grafts you cradled for a month. The organs were fine at first, then began to feel like a tumor, and then he'd get used to them again. He'd look in the mirror while shaving and not even notice the almost-harvestable spleen hanging off his neck like a fat, red slug.

But the lung was different. It didn't feel like a hitchhiker. It began to feel like a part of him almost immediately. The air he breathed was going into it, and the air it processed left through his mouth, tasting new and electric.

And his body! He felt energetic and invincible. He ran everywhere, not because he was in a hurry, but because he never felt tired. If he was breathing hard—and he was, it was undeniable—it felt powerful rather than exhausting. This was the way people were always meant to live, inhaling the world.

Now when he barbacked under the table, the bartenders actually thanked him. He'd shirked every time he'd worked before, taking smoke breaks every ten minutes, hiding in the back room to down a quick Lone Star when he was supposed to be restocking or collecting used glasses. But the new lung, now the size of a curled-up kitten, hungered and the only way to feed it was by burning through his blood's oxygen.

The new lung stretched to every part of his life. Women talked to him more. Men seemed a bit afraid of him. And when he saw the excitement or fear in another person's eyes, Jules breathed deep and proud.

A week later, the energy waned, like he was getting acclimated to a drug. He ran around his block for a solid hour, but he didn't feel like he could rip up a tree by the roots at the end of it. Instead, he felt normal, except that he wasn't tired. He wasn't anything. He was back to being Jules and Jules alone.

He tried to roll with it, but when the women who'd chatted him up at the bar only the night before wouldn't give him a second glance now, he couldn't stand it. He tried to lose himself in TV or computer games, but he couldn't stop worrying at the lung under his arm, holding it as it inflated and deflated like a paper bag.

He went back to the Body Farm and asked for another lung.

"I can handle it," he told the doctor. "I'm in perfect health, and the graft lung I've already got is just making me healthier. It's a win-win."

The doctor shook his head, his lips in the default no-frown frown doctors wore when they had bad news but didn't want you to feel bad about it.

"That's not the way it works," the doctor said. "You're providing a home for these organs. They're not providing anything for you, Mr. Juniper."

Jaclyn looked on kindly from the corner of the room, arranging supplies and being invisible, as nurses often are to doctors. And when Jules came back later that day, making sure the doctor he'd seen earlier was gone, Jaclyn looked on kindly as that new doctor let Jules down, too.

"Mr. Juniper," she said, stopping him from leaving the examination room. "Jules. You can't blame them. They're just following rules."

"Sure, sure," he agreed genially, but the extra lung felt like it was hyperventilating. "But the rules are stupid. I can handle it."

Jaclyn nodded, bunching up his paper examination apron and tossing it into the trash.

"If you're really interested in getting another lung, come back here at midnight."

The Body Farm closed at eight. Jules stationed himself across the street at eleven-thirty. At a minute past midnight, he knocked on the door and it opened at once. Jaclyn led him to a surgery in the very back of the building, leading him through the dark halls with the glow from her phone.

23

This doctor was different from the others. Older, more worn. *He's probably had a few organs replaced himself,* Jules thought. There was something sharp in his eyes when he appraised Jules, but it was an honest sort of greed — the only sort of honesty Jules really appreciated.

"Another lung, right?" the doctor asked, but it was all formality. He already had the nascent organ in hand.

Jules took off his shirt, and soon he had another lung under his left armpit, mirror to the first. And though he couldn't possibly be feeling the effects of it already, he would've sworn that he was more alert, more awake, more himself than ever before. Jaclyn smiled at him like the women at the bars had. Before Jules left, the doctor handed Jules a card that didn't have a name on it, just a number.

"Come only to me. Call this number and Jaclyn will make the necessary appointments."

The card was made of paper that felt like oiled leather. It was warm to the touch.

At first, Jules found it a little awkward to have both lungs. He loved the feeling of the lungs filling up and caressing the inside of his arms, but, if he wasn't thinking about it, he would let his arms hang at his sides and soon felt short of breath, as if someone was suffocating him. So he had to hold his elbows away from his body like a jacked bodybuilder. The lungs made it hard to barback because he was only ever needed on crowded nights, and crowds meant his lungs were squished all night.

But the benefits! It was like he was a new man with the extra lungs. Or, no, not a new man, but the man he was always meant to be. It wasn't even about the stamina it gave him. It was a mental thing, he realized. He was simply *more*. More interested in life and more interesting to others. He took up more space, people subconsciously giving way to him on the street. And those who chose to enter his aura, they lapped up his attention. He didn't lord it over people, either, the fact that he was better than them. Honestly, he was better than himself. He was best him that ever was.

Which is why, after the first lung was harvested, he immediately called the number on the card.

"I need them all," he told the doctor in the back room. Jaclyn wasn't there.

"I can give you ten, that's it."

Jules nodded, not trusting his voice.

Because of the distance the lungs needed to be from one another, they were attached all over his body. The armpits. The back of his neck. His thighs, front and back. His arms. All around his torso.

The doctor inspected his work as Jules stood nude in the cold, sterile surgery. A mirror on the wall showed Jules exactly who he was. A too-thin man quickly approaching middle age. Dark hair stylishly receding. And over his body, his new children, his new selves which would be him soon enough, given a day or so to feed on everything he could give them.

He left knowing he was never coming back. He worked every extra shift he could find, confident two weeks of that, plus the money from the first lung, would set him up for traveling to South America or Eastern Europe, somewhere cheap where he could live peacefully, content to simply better himself. Become the him he already knew he could be, permanently.

Three weeks later, a little after midnight, the doctor tracked the tracker embedded in one of the lungs. His hired muscle busted down the door to Jules' apartment, waded through a piled mess of dirty clothes and takeout boxes, and carried Jules down to the waiting surgical van.

"It's like trying to move a jellyfish," the muscle said.

The doctor had to work quick. The lungs survived a while after the body died, but the longer they fed off the dead, the harder they'd be to transplant. As he worked, the doctor couldn't keep from staring at Jules' face. It was gaunt from calorie loss and bluish from lack of oxygen, but the man somehow looked more alive than he ever had when he *was* alive. More handsome. Utterly confident. Complete.

Afterwards, the doctor rubbed the lung he'd had attached to himself earlier that week, scratched right where the lung joined his skin. That little bit of would-be scar itched like an old friend.

Jenny
Zachary Rosenberg

HAVING SPENT YEARS RESEARCHING THE INTELLIGENCE of portia spiders, Derek Feldman knew it was only a matter of time until Jenny found him.

Crouched beneath a desk, the arachnologist looked his partner in the eye. Samantha Gold flicked her head toward the door of the dimly-lit office. Since the catastrophe, nothing worked right in Laughton Peaks and Derek was convinced he and Samantha were the only ones remaining on the upper or lower levels of the subterranean station.

The needle-clicks of spindly limbs against the metallic floor touched Derek's ear and he put a hand over his mouth to keep from making any sound. The noise was distant at first, the sound of smooth pebbles thrown against the surface of an icy lake.

As it grew louder, a dawning sense of dread filled the scientist. Gnawing claws of terror spread out in his stomach, nearly making him forget that he had not eaten in days.

Trying for the cafeteria had been useless. With her intelligence, Jennifer Roberta Rosemary III, or "Jenny"—as she'd been affectionately named when no larger than a fingernail—had quickly discerned its importance to the remaining researchers and frequently patrolled the area. Derek had not seen Jenny since the last narrow escape, but he could still picture her long legs, the straight collection of black eyes, and the bristly hairs that had once led him to consider her so endearingly cute.

But that had been when her fangs were too small to pierce paper.

Click, click. Not the rapping of pointed legs on metal, but the scrape of mandibles together. From the sounds, Derek could tell Jenny had stopped wandering the halls. She was examining the doors. Assessing.

Deciding.

He prayed his stomach wouldn't growl like Ben Nelson's had just the other day. Jenny could not hear sounds, but she could sense vibrations. While Derek and Samantha had barely escaped into the labyrinth, Ben had not been so fortunate, tripping before they'd reached the door. Ben had not been a very big man and wherever his husk was now stored, Derek was certain Jenny was hungry again.

The clicks of walking resumed, the noises growing faint.

Samantha sighed in obvious relief.

"Can we go for the entrance again? You have your ID?"

"I do," Derek affirmed. He had not lost his keycard, nor his keys. He kept hold of the latter like they were swords, even though they'd be useless against their former subjects. "But you know the second we're out there, she'll feel it. We'll never reach the door before she has us." They had tried so many times to reach the entrance, but no matter what plan they made, Jenny was always eight steps ahead.

Laughton Peaks had been so well designed; no way in or out, save the magnetically-sealed doors, with vast atriums extending deep into the bowels of the mountains. A miracle of engineering and design, the upper levels were the tip of the iceberg compared to the subterranean city below.

But it all belonged to the spiders now.

"I always thought Jenny liked me," Derek admitted with the most hopeless of smiles.

Samantha shook her head.

"Derek. She's a spider. She doesn't like anyone."

"Portias are different. They're so smart."

This was an argument they'd had countless times. Many times, Derek had opened Jenny's terrarium to welcome her into a comforting palm. He'd allowed her exercise, to hop from one end of the lab to the other. But, by far, his favorite activity was introducing a new spider to her area. Jenny always observed it, sometimes for hours or even days, assessing its capabilities and behaviors.

Then she struck. Derek always provided her with good hunting. Portias were a marvel of evolution, far smarter than their pinprick-sized brains should ever allow. Jenny was one of the only portias at Laughton Peaks, culling other spiders who grew difficult to control in the growth hormone experiments.

It was fascinating when they were the size of a fingernail. Less so now. Derek caught himself clutching at the Star of David around his neck, staving off a prayer for safety and good will.

"When she's gone, maybe we can try to distract her. Look around the office for supplies. Something we can throw down a hallway. We can make for the front while she's busy searching."

"You think we can both make it?" Samantha lifted an eyebrow. "You know how she is. When we tried to lock her in the office, she webbed the handle to the wall before she went in. Nothing else has worked."

"I know that." He tried to keep the desperation from his voice, telling himself he could control the situation. This had all been about control, increasing the food supply. The hormones had worked on vegetation well enough, with the effects diluted in the insects who consumed it. The dilution should have been sufficient to keep it from transferring to the spiders.

"Should have" being the operative phrase.

"You don't need to tell me, Sam. But we're running out of options."

Samantha gnawed at her lip before acknowledging his point. "Get something heavy," she said. "A stapler, a paperweight. We'll need to be fast and have a lot of luck for this to work."

Derek was happy she saw it his way. He slipped out from behind the desk, reaching for a drawer to carefully slide it open.

"Didn't Brett always keep a paperweight here, Sam?" The lack of response drew his eyes to Samantha. "Sam?"

She wasn't looking at him. She was staring past him, to the opening of the room, her body shaking and her mouth open. The indescribable terror on her face made Derek reluctant to turn his own gaze to where she were facing. If he couldn't see it, then it wouldn't be real.

Click, click. Like switchblades sliding together, Jenny's mandibles worked as though in satisfaction. Her body was folded so that one half leaned through the doorway, her forelegs tapping on the walls. The size of a Great Dane, a steely gray, her legs like spears. One was wrapped about a small jar.

Jenny dropped the jar, marbles falling across the metal surface of the hallway. The gentle bounces were just like the sound her legs made against the same floor. Derek wondered how he could have ever found Jenny cute, with her waving pedipalps and gigantic eyes. Those eyes now reflected the light and Derek could see no emotion within them. No pity. No affection. Certainly no recognition. Nothing but hunger and efficiency, everything that evolution had left her with.

"Go," he whispered to Samantha. He clutched the other scientist's wrist and pulled her with him, just as Jenny sprang. A blur of motion, the portia kicked off the wall to land on a nearby desk. Some part of Derek's mind told him she was setting up her next move, as jumpers often did.

He grabbed something off the desk, maybe a stapler. He flung it at Jenny, ruining her next leap even as she sidestepped and let it harmlessly pound against the wall.

Derek turned with Samantha, running for the door and expecting to feel the hard embrace of Jenny's grasping limbs, the piercing bite of her fangs within his back. Would it hurt when the venom coursed into his bloodstream? Portias were so venomous that a flood of their toxin shut down a nervous system in seconds.

"Derek, come on!"

Samantha yanked him through the door. He slammed it shut, expecting to hear a furry body smash against it.

The quiet was even worse.

Derek and Samantha ran down the corridors, not bothering to mask the sound of their footsteps. Soon enough, he heard the slow, gentle noises of plinking limbs against the metal. This time, he knew they weren't marbles.

He turned a corner with Samantha, searching for some safe haven.

"There's the lower level!" Samantha said. She withdrew her badge, clutching it like a charm. "If we go through there, we might be able to lose her!"

Derek thought about taking another route. They could still double round to the front. If they split up, it would improve their chances. At least one of them might make it. He hated himself for the intrusive thought that came to his mind: he'd taken care of Jenny, he'd fed her and nurtured her. Surely it must be reciprocated on some level, spider or no. Maybe she would go after Sam, let him escape.

The sounds of approach grew louder. Then a loud clang echoed, like some wolf-sized body had just leapt to the ceiling, foregoing any hint of stealth. Derek's teeth rattled.

"The lower level?" he said. "That's suicide."

"We made it through before!" She ran to the door, lifting up her badge, holding it to the reader. "Come on. Come on!"

"Access granted," came the voice from the speaker, a light glaring emerald green. Samantha grabbed for the door handle, swinging it open. She held it for Derek, slamming it shut the moment he crossed the entry.

He turned back, wishing he hadn't. Like Lot's wife, he felt like his body had turned to salt. Through the translucent pane on the door, there was Jenny, hanging down from the ceiling on a thread of silk. Her pedipalps lifted slightly, like she was greeting them.

She reached out, tapping the window, her fangs twitching. He lifted his hand to the hard glass, telling himself Jenny couldn't break it.

"Hey, clever girl," he murmured, just as he had greeted her every morning for almost a year.

Jenny made no response, just watching.

Analyzing.

Then she descended to the floor, turned and walked back the way she came, vanishing around the corridor.

31

Jenny

"Derek?" Samantha shook him. "Derek!" Her voice was low, insistent, her nails biting into his skin.

"We got away from her. Todah Rabah," he muttered, the Hebrew comforting him. He thanked his deity and all his forefathers, every single angel and even some prophets. "What the hell do we do now?"

"We sure as hell can't go back there." Samantha turned from the door, the situation dawning on her. "We're in the lower levels."

The corridor was dimly lit, leading to only a single door that Derek knew went down into the greenhouse, a near city-sized atrium. It was also the place they had barely escaped with their life just days prior. Derek wondered if they had gone from bad to worse by fleeing Jenny.

"How many spiders do you think are in the lower levels now?" He hated to ask the question out loud. Acknowledging it would be to make it into reality.

"I don't know," Samantha admitted. Her eyes swam with tears as she faced the exit. "But we can try an alternate route. Go through the west wing and go upstairs, try for the south exit of the compound. Jenny won't have any idea where we are."

Derek glanced back through the door, as though Samantha saying Jenny's name might summon her.

"I'm not sure I like the odds," he said.

"You want to take it up with her on the other side of that door? She's probably patrolling right now, making sure we don't double back for the exit."

"Maybe she's too smart to wait there." Derek had once seen Jenny approach an orb weaver's web and play with the strands, simulating a trapped insect. The larger spider hadn't lasted five seconds after its approach. "Maybe she's angry we got away."

"Derek, I'm telling you one more time. She's a spider. She can't be angry, or sentimental, or anything. She doesn't recognize you, you're just food to her. She's smarter than the others, but that's all. She's no different than Betty or Harriet."

"I hope we don't run into them." Derek hadn't seen the female redback since he'd witnessed her broken terrarium, nor the ogre-face spider since her net had pulled Administrator Sturridge into the shadows. There were all manner of spiders, dozens of them likely claiming corners of the lower levels for themselves.

The insects had not had proper time to breed yet. The spiders would likely be hungry.

"Think we can wait until they die of starvation? They'll resort to preying on one another eventually."

"We'll go before they do. It's been a few days since we've eaten." Samantha's voice carried an edge of scientific practicality. "Derek, we can't delay this any longer. We have to try."

Derek knew she was right. When she opened the door, he walked down beside her, careful to keep his footfalls light. The lights still worked at the bottom of the stairs, the next door leading them into the atrium.

The hollowed-out section of mountain was covered in giant plants and towering trees. Derek felt fresh soil beneath his feet, avoiding stepping out too far into the chamber with its artificial sunlight up above.

Samantha pointed, making sure he saw. A section of loose earth lifted upward.

The glint of light across shiny eyes caught Derek's gaze.

"It's Nellie," he murmured. "Stay out of range. She won't attack if you don't get too close." Trapdoor spiders were ambush predators, striking at anything they detected near their burrows. Nellie wouldn't leave her den to stalk the two of them, not like Jenny.

Thick, massive strands of webbing covered the trees ahead. Derek couldn't see the owners, a blessing and a curse all at once.

"I think that one is a golden orb weaver's, which means it's Ophelia or Greta. Nellie being nearby probably means Rita is on the other side of the atrium. She hates the trapdoors." At least they didn't have to worry about the wolf spider. Rita didn't have Jenny's brains, but she was equally relentless.

"Keep to the perimeter," Samantha whispered. She began to walk, slowly, inch by inch.

Derek wondered what would happen if the spiders were allowed to escape Laughton Peaks. They were a distance from civilization and few males existed among the population—no male portias at all. At least there was no chance of a thousand hungry little Jennies descending upon the nearest town.

Sliding across the ground, Derek's attention remained fixed on Nellie. He tried not to look at the multitudes of dried-out body parts scattered all over the atrium, nor the webs up high, the bound-silk cocoons within.

One cocoon looked bigger than the others, making him think of a particularly tall security guard named Frank. The silk wrappings twitched, either in reality or in Derek's imagination. He muttered another prayer, his body moving again.

Almost there, he thought, hearing the buzz of Samantha unlocking the door.

She swung it open and Derek dared to tear his eyes from the atrium. He turned through, finding a wide-open, empty chamber. Samantha shut the door, slamming it louder than she had to. Derek winced, looking about the laboratory, the broken terrariums, trying not to look at the desiccated figures lying on the ground. The stench of death hovered in the air, a foul reek that burned Derek's nose.

"We get through the next door, it's just a short walk from there. We got lucky." Samantha sighed in relief, her eyes level. The corpses about them were just shriveled husks of flesh, tattered clothes bearing evenly-spaced twin punctures.

Soon they'd be out, Derek told himself. Soon.

Click, click. The metallic noise froze him in place. The sound of tapping on the wall. Derek turned in the direction of it, whirling about to see the vent drop out, slamming to the ground with the force of a bullet. Gray, pointed legs emerged, unfurling like a blossoming flower. From the vent, Jenny descended on a strand of silk, languid and gentle, like she was satisfied.

Derek turned to go for the doorway, ready to shout for Samantha. Jenny flew past them as if sensing their intentions, landing across the door. Her eight legs splayed out, a shield blocking them from escape. She began to rotate herself, adjusting her position.

Zachary Rosenberg

Grabbing Samantha, Derek ran to the side, some part of his brain telling him to shove her at Jenny and just run. The human part of him compelled him to pull Samantha with him. Derek's weakened body obeyed him somehow, sore legs pounding the floor as he saw the alcove. The open corridor beyond led somewhere that Derek couldn't remember.

Jenny landed behind him, where he had stood moments before.

All that mattered was getting away from Jenny. He and Samantha barreled through the alcove, already seeing the pathway to another atrium. Danger ahead, certain death behind.

"Left," Samantha wheezed.

Derek turned the corner with her, the winding passages their only defense from Jenny's leaps. Too fast to outrun, too smart to outwit. He knew in his bones that Jenny had known they would come here. She had already mapped out the route from the vents, knowing the timing and the location like any good portia.

As he turned the next corner, the ground suddenly gave way. Derek's feet skidded against dirt, unable to find purchase. He tumbled down alongside Samantha, a dark abyss gaping up around them.

Twisting as he fell, Derek landed on something soft, strong, and sticky. He tried to stand, but the strands held fast. He shook himself, the strands moving with him. A sickening realization set in, just as Samantha began to scream. He tried to shout to her not to move, to stay still, but she thrashed, the sticky network underneath them bucking wildly.

Above them on the ledge was Jenny, peering down and watching. Haloed by the single light above. She tapped a leg against the rim of the hollowed-out floor, then shrank back and vanished from sight.

Then Derek heard the clicking. Much louder than Jenny's own, a scuttling rustle from the shadows. He caught a flash of crimson in the darkness, the shape of an hourglass.

"Betty," he whispered.

The redback emerged from her hiding place, her legs carefully balanced on the strands. Her abdomen was bloated, her curved,

Jenny

sickle fangs leaking a dark fluid. Derek turned to see the wrapped forms in the—

—in the *web*.

He tried to be still, but he knew Betty had already felt the vibrations, knew that there was a morsel to be claimed. She climbed along the strands, descending toward them not with a bolting speed, but with the cautious confidence of a predator.

He tried to force himself to close his eyes, hoping her venom would work quickly, so he wouldn't feel his insides turn to mush.

Her body, polished obsidian in the light, came closer, the silk binding him in place.

Derek caught a glimpse of movement, from the corner of his eye. Jenny was peering down, gauging the situation, analyzing. A mad thought came to Derek: had Jenny hated him this whole time? Did she want to see him caught, devoured as recompense for holding and changing her?

Then Jenny's legs twitched. She sprang, a steely flash of lightning, as Betty drew closer to her prey. Betty reared up near Samantha, each of her eight eyes focused only on the bound victim in the web. Jenny hit her in the back, her legs enveloping the thorax of the larger spider. Holding Betty in a tight embrace, her chelicerae descended, fangs piercing through the black armor of the redback's head.

Betty did not twitch, didn't scream. She made no noise. The only motion the curling of her legs as Jenny's venom flooded her body. A death rictus took hold of the redback, Betty frozen in place. Derek thought he could read satisfaction in the dark band of Jenny's eyes.

Fluid leaked from Jenny's mouthparts, a slurping noise echoing as digestive enzymes turned Betty's innards to soup. Derek fought to free himself to no avail, knowing that when Jenny was through with her meal, he and Samantha would be next. Or worse, she would leave them, helpless, to return to when hunger took her over again, or as a meal for any wandering spider.

But then Jenny leapt nimbly off of Betty's body. She could not have finished her meal already, but she came over to Derek, so close that her legs brushed his chest. Her fangs clicked together. She stabbed her legs down, head descending. He closed his eyes so he didn't have to see the fangs.

Snip, snip.

Derek opened his eyes. Jenny had sheared the web beneath him, precise as a scalpel. She took hold of him, extricating him from the entanglement, curling him so he lay upon her back. Her hairs itched at him, stinging like little thorns, but no discomfort could overcome his relief, and his confusion.

Jenny moved and he was deposited on hard ground, back on the ledge from which he had fallen.

"Jenny?" he asked cautiously.

The portia looked at him, then turned, leapt back to the web, and emerged moments later with a shivering Samantha. Then Jenny leapt down again, returning to Betty's carcass.

Derek stared in nothing short of awe as the portia fed, something he had seen countless times when she'd been small.

"She saved us," he said in wonder. A smile came over his face and he knew he'd need a new pair of pants soon. "She—"

"Probably didn't do it out of the goodness of her heart." Samantha rubbed her wrists. "Derek, we need to go. While she's eating. Back the way we came, we can get out now."

"Sam, she pulled us out. She does remember me." Derek almost laughed, but Samantha tugged at his coat.

He turned, leaving the slurping sounds behind them. They passed cautiously through the atrium, back the way they came. With their shaking legs, Derek believed they must have been walking for almost an hour. He sagged against the wall to catch his breath and wiped his forehead.

He heard a dull thud around the corner. Sure enough, when he leaned around, he saw Jenny waiting for them.

She didn't make any aggressive movements. Derek slowly approached, stepping past her, and Jenny turned to walk alongside him, as though providing an escort. Derek reached out toward the spider, Samantha uttering a warning he ignored. He put a hand to Jenny's head, stroking her like he might a dog.

Jenny didn't shrug him off or bite his hand, but nor did she lean into it. She simply accepted the touch, continuing her walk.

"I think she's escorting us," Derek said. "Sam, she remembers me. She knows me. She knew where Betty was and she needed distraction, that's all."

Jenny scuttled ahead, pausing to wait for them.

"She's letting us go!" Derek felt joy spread through him, his feet quickening as the prospect of freedom overtook him. Jenny stopped in front of a corridor, turning to face them.

"Jenny," Derek began, "thank you."

He took a step closer. Jenny didn't move. He approached her, intending to step past her. But Jenny lunged forth, Derek leaping backward as her legs collided with the floor, her eyes locked on him. His mouth worked in shock.

"Jenny?"

Derek tried to step forth again, but Jenny reared up, flashing her fangs. He shrank back toward Samantha.

"Derek, out of the hallway!" Samantha held her badge to the side, opening the way to the cafeteria. "Come on!"

Derek followed Samantha through the doorway. Jenny started after them, slow and ponderous,. then stopped, framed in the entrance. She simply studied them, not pursuing.

"Doctor?"

Derek turned at the mention of his and Samantha's title. There, in a corner of the room, unshaven and bleary-eyed, was a still-living Ben Nelson, along with a smattering of other personnel.

"Ben? What's going on here?" Derek asked. His attention remained fixed upon Jenny as her legs gently tapped the ground.

"She got you too, huh?" Ben smiled bleakly. "She dragged me down into the atrium after she caught me. Made me walk along no-man's land." He laughed hollowly. "She snagged Vera before she got me. You know, the funnel-web? But Eric wasn't so lucky. Harriet got him before Jenny could make a move. Her record's not perfect."

There was food all about, packages, cans, a refrigerator, even a cooking station. Enough to last for weeks by Derek's estimation.

Samantha laughed, a hysterical and broken sound.

"Derek," she said. "You were right about portias. They are smart."

Derek only stared, numbly, at Jenny. She looked back at him, and he peered into those shiny, black-button eyes of hers. But all he saw in return was the mute reflection of his own horror.

"Look at her," Sam all but moaned. "She knows how to use us as *bait*."

Happy Birthday, Princess

M.W. Irving

I TRY TO MAKE CONVERSATION WITH KEN, the porter who has wheeled an enormous corpse into my lab through the swinging double doors. Everybody likes Ken, he's friendly with a broad smile, easy banter, and boy-band good looks. I get nothing but distracted, single-word answers from him. His eyes never leave the large window separating my lab from the one next-door— *Monster Development*. The neighboring laboratory is dark, the window is a mirror reflecting his nervous glances.

On his way out, Ken tells me the corpse he has delivered is a shock bear, gesturing with a nod to the lump on the gurney. Then he's echoing footsteps on the poured concrete floor fading down the hallway. The blue sheet covering his delivery is soaked through with blood. I can't blame Ken for his hasty retreat, knowing as I do what lurks in the darkness next door. During the infamous "Tentacle Period" I didn't see another person anywhere near my lab for months. People hate the smell of my work as well, industrial cleaner and chemical preserving agent, blood. I probably reek of it.

The sigh I let out as I peel the sheet back from my patient comes from down deep. Though it's agony to admit, the shock bear laying dead on my table is a magnificent scientific accomplishment. Sure, its very existence is a slap in God's face, using millions of years of evolution like a child in a playground, and the person who made it is the worst human being I've ever met, but the creature is beautiful. I've taken to calling this shock

40

bear *Dawn* because of the colour of her fur, glistening copper like the morning exhaust-haze on my commutes to work. Dawn is fifteen feet of obscenely enhanced animal, the highest danger score on the *Hunter Be Hunted* show—100 points. The clumps of muscle bunching around her shoulders give the poor thing chronic neck pain. Those muscles also give her the ability to swat a family sedan through a concrete wall. Genetic trickery courtesy of my asshole lab-neighbor, Dr. Sheila Allard.

Goddamn Sheila, that manic pixie, only a mind as sick as hers could conceive of a shock bear, let alone drag one into reality through a test tube. Not that I'm much better, really, but a giant, electric Kodiak? Jesus. They've amassed quite a staff here on the *Hunter Be Hunted* show. Fitting for the savagery we produce, I suppose. If she were alive, Dawn's fur would be standing on end, crackling with voltage. Whoever took her down probably won— if they weren't electrocuted and eliminated that is. Going for Dawn is a desperation move. I run my finger along the back of her claw, hooked and transparent like amber glass. My finger distorts, bulging and shrinking with the claw's contours as though underwater.

Time to get busy. I examine the wounds and recognize the work of a Buzzer. It's one of the more diabolical prize-weapons contestants can get. The Buzzer is a long, arm-mounted chainsaw with six gnashing blades that can dig through brick like it was cheese. A deep chasm has been dug into Dawn's flank. The deltoid, infraspinatus, and trapezius muscles are shredded and will need to be regrown. Four ribs have been mulched and the left scapula has deep gouges in it. The Buzzer has burrowed its way through arteries and into Dawn's heart. Vasculature is going to be tight for next week's deadline. The bones I can 3D print and replace while she's unconscious, but the muscles and arteries are going to have to be grown while she's awake. It's going to be a painful reanimation if they're to have her for the next show.

The first step is perhaps the most crucial—detox. I need to flush Dawn's system of the hyper-stimulants she's brimming with. She's been pumped full of what amounts to clinically-refined meth, bath salts, cocaine, and Adderall. A saint would eat their mother on that kind of cocktail, so unless I want this literal monster waking up on the homicidal side of the bed, I need to get it out of her.

The moment I finish inserting the drainage tubes Sheila bursts in through the door separating our labs. My throat constricts; that door is supposed to be locked. She's astride her office chair, kicking herself toward me, bumping into everything she passes. Tubes and records fall over and thunder rumbles in the wheels of her chair.

"Morning, Princess, how's the meat game?" She rolls herself to a stop next to me.

It's not even nine o'clock; she doesn't typically show up for another three hours, at least. I hope, as I always do, that if I ignore her she'll leave me alone. As always, she doesn't. When Sheila gets within arm's reach, she snaps her hand out to clip a tether to a beltloop on my chinos. The tether is the kind she uses to keep her abominations tied to their pens; when the clip locks it can hold back a bulldozer. It locks immediately.

Dread rises—she's going to make me look at one of her experiments.

"Sheila, no."

She pulls me along and my hips thrust forward with each of her tugs. We do an awkward mambo as she kicks us towards her lab, still sliding astride her chair. Her chestnut ponytail, held up by a purple scrunchie, bobs and swings in time with her kicks. Goddamn Sheila; who tethers people?

"Stop!" I shout and yank. It feels good for an instant before the fear of how she'll react takes hold. Her chair recoils at my tug and she spins towards me, eyes wide with surprise.

"I have to finish up with Dawn—" *shit* "—er, the shock bear, I mean."

"Oh, you've named your little pet?" she says like someone asking a toddler.

"I—"

"That shock bear ain't getting deader, Princess. Come check out what I made."

42

She gives the leash another couple tugs and smirks at my lurching pelvis.

"You're wrong, she's getting deader every second, I'm losing her to decay. The longer she's dead, the longer her recovery will be. Can you make a new shock bear in a week? No. They want her for the next show. I need to flush her out and fix her up. Now."

"Wow, did you rehearse that?"

I wonder briefly how she knows. Sheila looks over at Dawn lying on my table, glowing under the reaching arms of the medical lamps.

"I'm not surprised they want her for next week, look at her. She's magnificent."

Sheila rolls over to Dawn, letting out slack on my tether as she goes.

"I couldn't believe it when the eel genomes took. Woah-ho-ho! Look at that! I bet that hurt." She slaps the meat of Dawn's open wound with her bare hand. I fantasize about the shock bear coming alive and electrocuting her. The image of smoke shooting from her nostrils and her tongue bursting into flame brings a brief smile to my face. A millisecond smirk; I don't think Sheila notices.

"I bet she gave as good as she got, though. Fifty-thousand volts at least. You remember that pig when we were testing her?" Sheila makes an explosion sound, spit flying from her lips.

I remember the pig. Ham-smell lingered in my lab for days.

Sheila turns to the shock bear and crinkles her nose, putting on a cutesy voice as though Dawn was a little, shaking dog. "You did that to some crispy contestant, didn't you? Just like the piggy. I have a great idea, Princess. Let's bring ol' Dawn here back to life together. Huh? It'll be great. I'll just observe, I've always meant to watch you do your creepy thing."

She slaps Dawn's wound again; bear blood spatters.

"You think *my* work is creepy?"

After what she's forced me to look at, she has the gall to call what I do creepy.

"You're messing with death itself, killer, there ain't nothing creepier." She examines the equipment I've carefully laid out as

43

she talks. "Sure, they let me make science my bitch here, but you're playing with biblical stuff."

"There's probably something in the bible about not mixing porcupines with spiders."

She rolls her head back and laughs.

"If there isn't, there ought to be," she says.

With a scurry of feet she rolls her chair even closer to me, finishing with a few little thrusts of her hips until her knees are against mine. This is something she likes to do every now and then, and it's worse than all her other little torments combined. She gets up from her chair and, as close as she is, the two inches of height she has on my five feet, eight inches feels like miles.

"Come on, it'll be fun." Her voice is just above a whisper, deep and throaty. She peers at me through her eyelashes, lips thrust in a pout.

This little game of hers is the worst because of my weakness. I've sent multiple grievances to HR about Sheila's behavior, but I can't seem to list sexual harassment among them. The disgusting truth is I don't want her to stop. Sheila is undeniably beautiful; she would look more at home leading a cheer squad than hatching horrors in a lab. She is all the girls who spurned me in high school, college, and throughout my postgrad. I hate myself for the flush in my skin when she's this close. I try to step away but she has me pinned against my desk.

"Tell me, do any of your zombies come back craving brains?"

"No."

This is likely a lie. My resurrected patients have often gone on to eat brains, though I doubt the brains are specifically craved, as she's suggesting. Her hip is pressing into mine and it's hard to breathe.

"Do they ever bring anything back from the other side? Demons, maybe? Can you look into their eyes and see if there's an afterlife?" Her ponytail bounces with the enthusiasm of her questions.

"Um, no. Nothing like that. There isn't a Hell for animals."

"What if they're not 100% animals?" she asks, lifting her hand to her mouth so she can speak behind the back of it. *Our little*

44

secret, the gesture says. I want nothing to do with her secrets but I can't stop myself from asking.

"What do you mean?"

"What if a skootch of *people* got into a couple of my creations?"

"People?"

"Yeah, just a skootch. How much human DNA does it take to get you a ticket to Hell?"

"You mean there's human DNA in these things?"

"Human-ish, and only in a couple."

I don't know why I thought this was a line even Sheila wouldn't cross, but now that I'm faced with it I'm not surprised.

"Jesus, Sheila."

"No, no, not his. I'd love to get my hands on some genuine Christ DNA, though. Can you imagine? Half-God, half-ancient virgin?" She reaches to boop the tip of my nose. "Oh, please let me be your nurse, doctor."

I hate the thrill that rushes to the core of me.

"Fine."

"Ooh! Excellent. Should I go put on a nurse's outfit? I have one."

The blood filtration system dings; Dawn's blood is clean. I have to squirm to get away from the grip of Sheila's hip. She holds me in place for just a moment before releasing. The tether still dangles between us.

"Maybe your resuscitations are what brought all this Hell here."

She giggles at that.

"What is it with you and Hell today?" I say absently as I fire up the bone printer. The arms get to their intricate work and brand-new ribs begin to take form.

"Look around!" Sheila says, gesturing to the lab.

I take a moment to look. There are stop-frozen limbs, blood-spattered cages, a vast array of invasive instruments. There are throngs of people around the world desperate to watch the terrible things we create fight for their lives. The contestants get to have meat puppets, their true bodies safe and sound offsite. When contestants die, they're simply eliminated from the game and wake up with a headache and some grizzly memories somewhere else. When the monsters are horribly killed, they come to me and I bring them back for more. Over and over, I rob them of death's peace. Perhaps Sheila's right and this is Hell for monsters.

She turns out to be a spectacular assistant. Before I even realize I need a tool she has it for me. Most surprising of all is her silent attentiveness. It is the longest I've ever seen Sheila go without speaking. She even knows my favorite tea, Earl Grey, and brews us a pot. Maybe HR finally had a talk with her. With Sheila's help, I get nearly two days' worth of work done in just a few hours.

"Now it's time for the spark, isn't it, Dr. Frankenstein?"

I take a step back from the expression on her face. Her eyes are aflame in the way they get when she watches her creations kill something.

"Yes," I say, wheeling the Spark Unit over. Its plug gets briefly tangled with the tether still stretching between Sheila and me. I'd nearly forgotten about it.

Within the Spark Unit's aluminum casing, wires, circuitry, glass, and CPUs, is the digitized start-up sequence for life. The repaired brain will receive an instant of consciousness that will spark it into reanimation. Sheila watches closely as I attach the rectifying tubes.

"I thought it would be more dramatic. More lightning and sweaty shouting," she says, disappointment dripping from her voice. "Well, Princess, now that cause of death has been worked out we can get on with the fun part."

"Cause of death?"

"Yeah, this shock bear here, what did you call her? Dawn? She's gonna kill you."

She turns to me, laughing, and pulls something up on her palm display. Sheila begins reading aloud. When I realize what she's reading, dread sinks tendrils into me and I'm immediately covered in a greasy sweat.

"As director of Human Resources," she says in a nasal voice, "I am certain you are well aware of my case against Dr. Sheila Allard, but, if you are not, my chief complaints are these."

"Hey," I say, trying to interrupt. "That's supposed to be confidential."

"Princess, please, I'm reading. One: She will not stop calling me Princess despite my many requests." She looks up to my face. I don't know what to do. "Have you thought about not being such a Princess then? Two: I should not be compelled to see the things Sheila creates in her lab. I know it's her job to create nightmares, but she forces me to look at everything she makes, and I can't sleep any more. Oh, muffin. Last week she made me watch a cheetah give birth to a monstrosity with a shark's head and a scorpion's tail. I saw it kill and begin to eat its mother before it suffocated to death with frothing shark-gills. Nobody should have to see something like that."

She drops back into her chair.

"I'd read the other ten complaints," she says, "but I'm afraid saying these words out loud will turn me into a little bitch. It's a good thing I intercepted your emails or we might have a little bitch outbreak on our hands. It's contagious you know."

"Sheila—"

"I can smell the bitter essence of little bitch coming off you even now. It's like piss and sweat. I gave myself a little genetic enhancement courtesy of my dog, Burty. He can always smell a little bitch."

I've seen photos of Burty on her desk. He's a nasty looking chihuahua with bulging eyes and sparse hair like wires. I need to get away from her. Tearing at the tether attached to me accomplishes nothing, so I try to rip the beltloop right off. The little strip of tan fabric shouldn't be as strong as it is; I don't pop a single thread. I begin unfastening my belt, but panic has turned my fingers into useless sausages. Ultimately, I resort to tugging on my pants to get them off. They cling painfully to my hips and don't budge.

"Don't hurt yourself," Sheila says, observing my struggles with amusement. "How do you ever get laid? This is embarrassing to watch, and it's all for nothing anyway. Dawn here isn't *actually* going to kill you."

She pulls out a tablet and taps at it a couple times.

"What's that?" I ask, loathing the quiver in my voice.

"This? Oh, you're going to love this. I've installed an On/Off switch."

She shows me the screen. On it is an image of a switch, the kind that would be right at home channelling death into electric chairs from the 1950s.

"You installed a switch? In what?"

"In you, Princess. Nanites in your tea. I was kind of hoping you'd put up a bit more of a fight. Maybe a punch in the face to get the blood pumping, you know?"

She licks her lips and taps the screen. The switch switches and everything goes black.

***

"Wakey, wakey, Princess. It's your new birthday."

An instant and an eternity has passed. There's no grogginess as with waking from sleep; I'm simply back on. I'm no longer in my lab. Sheila really does have an On/Off switch for me. *Oh, God.* I go to speak but find I can't, I can't move. I'm not even able to blink. Well, my eyes blink, but it has nothing to do with me. Sheila leans close; my skin doesn't flush this time.

"You in there?" she asks, knocking on my forehead. She looks to a brain activity readout and reacts with delight. "There you are. Oh, you must be angry. Wait until you see the new background on my phone."

Sheila turns her palm to me. On her holo-screen is a picture of my naked body. It's not flattering. I'm unconscious, spread-eagle on a surgical table. My pale manhood, looking like an overexposed cashew, features prominently in the photograph's composition.

"It's an adorable piece of equipment you have there," she says. "I wanted you to see it one last time before I delete the evidence."

I can only look straight ahead, my outrage impotent. What has she done? My heartbeat feels strange. Slower, thicker. The monitor beeping out its pulse—my pulse—begins beeping faster.

"Oh, I'm sorry. Is this more unprofessional behaviour? Well, you've been reassigned to a new department of the *Hunter Be Hunted* show. You're talent now, so your concept of what's *appropriate*—" She does little bunny ears with her fingers at the word. "—is going to have to be readjusted a skootch."

Sheila wheels a large oval mirror in front of me.

"Don't ask what I use this for," she says with a wink.

She tilts the mirror so I can see myself. I'm unable to look away. It takes me a moment to understand that the grotesque mass of flesh in the reflection is me. While I'm still humanoid, but there is no other resemblance to what I once was. The head of a boar sits atop thickly veined muscles like hairy yams placed on both shoulders. I'm as broad as a dumpster. The face, covered in sparse, bristling hairs, ends in a snout above tusks, thick and yellow. There's a lobster claw where a left arm should be. There's more than a skootch of human in the DNA in the thing I've become. It's just enough to make me a truly uncanny horror. The eyes in this creature are mine. My mind crackles with a scream that I'm unable to produce in the thick, pork-throat I now possess.

"I've told them to name you Princess," Sheila says with a mischievous smirk. "You're going to be the deadliest thing on the show. They'll need something to replace the shock bear that killed you. This'll get her decommissioned for sure."

She cues something else up on her phone to show me.

I'm unable to turn away from a video of Dawn, very much alive, tearing into my body with her claws, teeth, and electricity. Sheila's shrieking laughter can be heard over the carnage.

"Thanks for showing me your little reanimation trick," she says over the cackling. "The producers will be glad you did before *Dawn* got you; they won't even miss a single show. I guess we won't see each other until some lucky contestant kills you."

She blows me a kiss and turns me off again.

***

I'm in the arena when I'm turned back on. It's different in real life, but I recognize it immediately. Seen from up close, the cracked concrete walls, dangling chains, oil-drum fires, and bloodstains both new and old, don't look like the set I've seen so many times. It looks like Hell. I can see the cameras zooming about on their wires and drones, filming from the safety above. The beast I'm imprisoned within is no longer sedated and strapped to a table. It's loose, drugged, and acting solely on murderous instinct. The power in its body is incredible—my body. I feel it but can do nothing with it. Only rage controls the beast.

When I first catch sight of a contestant wearing the clinging blue uniform and the familiar clone face, the beast charges blindly. A need to pull the person apart courses through me. Though I cringe inwardly, the thought of bathing in this contestant's blood —rip—bite—gorge on him—wakes something deep inside me and it feels good.

The contestant raises a Pooner and fires. The rocket-propelled harpoon-taser tears through the air. My lobster arm raises to deflect, a flex of unfamiliar muscles. Though my carapace armor cracks, the Pooner bolt glances away and I'm spared the jolt. Then I get a throat in my grasp. The life I take may not be real, but the terror in the meat-puppet's clone face is, and it's delicious. I hear laughing commentary from Clint Fistrick, *Hunter Be Hunted's* flamboyant announcer. Speakers mounted all around the arena give his voice an echoing, tinny quality. Nose cartilage crunches between my teeth as I chew.

I have an answer for Sheila now. Yes, the monsters we breathe life into crave brains. The anticipation of giving in to that craving thrills me. I will find her and I will rip her. It'll be Sheila's cartilage I crunch someday; I crave her brains most of all. I think only of her as I clip the head from another contestant and bellow under the torrent of blood that fountains forth. I will get control of this monster and we will come for you.

But first.

"Oh!" comes Clint Fistrick's professionally astounded voice. "Another kill for Princess!"

Ghost in the Machine
Ally Malinenko

THERE WAS NO REASON FOR ALICE TO BE NERVOUS.

She had done this before. She had laid topless, shivering, in the cold tube and waited for the noise to start. *There's no reason to be nervous,* she told herself, seated in the hard plastic chairs, one hand clutching the see-through bag on her lap that held her clothes. The other kept the gown closed at her throat. She didn't make eye contact with the other women in the waiting room. Alice had a superstition about that. Ever since her diagnosis, she told herself that if she connected to other women who were sick, she would only get sicker. As if the cancer was catchy instead of just shitty.

Because Alice was above this. She didn't participate in any of those walks or, heaven forbid, online campaigns to raise awareness. What was there to be aware of? She couldn't be more aware. From the moment she asked the doctor, during the biopsy, if he was concerned, and with a straight face, he said, yes, Alice, I'm very concerned, and then on the phone, the next day, told her news. Ever since then she has been acutely aware.

Raising that awareness was never something Alice needed to do. So, she didn't. She didn't go on the walks. She didn't call it a journey. Alice strapped herself to the conveyor belt of treatment and she kept her head down and that is how she got through it. Jeff, her husband, used to come to these things with her, but now that so much time had passed, it was easier to treat it like a regular doctor's appointment. Besides, it wasn't like Alice was getting results now. And, on top of that, it had already been so long. So many years without another scare. What were the chances?

That was the thing about a cancer diagnosis: you just got used to living on the edge of the worst news of your life. Because, otherwise, you would be wound too tight, a guitar string ready to snap.

And Alice was not the kind of person to snap.

She glanced at the other women in the waiting room. They were all older than her. She was used to that too. Most people with cancer were over fifty. Sixty, even. But not Alice.

Sometimes she thought about the Universe's finger—the way it circled around until it found her, picked her out of the crowd, trailed a line down her body, and decided her life would be derailed.

Except it wasn't derailed, Alice thought. Her life would only derailed if she let it, and she was certainly not going to do that. This was a hiccup. A bump in the road. This was just an afternoon—not even, a few hours—and then she would be on her way home, making a mental list of the things she needed to pick up at the store. Things she needed for dinner. Was she out of dishwashing liquid? She should add that, just in case. Doesn't hurt to have extra.

"Alice?"

Did she also need sandwich bags for the chicken she put in her salad? A salad she had been eating for nearly ten years now. After the doctor told her to lose weight. After she implied the disease was Alice's fault.

"Alice?"

She would never forget that surgeon's face. The way she raised an eyebrow after hearing about Alice's diet. The way she pursed her lips after hearing Alice had more than one glass of wine after dinner. Alice bristled. It was 2023. Science should have fixed this by now. She was still mad at that doctor, all these years later. The implication that Alice had done something wrong and that was why she was here, inconveniencing this surgeon. She had told Jeff that once, but he dismissed her as crazy and she never mentioned it again. The way he acted like she was paranoid. Sometimes it felt like everyone moved on but Alice.

"Mrs. Slade."

Alice jumped at the sound of her name.

"Yes, I'm sorry," she said getting up. Her fingers were sticking to the plastic of the bag holding her clothes. For a brief moment she let go of the gown, and, as she stood, it opened slightly and Alice felt panic rise in her throat. For a superstitious second, she was sure if that if anyone in the waiting room could see her body she would be sick again.

A sudden whiff of something caught her attention: the smell of burned flesh. The way radiation blackens and shrivels skin. The way it stayed gray long after treatment was finished.

"Follow me," the nurse said and, with a quick clip, headed down the hall. Alice shook her head. What was wrong with her today? She followed the nurse into the MRI room. It was always colder in here than anywhere else. She felt goosebumps up her arms and legs.

Don't look at it, she told herself. It was best not to look at the machine. Because no matter what, it always looked far too small to fit a human body. It looked like a mouth waiting to eat her; the tray she would lay on, its thick, hard tongue.

Instead, Alice kept her head down as the nurse prattled on about the contrast dye they would inject into her. She would pee blue later because of that dye. The nurse put the needle toward Alice's right arm and Alice yanked it back.

"The hand," she said, holding up her left hand. "Lymph nodes were removed so we have to do the hand."

The veins on the back of her hand were bulging, already looking like they belonged to someone twenty years older. And that was the way Alice felt. Like everything had fast-forwarded. Time added without memory or value or meaning.

A decade had passed in the blink of an eye.

The nurse slipped the needle into her vein. It was a feeling she no longer registered. She used to hate needles, but all these years later, they didn't faze her. She imagined someone could stab her with a needle in the middle of the bread aisle and she wouldn't notice. She'd just keep shopping. In fact, the needle in her hand almost looked like an extension of her.

It is …

"What did you say?" Alice asked.

The nurse looked up at her. "Nothing."

"Oh, I thought … sorry." Alice was going to explain more, but the nurse shoved two pink foam earplugs in her ears and the world went muffled. *Of course they're pink*, Alice thought, keeping her eyes down, trained on her feet, so she wouldn't dare look at the Machine.

That's how she thought of it: Machine with a capital M.

Mouth, she thought. *A Machine like a Mouth that is going to eat you all up.*

"Okay, let's go," the nurse said, kicking the step stool over to the tray. The tray Alice tried really hard to not think of as a tongue. A tongue that would slide her into the Machine's Mouth.

Stop it, she thought. *You're being ridiculous. You're thinking like a child.* And she was. She had done this for years. She knew the drill. She stepped up carefully, one hand gripping the gown.

This was the worst part. The part where she would have to open the gown, lay down on her belly, letting her breasts be slotted through two holes cut into the tray (*tongue*). Alice lowered herself carefully and the tech started moving things. Moving *her*. She bit down on her own tongue to stop the screaming as the tech rammed Alice's breasts back and forth to get them to dangle just as they needed through the holes. It was painful. It was humiliating.

Alice pressed her face into the padded plastic hole. She knew it would leave red marks on her face for the rest of the day. It always did. Just like she knew the contrast dye would change the color of her pee to blue. She tried not to think about what the dye was doing, filling her blood vessels, coloring her insides so the doctors could see if anything looked wrong. She thought of the diagrams of the circulatory system she learned about as a kid. How that was all she was now, lit up blue.

"Comfortable?" the tech asked.

The hard plastic of the tray cut into her sternum. Her breasts dangled through two holes, heavy, terrible things. Her arms were stretched above her head, like a deranged, flying Superman.

Comfortable? She would never be comfortable.

But she would also never say that aloud.

Alice, if nothing else, was a good patient.

She cleared her throat. "Yes," she said.

"You'll be able to communicate and we can hear you if you need us," the tech said. She carried on with the same speech, but Alice tuned it out. She inhaled and exhaled deep and long. *It will be loud, but you're okay,* she told herself. *And then it will be over.* And then Alice could go home to Jeff and whatever dinner he was making and she could think about nonsense things until her results came in and that was that.

The tech closed the door, leaving Alice alone in the room, laying on the tray (tongue) waiting to be slotted into the Machine (mouth). The tech had forgotten to put the blanket over her, but that was fine. Alice didn't mind the cold.

The tray below her jittered and started to back up. She tried very hard not to think about teeth. About cold, hard, plastic teeth coming down, breaking through the skin of her back and her legs, splitting her apart. Chewing and grinding her meat and muscle and bone. She also tried not to think about how small the tube was. How narrow. How if she exhaled her ribcage wouldn't fit.

"Breathe," the tech said as the intercom crackled to life. Alice almost laughed. Breathe. Sure. She was squeezed into the smallest of spaces and the tech wanted Alice to breathe.

Don't move, she told herself. The desire to kick a leg up was overwhelming, but she knew if she did, she would know, definitively, how small this space was, how impossibly narrow. How she shouldn't even fit. Then the panic would start and claw its way down her throat.

The squeal of the intercom filled her ears.

"Okay, we're going to get started."

The whole thing would take about thirty minutes. Less time than a washing at the laundromat—and yet it already felt like time was stretching away from her.

"Are you okay?" the tech asked.

"Yes," Alice said, hearing her own feeble and weak voice. So she said it again, louder. Clearer.

"*Yes.*"

She needed to sound okay because she had to be. She was always okay. Okay was her only state of being.

She took a deep breath, and then another, and the Machine whirled to life around her. Involuntary anxiety flexed Alice's fingers, her knuckles popping.

"Please try to keep still."

Alice wondered if the technician could really see that small a movement. Was she watching that closely? Did she see her fingers lift and resettle on the paper coating?

The Machine blasted an air horn. Alice couldn't help but jump a little. Then, remembering the tech's warning, she froze, her shoulders scrunched up at her ears.

Next came the steady knocking like a big fist pounding on her skull.

You're okay, she told herself.

And for the most part she was.

Until she wasn't.

There was a feeling, right at her ankle—a touch. Like a finger brushed over her naked foot. A tickle, even.

It's the air, she told herself. Still, she lifted her foot and rubbed it against the other.

The airhorn blast sounded again. She jumped even though she didn't want to.

It only took another moment before Alice felt something again. This time on the back of her knee. Another light brush, a finger trailing up her skin—and then a lone nail pressing, pushing deeper.

There's something in the machine, her brain screamed.

She remembered, when she was first diagnosed, the way she imagined someone lying beneath her bed, nestled in the dust bunnies, mimicking her positions. Each time she rolled over, they rolled over. She had strained her ears but couldn't hear anything over the fans that Jeff ran each night. Which was fine—Alice didn't want to hear her own breathing anyway.

Because if she heard hers, then maybe she would hear someone else's. Someone who lay still on the hardwood floor, staring up at the mattress listening to her breathe.

Someone who waited the way an illness waits.

There's something in the machine.

Hard, sharp plastic digging into her sternum, her face sweating against the cushion, Alice squeezed her eyes shut.

"Stop it," she said, her mouth moving without sound.

Before she could even exhale she felt it again. This time it was pressure, like a hand pressing down on the small of her back. She briefly thought of Jeff, when he would rub her lower back to wake her in the morning. But this touch brought no comfort.

"Excuse me," she said.

The airhorn blasted and her whole body jumped. Alice's teeth started to chatter. Had it gotten colder in here?

"Excuse me," Alice said, louder. "Can you hear me? I think something is wrong."

The tech's microphone squealed.

"Did you need to stop? If you need to stop we have to start over from the beginning."

Alice gritted her teeth and swallowed hard. She didn't want to stop, and she knew, in many ways, she didn't need to stop. It was impossible for anything to be in the machine with her. These were phantom feelings. Phantom touches.

They couldn't be real.

"N-no." Alice said. "I'm fine to keep going."

Keep going. That had been her mantra, ever since her diagnosis. As long as she kept her head down, her mind focused, she could avoid a recurrence. She could will "healthy" into existence.

Had it really been ten years?

It's just a matter of time, she thought. *Until it happens again.*

Alice squeezed her eyes shut as the machine started knocking. The sound moved in a circle around, starting on the left and then over her head and then back again on the right. She followed it with her ear, trying not to jump at the sounds.

You're fine, Alice told herself.

But this was a lie. The feeling was there again, just between her shoulder blades. The finest bit of pressure, like a hard object sinking into her skin.

A skeletal finger, digging down.

Alice felt her stomach turn over. For a second, she wondered if she was going to be sick, right here in the MRI machine. Then they would definitely have to stop. How embarrassing.

Yes, *embarrassing*. That was the word. She was acting like a child. This was not Alice. This was not the collected, buttoned-up woman she had become.

The airhorn blasted again and her whole body jumped.

Stop it, she thought.

There were hands on her shoulders. She could feel the individual fingers like worms, wiggling on her skin. And then the pressure as they gripped tighter and tighter.

A scream was born and died in Alice's throat. She froze, unable to move or speak. The feeling, the *thing*, settled across her back. She could feel the weight of it, lining up on the tray (tongue) of the Machine (mouth). Its legs mimicked Alice's. The hands that gripped her shoulders slid up her arms, aligning themselves with hers. She felt another skull on the back of her head. She could swear she felt it breathing in sync with her.

It's the thing under the bed. It's found me.

The air in Alice's lungs finally pushed through and a scream erupted. She spasmed and jumped, her heels slamming into the top of the MRI machine with a painful thud. She pulled her arms toward her body; whatever lay atop her lifted and vanished. With relief she barely had time to register, she realized she no longer felt the pressure of another body.

Still, her heart stuttered and tripped. What was happening?

"I need to get out," Alice yelled. But her voice sounded funny, like someone else was speaking.

She didn't care anymore about being childish. She only needed to move. To run. To get out. That was all that mattered. She arched her back, pressing up against the Machine.

"Hello, please help me," Alice said.

She wondered almost immediately if she'd really said it out loud. The tech's microphone wasn't squealing to life. But the Machine had stopped knocking. Everything was so quiet. Alice could hear her ragged breath.

"Please, let me out," she whispered. The tears came then, hot and fast.

The idea that she was trapped started small, but began to spiral hard and fast, spinning out of control.

She felt it again. The light tickle across her foot.

Dear Lord, she thought. *Please let me out of here. Don't let it touch me.*

But it was touching her. Crawling across her body, the weight and pressure of another living thing trapped inside this machine with her.

Trapped. Yes. She was trapped. Trapped in this machine with *something*.

The quiet felt oppressive—and in it she heard something that turned her stomach cold.

Breathing.

She could hear whatever was in the machine with her *breathing*.

"Somebody please help me," Alice screamed. "Please let me out."

There was a rustling down by her feet. Alice wanted to lift her head but she knew she couldn't turn over. She couldn't even crawl out. The tray (tongue) would have to be extended by the tech who clearly was no longer there.

The tech who left her in here with this *thing*.

The rustling moved to her left. Alice strained her ears. Whatever was crawling around inside the machine was coming up her side. It brushed another feathery finger across the back of her knee and Alice screamed. The tears threatened to choke her.

And then, to her horror, *something* appeared in her narrow field of vision. In the little plastic square cut into the tray. As she lay face-down, staring at what should have been the bottom of the machine, it appeared.

It was dark and shadowed and it took Alice a moment for her brain to snap together what she was seeing. To allow her vision to send pictures to interpret.

It was a face.

It was a woman.

But her skin was pitch black and speckled with stars like the night itself. She had no mouth. Barely a nose. But her eyes were two big starbursts. Like supergiant stars. Like White Dwarfs. Her face filled Alice's view and Alice started screaming. And then the woman (ghost? monster? demon?) reached a thin, long hand up towards Alice's face, and, without hesitation, shoved her fingers into Alice's mouth.

Alice could feel the reality of the woman, the bone and skin of her, against her teeth. She was too frightened to bite down. The woman slipped another hand into Alice's mouth and proceeded to pry her jaw apart.

Alice tried but couldn't scream.

She watched as the woman turned her face upwards, watched those bright, bright eyes nearing. And then the woman shoved her head into Alice's mouth.

Alice gagged and choked but the woman pushed through, pushing past her teeth, down her throat. Alice could feel the coldness of the thing filling her. Alice continued to scream, to try, as this woman, like a dark worm, wriggled inside of her. She could feel the woman's hair passing past her teeth, her tongue, down her throat. She filled Alice, filled her until Alice could feel herself getting pushed out and pushed away.

Until there was nothing but the dark.

***

The tray of the MRI machine rolled slowly out, clicking and groaning as it went.

"All done," the tech said, entering the room. "Everything okay?"

Alice couldn't speak, couldn't move. When the tech helped to lift her off the tray she blinked in the sudden bright light.

"Didn't—didn't you hear me?" she stuttered.

"Hear what?" the tech said, slipping the I.V. out of her hand. "You didn't say anything."

"I …" *I was screaming,* she thought. *Didn't you hear me screaming?*

"You okay?" the tech asked, already moving on to the next thing.

"I'm …" Alice shivered. She felt cold—as cold as space, one might say. "I'm fine."

"We'll be in touch in a few days with results," the tech said, offering Alice her bag of clothing. She plucked the earplugs out of Alice's ears roughly. "If we see anything, we'll schedule a follow-up."

"A follow-up?" Alice whispered, taking the bag.

She looked back at the Machine. At how small it seemed. She put her hand to her mouth, thinking of those cold fingers, the way the woman's hair caught in her teeth. She felt something move inside her, slithering around her organs, settling into place. She shivered again.

Alice climbed off the tray, holding her bag, unsteady on her feet. She walked through the room, suddenly aware that something would now, forever, walk with her.

And without knowing how she knew, she knew, with all her heart, that the tech would find something.

Even Mountains Are Worn Down

A.T. Greenblatt

THE SLENDER ONES ARE TAPPING ON THE DIVIDING GLASS.

It sounds like rain—if rain was sharp, insistent, and determined. I hunch my shoulders and keep scrubbing. The water in the utility sink is so hot my skin stings through the thick rubber gloves. I scour filthy food dishes, waste buckets, and containment boxes and my calves and feet beg for relief half an hour in. But I ignore my body, like I ignore the tapping on the glass from the experiment room.

I last another fifteen minutes before I cave.

The sole armless office chair that can support me is by the floor-to-ceiling windows. I put on my most confident self as I stride across the office space, head held high. Making eye contact with no one. I don't look out the windows as I grip the chair. I don't consider the fifteen-story drop as I wheel it back across the carpeted space with a clenched jaw.

I don't have to. I know it's there.

"Atta girl, Abby," Shira says from her desk, though her back is to me. And I know, then, she's the one that put the chair there. To help "desensitize me from my fear of heights." I want to remind her I'm not one of her subjects, but it won't make a difference. These scientists. They can't help themselves.

My knees thank me, at least, as I tackle the rest of the mountain of fouled-up dishes in the sink.

But even mountains are worn down, and, eventually, I can't avoid it. With a cart towering with freshly-cleaned supplies, I return to the experiment room.

The tapping of the slender ones against the glass barrier increases in speed and intensity as soon as I cross the threshold. I don't know who did it, but I hope whichever genius tapped on the glass once to get these creatures' attention has a special place in hell waiting for them.

Say what you want about the subjects, but they are quick to learn.

The fat ones inch up behind the slender ones when they hear my cart. All the subjects track me as I begin to refill the food and water bowls. Dozens of green or brown or bright black eyes observing and dissecting my movements. Intelligence in hideous faces. These ungodly children of slime mold and rats. Oozing, viscous, semi-translucent beings with their vertebrae, brains, and stomachs visible and twitching in their gelatinous bodies. Their hands, however, are human, or close enough. I'm queasy at the sight of them. The slender ones—the subjects who are either young, or unimaginative, or too stubborn to absorb—use these hands to great, annoying effect. Their tapping gets louder. And louder. Louder still.

I sound the chimes, a warning the subjects know. The floor they stand on will be electrified momentarily, but I wait until all the creatures flee to the inert part of the enclosure. Even for the fat ones, though they are slow and electricity doesn't affect them as acutely as the slender ones. When the safety gate is up between the corner they are crammed into and the rest of the enclosure, I tap the control panel, opening the glass barrier, and work on the filth within.

I do this as quickly as possible, holding my breath. The smell is nauseating. This wasn't part of the job description when I interviewed for the executive assistant role at the company a year ago. But here I am, making myself an asset.

The amount of foulness the subjects excrete on a daily basis is truly amazing. Mondays are the worst. For me. For them.

When the enclosure is significantly more clean, I distribute the food and water bowls throughout the space. It's not enough, but the scientists insist it's important to keep the subjects hungry. I step back and feel something squish, then clang and crunch under my boots. A stomach-turning sound I know well. It's only then I realize I'm not alone in this space.

Grimacing, I lift my shoe. It clings to the floor for a moment, then reluctantly releases. The goo reforms into a familiar shape.

Subject 101 stares up at me. The oldest and fattest of the scientists' creations. Its human-like hands are so armored in bits of plastic and putty and dirt that they have become immobile. It can no longer tap against the glass like the slender ones and it moves slowly, when it deems to move at all. It is one of the most resilient subjects that the team has ever created and its continual survival is a point of pride for Bennett, Shira, and the others.

Even crushed under my weight, the subject is unfazed. And I am, if nothing else, a big woman.

But Subject 101 seems to feel nothing anymore. I pity it. I envy it.

✻✻✻

"Soon we'll be able to launch them to the moon. But without the shuttle." Bennett chuckles as he plucks another pretzel from the bag and tosses it in his mouth.

He's always eating. When I first started working here, I thought it was a sign of genius. A mind constantly working, thinking, using the lion's share of energy so the body remains gaunt. Then it dawned on me that my brain doesn't shut up either, so much so that by the end of the day it's a relief to become a blank slate in front of some cheap-thrills TV. But unlike Bennett, I'm judged when I eat a cheese straw.

"Everything should be good to go," I say with a twist of guilt. Lab assistant wasn't part of my job description either, but here I am. "All you need to do is run the program." I nod at the laptop.

I've been in the office since 5:45 a.m. setting up the experiment, and the large conference room for a staff meeting in the afternoon. Also the coffee makers, lunch delivery, and answering all the emails I was too exhausted to reply to with any semblance of professionalism last night.

"I think this crop is going to work," says Bennett, leaning down to stare at the creatures behind the glass. He says this with every new experiment. With every new batch of test subjects. Today, the youngest, freshest is Subject 2324. Its hands are spindly. It looks unsure, blinking in the fierce fluorescent lights. The older ones undulate, stressed. They know what's coming as Bennett funnels them into the experiment chamber with chimes and electrified floors. Except Bennett's impatient and the subjects that are too slow jump and seize with shocks.

The experiment chamber has been set up to look like a collapsed basement with a gas and water leak. Cement floors are shattered and the ceiling's caved in. There's boxes in the corner, shelves with aging paint cans along the wall. Metal and PVC pipes run the length of the chamber, bent and cracked. It looks almost real; our design engineer, Casey, is quite proud of it. Only difference is that ours is well-lit.

The older ones vibrate with anxiety.

I asked Shira once if the lighting was a design flaw in the experiment. Because, in reality, collapsed areas are dark, and if left to their own devices, the subjects want nothing more than to eat, sleep, and fuck in an unlit corner. Even in dire situations. She didn't answer.

"And here we go." Bennett pulls up the run file on his laptop and hits enter with a flourish.

Nothing happens.

"Abigail, you forgot to turn on the gas. Again." He says this like it's the most obvious thing. And, yes, it's not my first time making this mistake. But wasn't there a fresh cappuccino with hemp milk waiting for him when he ambled into the office at 9:15? He shouldn't be making me feel guilty.

It still works.

I hurry to the utility room as fast as my messed-up lungs will let me. It's a converted janitor's closet and the gas line is a makeshift addition from the office kitchenette, absolutely not approved by the building management and, I'm fairly certain, completely unsafe. I've begged Casey to redo the installation. He keeps promising, but it's been months.

I turn the valve on the gas line. The familiar hiss is followed by the smell of rotten eggs. My palms sweat and my chest tightens.

In the office stairwell there's a sign: "Disabled people wait here in case of emergency." I asked Bennett if there was a rescue plan for me if something goes south. He told me not to worry.

From the experiment room, I hear Bennett cheer the subjects on.

I reenter. Behind the thick glass, the chamber is filling up with water from some of the damaged pipes, while others leak gas. Death from above and below. On the shelves, near the old paint cans, are putty, pipe cutters, quick-dry cement, and all the tools they need to fix this situation.

The subjects have their task.

But they are scrabbling at the chamber's exit. They're fighting for the simple way out. Because just beyond the experiment chamber, there's a dark room filled with food.

The scientists like to keep the subjects hungry for a reason.

I remind myself, again, that these creatures will one day save lives. That the growing epidemic of collapsing houses throughout the country needs resilient workers to make them safe again.

It's only when water rises to their soft midsections that the subjects begin to gasp and heave. The slender ones take fistfuls of putty and smear it on the cracked pipes haphazardly.

"I don't understand," mutters Bennett. "We showed them how to do this."

But I understand. Sometimes you'd do anything to get out.

Subject 101 is the only one that moves methodically. It slithers slowly from leak to leak, dragging tools and materials within its opaque body, like half-consumed tumors. It engulfs the broken sections of pipe with its gelatinous, malleable body. Carefully, it unbends, patches, and replaces damaged sections.

The cleverer subjects catch on. Though they don't have the mass—or tools—Subject 101 has, they use what they can. From the office down the hall, Shira squeals in delight. She always watches the experiments remotely, preferring not to interact with the creatures she and the others created. But, this time, even I'm impressed.

The subjects manage to fix the leaks in thirty-five minutes and twenty-four seconds. It takes another five minutes for the chamber to drain and the air vents to do their job. Afterwards, the ones who can, slink and claw into the lightless room beyond the experiment chamber.

On the faux-basement floor, a great many slender ones and a few fat ones do not move. Dead or comatose, I can never tell. I'll give it twenty-four hours before I clean up and incinerate the bodies, just in case. The next experiment is not scheduled for another three days.

I use the control panel to open the dividing glass as Bennett lopes out of the room, long-limbed and light-hearted. Suddenly, my entire body hurts. I step with care around the incapacitated, limp form of Subject 2324 and begin putting the tools away.

One of the pliers is missing.

I turn around in time to see the pilers slide into Subject 101's body. Sucking and squelching, spilling slime and dirt as it reconfigures its organs to accept this new addition. I briefly considered trying to reclaim it, but we both know I won't. Subject 101 practically has a complete tool kit within it now, and I suspect I'm the only one in the company who knows.

"It's good to be prepared, I guess," I tell it.

It simply watches me with impassive eyes.

✱✱✱

I leave the office around 7:00 that night and take the elevator that rattles like phlegm in a sick chest. I bite my lip so hard, it almost bleeds. I hate this fucking elevator. I hate that my stupid, scarred-up lungs won't let me take the stairs. I hate that no matter what I do for this job, it's never enough.

I realize I am hungry. I planned on making myself a nice meal tonight because experiment days always need a bright spot. But I'm too tired and hungry to even do a basic chicken basil rice dish.

67

So I stop at the southern-cooking fast-food joint at the corner and eat the combo meal on a bench outside. It's too salty and overcooked, but the fried thighs are crispy and fatty. I haven't eaten enough today and somehow that makes the meal taste ungodly good.

It's the mashed potatoes and gravy that ruin it. They're the consistency and color of the subjects' food. Which reminds me of the slimy, flaccid bodies I left on the experiment chamber's floor. Which reminds me of the growing, gnawing hole that guilt is chewing in my stomach. Reminds me of how expendable I feel.

My appetite vanishes. I dump the half-eaten potatoes in the trash and walk to the bus stop. I'll apply to ten more jobs tonight, I promise myself. Things will get better. Eventually.

Onboard, the bus is nearly empty, leaving me with a prime choice of seats close to the rear exit. Small comforts. I like having an escape route if needed. Through the window, I study the passing houses, erect and collapsed. Every month there's a few more ruined ones along the route, the land underneath it inexplicably giving out. And no one knows why.

I tell myself that the office is safe, that high-rises have deep foundations and are routinely checked. But it rarely makes me feel better.

God, I should have never taken this fucking job.

I check my personal email when I get back to my apartment. It's a small, but cheerfully decorated, one-bedroom on the ground floor. Cozy. My inbox has nothing but promos and more blanket application rejections.

I sink into the couch, but refuse to let in the creeping despair. I'll hold out at this gig a little longer. Air conditioning; a boss who's willing to hire a fat, chronically-ill woman with a BA in philosophy; and health insurance is a rare and holy trifecta in this economy.

Then I see it; an email from the law firm that made me go through six rounds of interviews two weeks ago. *Dear Abigail, thank you so much for your interest and time, but unfortunately …*

My dad had this saying: "Things will probably get worse before they get better, but they'll get better." I've clung to that mantra, though it never did get better for him.

Suddenly, my apartment is tight and airless. I have to get out. Get out, Abigail, get out. I grab my keys, but forget to lock the door. I don't care.

Tonight, like most nights, I find myself at the old quarry down the road. I lean over the railing and try to see the bottom. I never can; it's too deep, the ground gave way five years ago and maybe there is no bottom. Still I stare down, down, down.

The scientists are wrong about me. It's not heights that I'm afraid of.

✳✳✳

"It's a terrible idea," I say to anyone who will listen. No one's listening. It's been three days since the last experiment, since Subject 101 swallowed the pliers. Two days since I cleaned the experiment chamber of bodies and sent out another twenty resumes.

The scientists want to add fire to the mix and I've been here since 6:30 a.m. writing emails and making phone calls.

"We need to show progress," Bennett says, tapping the dividing glass. "Progress equals money. And we need money." The subjects are already in the experiment chamber and they jump at every sharp tap of Bennett's fingers.

One of the younger ones, Subject 2320, slides up to the glass, and stares directly at Bennett. It raises one of its eerie human hands. Bennett grins.

"Aw," he says.

It tightens its hand into a fist and, with surprising force, pounds the glass.

"What the hell!" Bennett jumps back in surprise.

More subjects crowd the glass. The slender ones begin to pummel the barrier, making the experiment chamber vibrate. The fat ones throw themselves against the divide for the same effect.

"What the hell?" Bennett says again, but hushed.

"They're quick," I say. "I think they've figured out the tests get harder." I omit that I accidentally taught them that when I slammed my fists against the experiment room wall this morning, reading through the test plan in plain view of the subjects.

"Is that your expert opinion as an executive assistant?" Bennett snaps.

The slender ones' pounding gets louder.

"Run the experiment, Abigail." He points to the laptop.

Really, it's a small slight.

But it's enough.

"I called the building management about the gas line," I say, not moving.

"What?" Bennett's face turns pale. "When?"

The pounding sounds like a hail storm.

"This morning."

"What's happening in there?" Shira's voice is barely audible from down the hall.

"For fuck's sake." Bennett grabs the laptop. A moment later, there's the familiar hiss and smell of sulfur. The pounding stops as every face, human and hybrid, turns towards the broken pipes within the experiment chamber.

Then everything erupts in flame.

This time, the subjects are expected to make repairs as everything burns. It is too much. For them. For me.

When I was fifteen, my childhood house was one of those that unexpectedly collapsed. One day the ground was solid, the next it was quicksand and mud. I was in my bedroom when it happened. The window was stuck. Something in the kitchen was burning. The air became smoke. And dust. I couldn't get out. The ground—it was too near. Too far.

The subjects shriek as the tools burn their hands.

"Turn it off," I say. But the scientists aren't listening.

It is too much. I reach over to the control panel and open the dividing doors. The subjects come spilling out. The slender ones scurry to dark, safe areas, and the fatter ones follow. Behind them, the flames are still raging.

Horror seizes every cell of my body. Opening the glass divide should have killed the experiment and automatically shut off the valves.

"It didn't work," says Bennett.

"Turn the gas off!" I shout and rush over to the sink. Bennett runs to the utility room. Where the fuck is the fire extinguisher?

"It's stuck!" His voice is muffled from the next room over, but his panic is clear. The flames have found a stack of paper towels.

I hurry over to the utility room expecting to run into Bennett. But he's not there. I scream as I strain against the gas valve. It takes both hands, but I do it. I turn it shut.

I sit down hard on the floor, gasping.

The hissing sound is still there.

Oh, god, there's holes and cracks in the line.

"Help!" I shout and scramble into the office. But my co-workers are streaming towards the stairs.

When I was fifteen, my house inexplicably collapsed and I was trapped. Until my dad knocked down my door and carried me out. My lungs were never the same from the smoke and dust. But he didn't survive.

I promised myself I would never be trapped again.

Subject 101 is watching me from the utility room entrance. I'm not even surprised.

"Nothing bothers you anymore, does it?" I say, getting to my feet. I pick it up, feel its oozing, grimy body drip through my fingers and I want to recoil, even now. Instead, I say: "We've been in a trap all along, haven't we?"

It blinks at me.

It's heavier than it looks, but I suppose that's all the tools it carries within it. I place the creature down near the leaking pipe. I smell the experiment chamber burning, feel the heat through the wall.

"Please," I say. Subject 101's eyes are unreadable as I leave.

I go to the stairwell's rescue area to wait.

I wonder if help will come.

Evergreen
Robert Perez

SNOWFLAKES COLLECTED ON CHLOE'S EYELASHES as she searched the cloudy sky for the moon. She imagined her little brother Silas staring up at the same moon, expecting the silhouette of Santa's sleigh to dash across like a wishing star. She pictured her mother reading a poetry book on the sofa and drinking a cup of valerian tea.

As Christmas Eve crawled toward midnight, the group of strangers continued marching through the winding neighborhoods. They passed a lawn with a family of snow-people and Chloe shivered under the scrutiny of unblinking coal. It was as if the figures of ice were silently taunting them with a shared ephemeral fate; had they already outlasted the hands which sculpted them?

The end of civilization had many names—Hollylock, Ouroboros, The Devil's Halo—but it was originally called Evergreen. The most popular holiday decoration to hit the shelves since fake snow was a super GMO: an instant wreath, a Christmas tree in a can, moss in aerosol form. The product was resistant to temperature extremes and flourished on everything. The instructions on the can warned against skin exposure and inhalation. Within a month people started bathing in weed killer, and many died of drinking it. Verdant hills rolled into the distance as the heaps of bodies grew. Cities became giant hedge mazes where all who wandered were lost. The world synchronized in artificial spring.

Not long ago, the group would've been mistaken for carolers, and now they would forever be refugees. All the holiday songs

72

had become dirges. Chloe had sheltered at home for weeks, praying for the safe return of her mother and brother. The last time she saw Silas he was running out the door, excited for the upcoming school day. The last time Chloe saw her mother she was standing in her bedroom doorway, backlit by the hall light. She remembered her mother saying goodnight and gently pulling the door shut. Chloe had never seen or known her father, but she hoped for humanity's sake he was somewhere out there, surviving.

Eventually hunger and desperation pried Chloe from the safety of her home. She covered up her exposed flesh and ventured out into a transformed world where plants moaned, screamed, and begged to be burned. The nearby grocery store had been ransacked for most of the non-perishable food, but she did end up finding other people to band together with. The group started out as twelve, but over the miles and days their number dwindled down to six. Some days they'd wake and find a member or two had vanished in the night. No one needed to ask any questions. It was easier to keep moving. There were rumors of places where Evergreen had not spread. Some believed there was hope in Death Valley.

The group trudged south through brightly lit cemeteries that were once suburbia. They crossed paths with a deer covered in Evergreen; it ignored their presence, nuzzling into its grassy hide, eating itself. The snow was relentless and hindered their progress. The longer they traveled, the deeper their footprints became. They had to find shelter soon. Chloe was cold and exhausted, but the group could not stop. Each house they passed was marked by a wreath on the door.

As they pushed through the drifts, Chloe tried to ignore the creeping ache in her hand. She prayed it was just frostbite, but fell back from the others all the same. She watched the group walk away from her as if in slow motion, realizing she might not ever touch another human again. She held up her aching hand and tried to remember her last embrace. Before she removed the glove, memories of hugs and kisses flooded her mind. Trying to hold back her tears and failing, she laughed bitterly. If from this moment forward her touch resulted in a death sentence, then at least her life would be short.

She carefully pulled each finger of the glove loose, took a deep breath, and revealed her hand. Chloe had a green thumb. The discoloration spread to the center of her palm, a tingling sensation dancing along the edges of her hand. The affected skin was dry and cracking, with tiny hair-like green needles sprouting painfully from the fissures. She rewound her days trying to remember anything she'd touched that might have been tainted, or if she had shared anything with the others. Earlier this morning, before she put on her gloves, her hand had been fine.

In a way, it was a relief. Surrender meant sleeping in a warm bed. Doom was her key to a lost world. Chloe thought of all the holiday presents that would remain wrapped forever and vowed to open as many as possible while she still had time.

As the distance between her and the group stretched, she found it difficult to speak. It would be so easy to slip away unnoticed into the swirling snow, but she felt that she owed them a warning. Her voice cracked on the first try, and was stolen by the wind on the second, but she finally managed to call out.

"Hey!"

The group turned around.

She waved at them with her ungloved hand. "Good luck!"

They ran when they realized the truth; no goodbyes or backward glances. She couldn't blame them. Her tears were freezing on her cheeks, but she didn't have to be cold anymore.

Chloe picked the nicest house on the block and walked up the driveway. She could buy herself an extra week if she cut off her hand, as long as she didn't botch the self-amputation; she had seen it done before. She used to cling to the hope that great minds were working on a way to stop the green invasion they'd started, but she was beginning to doubt if anyone would live to see the New Year.

She would become a garden. Chloe considered which seeds should fill her pockets. She wondered what it would be like to be a dandelion.

Muscle Man
Lena Ng

THE STAGE LIGHTS REFLECTED OFF THE FINAL TWO COMPETITORS'
SKIN, accentuating each curve and ripple of tanned, honed muscle.
Like living sculptures cut with God's own chisel, they had worked
for months, every day in the gym, to tone, bulk, perfect flesh as
clay. Bobby Delinger on the left, the reigning 1984 World
Champion Pro Level Mr. Muscle Man, versus up-and-comer
Frank Testaroni on the right.

The spotlight shone on Bobby. He was known in bodybuilding
circles for his commitment to both size and symmetry. Usually,
guys had one or the other. But what set Bobby apart was the
whole package. Bulky, but with a clean, tapered waist. Tall with a
heavy-set jaw, too brute to be handsome, but faces weren't judged
in this type of competition. Bobby started his final pose sequence
with a front lat spread, curled fists on his hips, showing off the
width of his shoulders. From there, he transitioned into back
double biceps, then side chest, then vacuum pose. He brought
each of the classic poses to the next level. Not only physically
flawless, but he was a genuine guy, as well. Hard-working,
focused, quiet in speech and manner, despite the showmanship
needed during competitions. He ended by flexing both his front
biceps. The three judges looked impressed.

That's not to say Frank Testaroni wasn't a worthy contender.
He wasn't yet taken seriously in bodybuilding circles—he had
placed seventh three years ago in the Easton Pro Cup, his debut
at pro level, and had only placed fifth in last year's Mr. Muscle

Man. He worked hard however, and anyone who followed bodybuilding could see his potential.

The judges took notes and whispered amongst themselves. Finally, the head judge crooked a finger and passed an envelope to the jovial, black-tied host for the night's event. The drum rolled with a moment of high drama.

"And the winner of the 1985 Pro Level Mr. Muscle Man competition, located here in gorgeous San Francisco, is ..." The drum roll stopped and the host cracked open the envelope. "... Frank Testaroni!"

There was an instant of disbelief before Bobby's body deflated. He took a step back on the stage. The spotlight shifted to focus on the winner and Bobby was left standing in the dark. The host put out a hand and Frank shook it, his head tilted to look at the flashing camera lights, his smile a bright, white beam.

Bobby's thoughts were churning at the required press conference after. He had no idea why he had lost. This year he had added an additional twenty pounds. A little thickening in the abdomen? His muscle striations weren't as prominent and cleanly defined as he had wanted them to be. Was that the issue?

The questions were now directed to his competitor.

"Mr. Testaroni, wuddya think you did differently this year?"

Frank ran a hand over his blonde buzzcut. "No offense to Mr. Delinger, but he's a bit, you know, old school. I've been trying some new techniques, new supplements. I've been drinking a tablespoon of Ready's High Protein Powder every day before my work-out. They're not paying me to say that, by the way, but if they want to get in touch with my agent, I'm open to representing 'em. Then there's—"

A high whine seemed to fill Bobby's ears, drowning out whatever Frank was saying. He looked at the thick gold ring on his pinky, the winner's ring from last year's competition.

He couldn't be a has-been already, could he?

***

The coach dropped a clean towel around Bobby's neck.

"Them's the breaks, unfortunately. Can't win 'em all." At Bobby's silence, the coach continued. "Maybe, just maybe, you'll now listen to some of the new techniques I've been talking about. That protein powder Frank was blathering on about, there's something to it, you know. Then there's amino acids, creatine, citrulline. Times are changing, science advancing. Diet and exercise, yes, but also supplements and medical supervision.

"Look, I know a good place to get you started."

***

The girl didn't look like she'd be someone working at a supplement shop. All these big guys, guys whose arms didn't touch the sides of their body, milling around, and there she was, a tiny thing who looked like she'd blow over if one of them sneezed too hard.

Bobby was always bad at talking to women, especially to the ones he thought were pretty. And this girl was pretty, in a kindergarten teacher sort of way. He'd rather talk to another guy. But she seemed to be the only employee, so silently Bobby gave her his list. He glanced at her red nametag—Ariana–and thought it was a nice name. She studied his list, carefully went to each shelf, and soon his basket was full.

When she rang him up, he was able at least to murmur, "Thank you, Ariana," glancing down at the top of her head.

***

Bobby grabbed the bar with a hook grip, bent his knees and lifted the three-hundred-pound weights. He straightened his arms and held up the bar for two seconds before dropping the weights down on the mat.

He practiced five reps each, adding weights in fifty-pound increments. He topped out at five hundred pounds and bent over his knees, puffing. A pounding started in his temple. Sweat dripped over his checks and off his jaw. He threw himself on the bench, rubbing the bridge on his nose. He was done. Who was he kidding? He'd never get better. This was the end of the line for him.

Bobby could hear his father's voice. "What, you think Daddy is going to solve all your problems? The big pick on the small. That's the way things work. You don't want to get picked on, you got to get big. In the meantime, stop your snivelling."

Bobby gritted his teeth and got up from the bench. He signalled for his coach.

"More weights."

Five hundred and fifty pounds.

He gripped the bar with both hands, took a deep breath, and lifted.

"More."

Six hundred.

"More."

Six-fifty.

He'd never pushed himself this far. One more go. Seven hundred. With a grunt and a snap of technique, Bobby held the weight for a second above his head before he had to let go with a crash.

His coach was hollering. "Way to go, man. A new record!"

To celebrate, Bobby had a protein shake for lunch.

***

After a few weeks and a few mores times in the store, Bobby finally got up the courage to mumble, "How come you're working here anyway?" At least Ariana knew his name, and she greeted him pleasantly each time he came in.

"My uncle gave me this job," she said. "He owns the store. Mom said what better place to meet a man than here."

Bobby's heart sank. "So you have a boyfriend?"

She shook her head.

Bobby was shocked and felt a hopeful flutter in his chest.

"All these guys and none of 'em asked you out?"

Ariana gave a slight shrug. "Not their type." Which was likely true since she didn't have any figure to speak of. "Not anyone's type."

Bobby's heart seemed to bloom in his chest and the burst of feeling gave him the bravery to ask, "Can I take you out sometime for coffee?"

Her smile answered his question.

***

More than a few glances shot their way as Bobby and Ariana entered the coffee shop. They made for an odd pair—one hulking man with a thick neck and built like Thor, with a girl who looked like she'd need help shelving encyclopedias.

At Bobby's urging, Ariana took a seat at a table in the corner. He stood in line and soon joined her, a large black coffee in one hand and a caramel latte in the other. He briefly worried that the chair wouldn't hold his weight, but he was used to being careful around furniture.

They sipped their coffees in shy silence. Finally, Bobby blurted out, "How come you're still single? Pretty girl like you."

A shade of red started at the base of Ariana's neck and flowed into her cheeks.

Bobby hung his head. He did it again. He always said the wrong things to women. That's why he preferred to stay silent, hoping one of them would approach him, impressed by his size or achievements. But whether they were intimidated or freaked out by his size, or just thought he was a meat-head, none of them ever did. Ariana, he thought, would be used to seeing muscular guys, so that was one of the reasons he took a chance at asking her out.

"I'm sorry," he said. "I shouldn't have asked such a personal question."

Ariana smiled ruefully. "It's not that. It's just that when you asked that question, I had a flashback to Christmas, when Aunt Cupid said she knew a nice guy I should meet. He turned out to be a jerk. Or Thanksgiving when Uncle George said he was still waiting on a wedding invitation."

"I'm not good at this."

"What?"

"You know, talking to women."

"Really?" Bobby could see she was teasing.

"You don't mind dating a has-been?" he asked. "Not like I'm a winner these days."

Ariana's expression turned to puzzlement. "Do you think that would affect me dating you?"

Bobby scanned her warm soft eyes and honest, open expression.

"No, I don't think it would," he said.

But inside he wasn't sure.

✳✳✳

Bobby switched up his meal routine and experimented with supplements. He tried to change this workout routine by increasing the reps, weight loads, and muscles exercised. At night, his body ached and he would alternate ice packs and hot baths to try to relieve the pain. Every three to six months, as he did the competition circuit, he was rewarded for all his efforts by hearing:

"And the winner for this year's WBBO competition … Bill Tiller!"

"And the winner for this year's Easton Pro Cup … Skip Johnson!"

"And the winner for this year's Mr. Galaxy competition … Alex Hughes!"

Each competition was another humiliation. Bobby had taken his previous victories for granted. He was getting complacent. He was hungry to get back on top, for the journalists to ask him how he did it, to have people at the gym congratulating him instead of watching what they said so as not to offend him. Now they rushed by him to the new winner as though Bobby was invisible.

"Look," his coach said. "Why don't you hang up the towel? You've had a good run, let someone else take the lead."

Bobby looked at him with red eyes.

"You don't believe in me anymore."

"It's not that, Bobby. But every athlete has their time. For some, it's a long career. For others … it's a short one."

"I'm not done."

"Just think about it."

"I'm not done."

The coach took in a few deep breaths. He'd seen what happened when guys stayed in too long. They got injured, sometimes permanently, with spinal problems or with pain from sciatica that could make a grown man scream.

"We'll get you a new doctor," he said, "someone specializing in athletes." At Bobby's glance, the coach lowered his voice. "You're a good guy. You want to do things by the books. It's the other guys, though … they're willing to do things that give them an edge. And there *are* ways to get an edge, all aboveboard, all within the rules."

"What to do you mean?"

"Basketball players are tall. No one complains that they have an advantage."

"What are you getting at?"

"The competitions screen for doping. They don't, however, screen for genetics."

Bobby put his head in his immense hands. This was not the route he wanted to go. But he was tired of losing, of being a loser.

Quietly, he asked, "Does it come with any risks?"

The coach shrugged. "With everything, there are risks, unintended consequences. But there are no drugs involved. It's currently being tested on cattle to produce more meat with less fat. Scientists remove a gene that produces myostatin. No myostatin means more muscle growth. Technically, it's not cheating. And even if it is, how do you know your competitors aren't doing the same?"

Bobby thought about it. Maybe it was true that his competition had already gone through this procedure. He was always late on the uptake. That would explain Bruce Kellar, taking home the North Division title, and even ninth-ranked Tom Murray, who unexpectedly won the Crown competition. He needed this procedure just to be a contender.

"I'll think about it," he said.

✳✳✳

After his workout and shower, Bobby walked back to his fifth-floor apartment in the Hunter's Point neighborhood. It was one of the poorest neighborhoods in San Francisco, but the only place he could afford and still be able to eat the number of calories a bodybuilder needed. He had a couple hundred left from his previous winnings, but unless he was able to get more endorsements, he wouldn't make rent.

He glanced at the pictures on the table. Beaming, arms up, first place medal around his neck. Why didn't he appreciate his victories more? Why did he feel only relief at the time? He looked at the card his coach had given him, dialed the number, and made an appointment.

✳✳✳

In the darkness of self-doubt and second guesses, Bobby stared at the water-stained ceiling as he lay on his bed. Bodybuilding was where he could have some semblance of control, where hard work was made visible in every line and curve of his physique. Wasn't what he was about to do just another extension of this? Only in his case, it would be on a permanent level. But he was committed to following his dream. Who would he be if he wasn't a bodybuilding champion? He'd be a guy shining shoes or making burgers or parking cars. He'd be one of those guys that no one sees, invisible, someone to make other's people's lives more comfortable, only to struggle on minimum wage in his own life. Only with bodybuilding and getting bigger did people see him. How could they not?

Ariana, with her soft eyes, seemed to be one of the few people who saw past the form and into the person inside. Would she like that person? Would he? Without his muscles and awards, was there anything left to like?

The next day, after Bobby had listened to the spiel and signed all the consents, the doctor hooked up the IV. During the three-hour infusion, Bobby tried to relax and visualize victory while the genetics-altering material flowed through his veins.

***

Ariana's face lit up when she saw Bobby as he walked into the store.

"Hey, haven't seen you for a while," she said.

Bobby unloaded his items on the belt and she scanned them in.

"I won't be back for a bit," he explained. "Gotta work on my form, get serious again." He started to place his items in a bag.

"Oh." She couldn't hide her disappointment. "You need supplements, though, right? And you need to eat. Don't tell me you don't need coffee. We can always go out again."

Bobby focused on putting away his items. "Can't afford the distraction."

He felt awful seeing the drop in her face. He didn't want to hurt her feelings, but he didn't want to drag her into whatever was happening with him.

He tried not to hurt her. "It's not you. It's—the timing's not right." He picked up the bag. "Maybe I'll see you around."

***

"Whatever you're doing, keep it up." The coach nodded his head in approval. The muscle striations were well-defined and clean, the thick veins prominent. "Man, you're a giant now. Let's get you on the scale."

It was a groundbreaking three hundred and ten pounds of sculpted muscle. Bobby was shocked himself. After the procedure, he had put on twenty pounds in two weeks. Easily. Not having to gulp down ten thousand calories from eggs, chicken breasts, and lean steaks. No more powders or shakes. He hadn't even increased his workout time. The muscle just kept coming, as though growing in his sleep.

✳✳✳

Bobby sat uncomfortably on the couch. He'd tossed and turned on the bed, but sleep eluded him with the pain in his back. He felt slightly better upright on the couch. He turned on the TV, but nothing was on this time of night. Finally, he settled for an old black-and-white movie. King Kong was climbing the Empire State Building, holding Fay Wray, while the choppers circled and shot at him. Bobby fell asleep to the quiet staccato pops of gunfire.

After two hours, a twitch awoke him, and after several minutes staring at the wood panelling, Bobby flipped to a news channel. This time, demonstrators were protesting the use of what they called Frankenmeat. The word had leaked about genetic modification of beef.

"What will happen if we eat it? How will it affect us and other animals in the food chain? The meat is not fit for human consumption," a protestor told the reporter.

A shaky night-vision clip was aired: shocking footage, the animals growing to gigantic proportions, but developing health problems, knees buckling, suffocating under their weight, ribs crushed as they hit he ground. Carcasses that looked like cows, if cows were giant melted balls of meat thrown in a fire.

What would happen if this meat got into the food chain? Bobby thought. It was too late for him, but he wasn't on the menu for consumption.

He was drifting off to sleep when another twinge woke him. A muscle in his left arm twitched like it was attached to a voltage meter. As he watched, Bobby could see a muscle enlarging. Swelling like an expanding cord of rope, rippling and thickening.

A muscle twitched in his right arm. The eerie reflection of the television glowed in his eyes as he watched the muscle wriggle and bulge. Bobby felt a twinge on his face. He touched his cheek and it swelled under his fingers. He got up from his chair and had to stoop to avoid hitting the ceiling. He ducked into the washroom to see his reflection in the mirror. The muscles around his eyes, his forehead, his chin wriggled and welled. His brow thickened and grew heavier. His eyes looked more deep-set against the deepening flesh. His neck seemed to meld into his shoulders.

The muscles on his legs writhed like a den of snakes. Skin raised and rippling. Not only moving but growing. Bobby's legs widened to double their thickness. Soon he wouldn't fit through the bathroom door. He pushed his way out, cracking and splintering the door's wooden frame.

✳✳✳

The next day, after her shift at work, Ariana made her way to Bobby's apartment building. She walked slowly down the shabby hallway, checking the numbers on the doors under flickering lights, the plastic bag she carried rustling with the weight of the plastic containers.

Ariana reached apartment 507. She gave a light tap on the door. No answer. She tapped again. She was about to leave the bag of supplements outside when she noticed fluid seeping under the door. She slowly turned the handle.

Don't come in, Bobby wanted to say. But the muscles had overgrown his larynx and the words came out as incomprehensible grunts.

Ariana didn't know what she saw, but she screamed and screamed and screamed. Later, she could recall little of what she had seen; the horrifying sight had snapped her memory. She could remember only flashes of something monstrous. Flesh. Flesh everywhere, filling the apartment to the ceiling. Glistening, bulbous skin. Damp, gelatinous skin with twitching muscle rippling beneath the expanse of pink. Muscle that bulged and pulsed and seized like electrified worms. Tiny eyes in the centre of the mass of what was once a face.

The mass was moving toward her like a monstrous slug.

A cord of flesh shoved her back out of the apartment. The door slammed in her face. In her terror, the only thing that Ariana could do was run.

✱✱✱

The choppers were circling. The buzz of rotor blades dipped and fell like metallic mosquitos. There was something hideous in San Francisco Bay. Something large and alien, pink-fleshed and wider than Levi's Stadium, standing taller than the Salesforce Tower. It might have once been human, if a massive candle-shaped human had been melted into a gigantic mound of pink, oozing meat.

A pop and flash of light. The *rat-ta-tat-tat* of machine guns firing. The flesh monster roared and waved swollen arms, flicking the choppers away like flies, churning the water with its weight.

Another wave of its arms and the Golden Gate Bridge snapped like it was made of popsicle sticks. Cars zoomed and swerved, leaving tread marks on the concrete. Some fell into the heaving water, swiftly sinking into its depths.

Someone stood watching, her hand over her mouth, on the sidewalk. Ariana stared at the monster and recognized familiar eyes, a flash of the thing in Bobby's apartment. She jumped up and down, waving her arms.

"Bobby, Bobby, no! Bobby, stop!"

His immense blob-like face turned, the sight of Ariana focusing his still-human eyes. Beneath the rippling cords of muscular flesh, she could see that Bobby was still there, still inside the gigantic mound.

The waves rolled with each movement of Bobby's legs. Ariana watched as Bobby moved across the waters of the Bay. The ground shook with each underwater earthquake from each giant step. Neither seemed to be aware of the danger. The shifting of the earth created a giant tsunami.

Before he could reach her, a wall of water crashed and swept Ariana away.

Bobby moved closer to the shore, but his steps created another wave that pushed her further and further away from him. He bent and began to crawl on colossal hands and bloated knees.

Ariana was caught in the branches of a tree, her face slack, her hair a soft brown tangle. She was pale and unmoving, limp. Bobby held her body, to him the size of a caterpillar, in his giant palm. He tried to rub her chest with the tip of his little finger. Water gushed from her mouth. He turned her to her side with a slow move of his index finger. Her body slipped between his fingers and fell into the water.

She didn't resurface.

Bobby crouched and put his face below the water's surface. He caught a glimpse of Ariana's body pulled out with the receding wave. He crawled out, following her, but each move pushed the water and her body further out to sea. Bobby knew if he moved too far away from shore, he would sink and drown.

But he had to find her.

Bobby crawled further from the shore. Soon, he could no longer touch the bottom. Underwater, he caught a glimpse of a tangle of brown hair. He stretched and reached until he caught her. He cradled her body in the palm of his hand, clutched against his bulbous chest. Bobby turned and struggled to swim back to the shore. He kicked his legs and thrashed his arms, his palm in a loose grip so as not to crush Ariana's body. But the tides moved relentlessly and drew him deeper into the ocean's heart.

Eventually, his hand relaxed and Ariana drifted away.

✳✳✳

Bobbie's body travelled, currents pulling it further and further offshore until it sank to a depth no man had yet explored. Despite the darkness, despite the pressure, despite the lack of oxygen, there still was life. Giant isopods resembling sea beetles, with rows of claws and armoured, ghost-white bodies, tip-toed over the fleshy underwater mountain. Spider crabs with spiny legs and shells joined them. Scavenging fish–barracudas, hagfish, even a juvenile great white–plucked mouthfuls of meat from the decaying body, tearing and swallowing the chunks whole.

All these creatures picked and scraped and feasted on the giant mass of muscular flesh. Like whale fall, Bobby's remains fed an entire ecosystem. His mass of flesh had no bones remaining since they had been pulverized by the invading muscle growth. The sea creatures feasted, tugging with claws, twisting off chunks of flesh with serrated teeth, until, after the passage of many days, nothing remained.

***

The battered trawler, white paint peeling, rocked on the rhythm of the waves.

"Haul 'er up," said the grizzled fisherman in the yellow rain-slicker. Another younger fisherman turned the crank handle until the day's catch hung in the nets over the deck.

The grizzled fisherman's mouth gaped open as he looked at the net's contents.

"That's one ugly fucker."

It was definitely ugly. Big and ugly. It had extended jaws like a giant barracuda; eyes blacker and larger than a deep ocean squid; long, sensing whiskers like willow switches hanging from each cheek. But its body … its body was unlike any fish the grizzled fisherman had seen in his forty-plus years hauling catch. The body, larger than a great white shark, but with rippling cords of muscle snaking down the length and width of its body. Muscle that twitched and spasmed like it was hooked up to a voltage meter.

As the two fishermen stared at the catch in horrified wonder, the net started shaking. The monstrous, muscular fish starting jerking from side-to-side, before clamping down on whatever else had been caught in the net. Rivulets of blood ran down the netting and dripped onto the deck.

"It's eating the catch!"

The grizzled fisherman grabbed a harpoon and starting jabbing. The muscular fish jerked and thrashed. A cord of muscle flew from the body, lashed through the net, and whipped the grizzled fisherman across the face. The older man was flung backwards, sliding across the deck.

One rope of the netting snapped. The jaws broke through the hole and the older fisherman could see it had three rows of serrated teeth. Another rope snapped. Soon the monstrous fish would be freed onto the deck. Despite its easy meal in the netting, it still looked hungry.

"Throw it back in! Throw it back in before it gets us next!" screamed the grizzled fisherman.

The younger fisherman turned the crank and yanked the rope. The net pivoted once more over the open ocean. He pressed the release button and the net opened, releasing the day's catch, and the monster fish slid back into the sea. They watched with racing hearts as its monstrous silhouette disappeared back into the ocean's void.

Later, when recalling their story over a couple of beers, the fishermen tried to convince themselves it was only a hallucination, the result of hot sun and too many days at sea.

Sincerely, the Guy Who Saved Your Asses
Pooja Joshi

THE PROBLEM, AS IT SO OFTEN IS, was our apparent inability to just sit down and be fucking grateful.

If only we could have weeded that out of our DNA.

I guess it's best to start with when Bangkok went underwater. That was the real *oh, shit* moment. It wasn't so bad until then. Amsterdam pushed their expiration date out with some ingenious levee construction. Venice just became a houseboat city full of half-submerged ruins—the marketing was *chef's kiss*. The resorts all hightailed it out of the Maldives, and everyone else drained out pretty soon after. And no one really gave a shit about Basra. So it was Bangkok that really lit everyone's pants on fire.

Everywhere was sinking. At least the Thai prime minister had a plan. Sea walls and the like. There were conferences with the Americans and even an agreement with Japan to help with all the construction. But two back-to-back typhoons and the tsunami? Well, that really forced their hand, didn't it?

Really, they shouldn't have turned to the Americans or the Japanese at all. The solution was right there in Thailand the whole time. Dr. Chankimha told me he'd been working it out for years, ever since it became pretty clear to him that the engineers weren't going to be able to solve the problem fast enough. He was the head of genetics at Chula at the time—super sharp fellow, obviously.

I met him at a conference in Osaka two years before he died. He told me his whole theory, and I couldn't understand why he was struggling so much to get funding for it. The fundamental idea was to stop trying to fight nature and learn to live with it. To cut the arrogance out and coexist with the planet instead of trying to tame it. Guy was ahead of his time. Apparently, I was one of the very few people who had listened to him, because, when he died, he left the notebooks containing his life's work to me. You can imagine my shock when I showed up at my office in Cambridge one morning to see a pile of heavy boxes and a super pissed DHL guy.

So, anyway, it was Dr. Chankimha's idea to start, but I'll take credit for actually executing everything. The science wasn't even the hard part—again, I have Dr. Chankimha to thank for figuring all of that out. The hard part was the politics. Pretty much every institution I talked to laughed at me when I explained the need for—these are their words, not mine—"radical human experiments." My department head at MIT ended up putting me on forced sabbatical—basically, I had turned into a liability for her.

Right before I was booted out of Cambridge, I was able to get in touch with some folks in Bangladesh, and they were okay with me running the first experiments out there. I mean, down in Cox's Bazar? That's where they put all the refugees from Myanmar. Desperate people. People ready to do pretty much anything that promised some respite. The place was flooded every monsoon season. I didn't meet anyone who hadn't lost someone to the floods. So, yeah, I could see why they all wanted in on the serum.

The administration process was quite straightforward. Chance of failure was obviously high, given the early stages of it all. But if it worked? The first few days were a little painful. It's not easy for the human body to let itself get infected in such an invasive way. But once you got past that hurdle and all the phenotypical changes had manifested, you were good to go. Usually.

My team was in the process of running a (somewhat surprisingly) successful experiment in Cox's Bazar, pretty much out of sight, out of mind from the ivory towers of the world, when it all went to shit in Bangkok. Some wily American researcher went and spilled the beans to the UN—that he'd traveled to coastal Bangladesh and found a "colony of merpeople" happily living in a bunch of mostly submerged villages.

Hated that guy. *Merpeople*. Glad that never caught on. They were huphins. A genetic hybrid of humans and dolphins. It was the perfect adaptation to counter the relentless rise of the sea. When the waters came in, huphins could survive under the waves. When the waters receded, they could survive on the land. Every single huphin who'd taken the serum was thrilled with it. Well, I should caveat that. We did lose some people, so, obviously, we weren't able to get any feedback from them. Science isn't always a sure-fire thing, you know? But we worked out the kinks over a few months. Way faster than most scientists work. We had to, didn't we?

Obviously, the UN had something to say about the whole thing, citing "inhumane experimentation" and "war crimes" — what war they thought I was waging, I don't know. It didn't make sense to me. I was a bona fide superhero, not some diabolical post-modern Mengele.

But before anyone cracked down on me, the Thais called and told me to make a beeline for Chiang Mai. They gave me asylum and said I could have whatever resources I needed to start mass-administering the serum in Bangkok. I must admit, I was giddy about the prospect. Cox's Bazar had been a good start, but it was a small achievement, on the fringes of society. This was one of the world's biggest cities, and I had an official green light this time.

We were able to get the serum to over a million people in the first three months. Huge success, if you ask me. Obviously, a lot of people had doubts about turning into something that felt very *other*. I instructed my teams not to spend too much time convincing them. If they wanted to drown, they could drown. Everyone who was committed to surviving would survive first.

They started building the Marine Sector soon after that. Most of Tha Kham was already abandoned and underwater, so we started there, rebuilding the structures to be adaptable under and above water. And then the huphins started moving in. Honestly speaking, it was insane for me to see it happen. It was like building a new civilization, an entirely new species, in under a decade. We even inaugurated a university down in the Marine Sector—Chankimha Technological University, in the old professor's honor.

The UN couldn't really keep being a bitch-baby after seeing the success we were having in Bangkok.

People across the world were talking about it. A couple of Russian billionaires snuck their families into Thailand to get the serum illegally, and then all hell broke loose. I don't know why they even wanted it. It wasn't like their Moscow mansions were at risk of flooding anytime soon. We obviously had production issues with the serum after demand shot up. Couldn't churn it out fast enough once the Philippines, India, and Italy were all begging us for new batches on the daily. I got a couple of facilities to start manufacturing in China, but someone cut some corners at some point in the process, and before I knew it, there were twelve thousand dead people in Dandong.

I was furious.

While we were dealing with all of that, all the instability in Bangkok started. The government had pretty much siphoned off the Marine Sector, forbidding the huphins from mixing with the human population. I couldn't understand why. These were the same people that had been human right up until the serum was administered (obviously not including the babies that were born to huphin parents; we were still studying them for any substantial differentiation). But, for some reason, the humans all thought it was best to keep them contained, just in case.

The huphins were understandably pissed about the whole thing. They had pretty reasonable concerns, if you ask me. Why did they need to pay taxes if they couldn't vote? How was it fair that they had no representation in Parliament? Why did they have to carry around identification everywhere they went? I got it. Way back on my dad's side, I've got a bit of Jewish ancestry. Trust me, I got it.

I'm not sure if the huphins' decision to not handle things like Gandhi was the right one. I guess their thought process was that the nonviolent guys always end up getting assassinated. I really thought there was a diplomatic solution to the whole thing, that it could be resolved soon enough. I trusted the politicians to handle it.

Mistake.

The huphins actually won in Bangkok, in the end. They declared Tha Kham independent from the rest of Thailand, and then they started reaching out to the other Marine Sectors from around the world. New Orleans was an easy win since everyone and their mother had a gun. It was bloody, but they separated and joined up with the Marine Sector in Miami. The Independent Marine States of America, they called themselves, picking up pieces of the Gulf of Mexico's coastline as they went. Port Said, out in Egypt, proved to be a big problem. The huphins took over the whole place and then shut down the fucking Suez Canal. That threw everyone for a loop. Kolkata was next. Then Nagoya. Sydney. Rio.

We were confronting a new reality, where there were suddenly two species fighting for dominance on Earth, with turbulent fault lines in every major coastal city. Personally, I was still holding onto the notion of a precariously balanced version of peace. They had their independence. They could have stopped at that.

The problem was the huphins had been wronged. They'd been caged up like animals in some places. Told they were unnatural. Looked down upon because they took the serum to survive. Easy to say when you're an elite with the resources to just pick up your life and move. They did what they had to do. And they didn't like being told otherwise.

That's when things got really bad. The Americans took it too far first, as they always do. Most of downtown Seattle was Marine Sector, and Washington decided the best way to show the IMSA who was boss would be to bomb the shit out of it. When the dust cleared, they had just ruined a perfectly good marine city. The huphins mostly managed to evacuate—all they had to do was swim out into the ocean and wait. When they came back, most of them were still alive. All of them were pissed.

94

Wasn't just them either. A lot of humans were sympathetic to the huphins. The second-class citizenry situation was pretty unsavory. I mean, America wasn't that far removed from the First Civil War. They hadn't forgotten what it was like to have some people thinking they were better than others because of their skin.

So that's how the Second Civil War broke out in North America. Canada and Mexico and their respective Marine Sectors were pulled in too. I left Bangkok—fucking wasteland by that point. A lot of places were. Made my way to Japan and rented a little house outside of Morioka for a few months, just to clear my head.

I should have seen it coming. I could feel them watching me for weeks, someone staring when I'd get my morning coffee or walk to the grocery store, but I kept shaking off that feeling and telling myself everything was fine. Always trust your intuition.

I got taken in by the UN tribunal in Tokyo two weeks ago. They're saying I'll probably be slapped with the death penalty any day now. I'm giving these pages to Osamu, one of my guards. It was his idea that I write all this down. He says it'll be valuable when I die, and he can save up for his family to get the serum. I didn't realize they were charging for it now. They weren't supposed to do that. But I want to help him. Really, from the beginning, I just wanted to help. I thought I was saving the world. Osamu says that Jesus got killed by people who didn't get what he was trying to do. I'm not going to compare myself to Jesus, but, well, yeah. Anyway, I just thought everyone—humans and huphins alike—would be a bit more grateful.

But I guess it's not in our DNA to just sit down and be happy that someone stuck their neck out for us. At least, not yet.

I suppose that'll have to be the next guy's problem.

Soulless
Wade Hunter

MY NAME IS SIMON.

Simon Bullstein.

Dr. Simon Bullstein.

My name is Dr. Simon Bullstein.

My colleagues call me Dr. Frankenstein.

The police are looking for me. I am wanted for arson and murder. I know that at least fifty people are dead. I am wanted for these deaths, but I did not commit them. They are my fault. I created what killed them. I am a genetic engineer. I am *the* genetic engineer, to be exact.

Why haven't you heard of me then? Simple. I'm one of the country's best kept secrets. To the public, my job does not exist. In my head I hold information that could damn humanity. With all my neurons clicking, I could change humans forever. As a matter of fact, I may have already.

I was recently let in on this last part.

Some people dream of being as smart as I am. It's a curse. With the knowledge in my head someone could become extremely dangerous.

Someone already has.

I close my eyes and swim in the darkness. It's nice. It's peaceful. It's a farce.

Outside a siren wails. I feel myself tense.

They—the police—won't find me. It's not because of how smart I am. It's because someone doesn't want me to be found. The government? Not quite. They want me found, yes, found before the police catch me. More importantly, they want me found before I fall into the wrong person's hands.

It's too late for that.

The police are looking for the person that killed all those people, but it's not me. They don't know that, though. I have a vague feeling they wouldn't listen if I tried to explain it. Like I said, my job doesn't exist in the real world.

✳✳✳

"You did this all to yourself," he told me in a mocking voice.

All to myself? What about all those people that burned? Didn't I do it to them also?

I wonder where things went wrong; at what point did I lose control of the situation?

I hear footsteps on the floorboards above me.

It's him up there.

"I am just an animal," he said. "Man condemns himself for what are truly natural acts. Man does this because he thinks he is above all other life. Man thinks that he is special because he believes that God created him in his image. Man thinks this makes him supreme."

I try to disagree, but deep down I know he's right.

I try anyway.

"We are what we are because God has made us this way," I said.

He spit in my face at that point.

I close my eyes and swim in the darkness.

Footsteps beat like ancient war drums above my head.

He's playing with me. He wants to control me. I know this because I did it to him. He's pissed. It's all my fault. I should have never shot him.

Twice.

The sirens die off in the distance.

"Don't speak to me about God," he said.

When I left work yesterday, everything was fine. I was in

control. He was locked away in a room with IVs feeding him drugs to keep him complacent. When I left work, the sun was blazing in a sky the blue of a robin's egg. When I left work, I expected to see the faces of my colleagues again.

I did see some of them this morning.

They were all melted and gooey.

On my way to work this morning, I walked past a police car parked on the street. I walk to work because it is easier for me to lose someone that may be following me.

I must be conscious of this.

As I passed the police car, I saw a crowd of people ahead of me. This was just before I turned the corner to see the circus of fire trucks, policemen, and ambulances in front of what used to be my workplace. The building was made to look like an office complex, but it was one of the most high-tech research facilities in the world. As I walked past the cruiser, before I saw the burned wreck that used to be my second home, I heard my description crackle from the police scanner.

Male. Caucasian. Approximately forty. Short brown hair. Brown eyes. Six-feet tall.

Pretty vague really, but, somehow, I knew it was me. Call it the smell of roasting flesh in the air. Call it the parade in front of my secret workplace. Call it what you want, but I knew for sure that it was me that the phantom police voice was describing. I knew when I saw the charcoaled bodies being wheeled from the burned-out building that acted as my research facilities.

I knew what had happened.

He warned me.

"I'm going to burn it all down," he said. "This building. This project. This world. You."

He warned me, but I didn't listen.

I close my eyes and swim in the darkness.

"We are what we are because God made us this way."

"Don't speak to me of God. You think you are God."

I'm not God.

I'm a genetic engineer.

I am *the* genetic engineer.

I only play God.

"I'm going to burn it all down," he said, and a hard lump formed in my throat. It was gone the moment I heard the lock engage behind me. The moment I left him lying in that bed with two gunshot wounds. I left work knowing when I came back in the morning it would all be as I left it.

My project. My workplace. My co-workers. My life.

Nothing was supposed to change. I said goodbye to Jimmy, my assistant, on the way out the door. Good ol' Jimmy with his bad haircut and unshaven face. Good ol' Jimmy with eyes that could melt any girl's heart. I patted him on the back and said, "See you tomorrow."

I saw him. He had plastic pens where his eyes should have been. They had melted in the fire and filled the sockets. He looked like a demon.

"I'm going to burn it all down."

I hadn't believed it possible.

"You think you are God."

I was God. His God. I created him in my image.

I am *the* genetic engineer.

I close my eyes and swim in the darkness.

As I watched them roll Jimmy out of the building, I caught hints of recognition across the faces of the people standing around, the people that I passed every day on my way to work. The shopkeepers. The waiters and waitresses at the surrounding cafés and bistros. These people don't know me, but they recognized me. They have heard my description. They know where I work, just not what I do, and they recognized me. They heard my description on the police scanner, and slowly their minds bent it to match my face. Standing there with the acrid smell of burning flesh and smoke filling my nose, I looked around and saw more and more faces turning my way. I turned and walk away. I passed the police car from which I heard my description, and it crackled again.

Suspect identified as Simon Bullstein. Consider him armed and dangerous.

The most dangerous thing about me is my mind.

I did not kill these people, but I am responsible.

"You think you are God," he said.

I stared back at him blankly. I was his God. Flesh of my flesh. Blood of my Blood. I created him in my image. He is my child. He is me.

"Why did you kill all those people?" I asked him.

"I am just an animal," he said.

I walked faster after hearing my name on the police scanner. I left the smoldering ruins of my friends and colleagues behind. I left the suspicious stares behind. I left the flashing red lights behind. I left my life behind.

I close my eyes and swim in the darkness.

I understand why the police think it was me that did all these things. The man that did them looks exactly like me. He is a bit slimmer in the face. Me fifteen years ago, but me, nonetheless me. He has the exact same DNA, enhanced, but the same.

He is my child. Flesh of my flesh.

I am *the* genetic engineer.

How he got out, I will never know.

✳✳✳

"Why did you kill all those people?"

"I am just an animal."

"But it's wrong."

"Does God tell you it is a sin?"

"Yes."

"Do people burn for your sins?"

"Yes."

I created him to be the ultimate soldier.

Flesh of my flesh.

I used my DNA as a precursor for what he would become. My DNA that gave me so much in life. My DNA that enabled me to accomplish all that I am. I gave it to him, and he was born.

The word *made* comes to mind.

The word *grew* replaces it.

The word *engineered* replaces it.

His DNA is vastly advanced. He is perfect. He can regenerate tissue tens of times faster than any human. His reflexes are faster than any man ever to walk the planet. His strength is something out of a comic book. He can take two slugs in the chest from five feet away and live to tell the tale.

I know this.

I shot him twice to see.

"I'm going to burn it all down."

He is perfect–too perfect, if I say so myself.

"Do people burn for your sins?"

"Yes," I said, and my mind filled with the image of Jimmy. Jimmy with his eye sockets full of molten plastic. Jimmy turned into a gooey demon of black and red. Jimmy sizzling and reeking of burnt flesh.

I looked at him then, my child, and he leaned into me.

The look in his eye was savage.

"Yes," I said, and I believed it.

For creating this monster, people burned.

I think I will join them in the end.

He paused a minute, and I had the oddest feeling that he was going to bite my face.

"I am just an animal," he'd said earlier.

I wriggle against the restraints holding me. He brought me here. Not that I know where here is. I woke up tied to this chair in some basement. One minute I was on the street, running from something that I did not do, the next I was here.

"Will people burn for your sins?"

"Yes."

"I am what *you* made me. You are more God to me than anything, and I am more than you. So what should I fear?"

"You have killed ruthlessly."

"It is what I was made for."

"It's different than that. There have to be morals, limits."

"Do you punish the lion when it kills?"

"When it does it for pleasure, yes."

"It doesn't matter." He said this with such indifference that I was shocked. He was still in my face, breathing hot, sticky breath into my eyes. I couldn't even manage to blink.

"I kill," he said, staring deep into my soul, "because you made me. It doesn't matter because you made me."

"I don't understand," I said, trying to turn my head away, but his hand was on my cheek before my chin moved two centimeters, holding my gaze to his.

"It doesn't matter because you made me. You'll burn. Not me. Your God will have his vengeance on you. Not on me."

He paused. His hot breath robbed me of oxygen.

"I am untouchable by your God."

"But no one—" I began, until I saw the smile spread over his face, stopping my words in my throat.

"I am," he said, and the words made me cringe. They were full of unbridled lust, of hatred, of excitement. What words would sound like if they were an orgasm.

"You made me in a petri dish. I wasn't born. I was engineered."

My words in his mouth.

Fitting.

"I lack the leash that binds you."

I said nothing, but he waited to see if I would. He turned my head so that he could whisper into my ear. He go so close I could feel the stubble on his chin rub against my cheek.

"I'm soulless," he said softly into my ear.

That's when he turned and left. That's where we are now.

With me sitting in the basement tied to a chair, and him stalking the floorboards above me.

I listen to his footsteps.

I close my eyes and swim in the darkness.

It started as a simple thought, really. He'd passed every test that we ran on him with amazing ease. The only thing left was massive trauma.

Bang. Bang.

Two in the chest, and he went down.

The footsteps above me get louder as if God himself is banging around the floors of Heaven.

Bang. Bang.

He went down, and the blood spurted from his chest. It spurted four times, throwing deep black flashes of coronary blood onto the ground around him. I watched, not in remorse, but with the cold, hard eye of the scientist watching the results of his experiment, thinking *back to step one.*

But the blood stopped spurting, and he groaned.

Flesh of my flesh.

He is my child.

I am his God. I made him this way.

There in a pool of his blood, he stared at me with bloodshot eyes. At first, I believed him to be in shock, but now I think differently. Now I think he was measuring me.

"I'm going to burn it all down," he said to me as I was leaving. "This building. This project. This world. You." I latched the door behind me and patted good ol' Jimmy on the back. That was the last time I saw anybody that I worked with, alive.

I shot him twice, my child, and the next morning he was not only alive but strong enough to escape an inescapable cell and destroy a military research facility and everybody in it.

He is perfect.

He is soulless.

You think you're God.

I am his God. He displayed that in the order of words, but I fear the roles have changed hands.

I listen to him, walking above me.

Judging me.

Deciding my fate.

I close my eyes and swim in the darkness.

I started my work, trying to find a way to cure disease, all of it, to end human suffering. I was so close. I found a perfect method of using a person's DNA and forging it into something more. The method was exact and extremely fast.

I am *the* genetic engineer.

That was when the government found me. That was when my life's work went totally FUBAR.

I think of Jimmy. Jimmy with the eyes that could swoon any girl. Jimmy with the eyes full of melted plastic. I did that. It's my fault.

I am just an animal.

I damned Jimmy.

I am untouchable by God.

I thought I was God.

I am soulless.

What have I created?

I listen to the footsteps above me.

The word Antichrist comes to mind.

I created him in my likeness. Flesh of my flesh.

Soulless.

No leash.

No conscious about consequence.

I close my eyes and swim in the darkness, and now more than ever it is a farce.

The government told me that they wanted a genetically-engineered super-soldier. I made an off-hand remark, asking if they had the spandex and the red, white, and blue shield already made.

Blank stares.

"Captain America," I said in return to their silence.

"No," they said. "More like Michael Myers."

And so went my aspirations about saving mankind, and so came the first steps to damning it.

When I think of what I could have accomplished compared to what I did accomplish, the word Horseman comes to mind.

Flesh of my flesh.

How could things go so wrong?

I am an animal.

He'll never stop.

I kill because you made me.

What have I done? I am the moth, and he is the flame. I try to think of just one of the seven deadly sins that I don't represent.

I hear the footsteps above me again.

You think you are God.

No. Not any longer. Not now. Now I only wish I were God so that I could fix everything.

The cellar door opens. He is coming.

The last thing I said to him before I pulled the trigger and opened two geysers in his chest was "See ya on the flip side." *See ya on the flip side,* like I was some crazy radio announcer. *See ya on the flip side,* as if it were all that easy.

Well, here we are. The flip side, because he has the gun and the control. I have nothing. I see the gun tucked into his pants as he descends the steps. I taste the irony of the whole situation like saltwater in my throat.

Who says that God doesn't have a sense of humor?

He is in front of me now.

I close my eyes and swim—

He slaps me so hard I feel it in my arms. My eyes water, but I can see that the gun is pointed at my chest.

Flesh of my flesh.

Only my flesh doesn't have an extra few peptides that accelerate healing.

The end of the barrel looks like a big black eye.

I think of Jimmy.

I am just an animal. I kill because you made me.

"Do it," I scream at him.

He says nothing. Until, after what seems like minutes, I hear a low laugh coming from him.

"Will you burn for your sins?" he asks.

"Yes," I say, as if it is my last confession.

It is.

I hear the hammer of the gun click back.

I shot him twice.

He lived.

I won't.

I *was* the genetic engineer.

"See you on the flip side," I say. It seems like the appropriate thing to say. "See you on the flip side," I say again in a small voice, staring into the black eye, reliving the nauseating smell of Jimmy on his gurney.

"No," he says lightly. "No, you won't."

The gun sounds twice.

I see the blood gushing from my chest before I feel the pain.

I try to close my eyes, but I can't.

Suddenly I'm swimming.

Swimming in the darkness with my eyes open.

And this time it's not a farce.

The Mad Successful Doctor
Violet Schwegler

THE AMPHITHEATER WAS FILLED BEYOND CAPACITY, employees standing along the back walls, sitting in the aisles. Most of them were unaware of the sheer size of the workforce—of each other. A good ten thousand scientists and assistants and administrators, all gathered together for the first time. Maybe even more, a zero missing somewhere in the tally. Employee interaction was going to be at staggeringly high levels after this event.

Backstage, Claire Reed bit off a hangnail while continuing to pace around the green room. She looked smart in her business suit, the one she'd bought for business things, those handful of times she'd had to leave the lab. Just a couple years ago, this was nothing but a hope and a wish, something poetic. But this, now, was reality—and it was about to smack her right in the face.

There was a knock at the door of the dressing room.

"Come in," called Claire.

Claire's assistant, Matilda, poked their head in. "Everyone is ready for you."

Claire nodded in reply. This was it.

Showtime.

Claire walked out onto the stage to thunderous applause. She could see so many faces that she recognized and even more she had never seen once. Long gone were the days when she would personally interview every applicant, every janitor and grad student and test subject that set foot in the building. Long gone were the days when there was even only one building.

"I," she began, "am in awe of the sheer amount of you. You're all amazing and I thank you for taking the time out of your lives to be here today. What we are announcing at the end of this presentation will blow your minds. And I, for one, cannot wait to see all of your reactions.

"But, before we get there, I feel we should take a look back into our history. Some time ago, we commissioned a small documentary team to do just that." She turned, held her arm up vaguely to her side. "Let's watch!"

A video began playing on the giant screens set up throughout the venue: candid shots of employees enjoying themselves, working at stations, taking massive shits; interviews talking about the history of the company, the sweeping scope, the most sordid sexual rumors, and even some hints of things yet to come. All set to rumbling percussion and triumphantly swelling strings.

The video came to an end and triggered, as Claire had predicted, a standing ovation from the "worker bees."

"I think you can clearly see," Claire said, back at center stage, now wearing what appeared to be an obsidian crown, "that we mean business, but that we can also be friends, too. Eventually, I'd like us all to think of each other like family. I know some of you feel that way already. Don't worry, psychiatrists have been assigned." She forced herself to smile. "Kidding!"

The employees chuckled. Some a bit more than others. Overall, the joke went over fine.

"Now, there are going to be some hard times ahead. We all know this. Doing what we do, making the enemies we make, it was an inevitability, really. But if we all just pull together, we can get through with as little loss of life as possible."

A murmuring rose out of the darkness of the amphitheater.

"Listen," Claire said, "I can see some of you are a little concerned and I don't blame you. It is disappointing when you realize that your neighbor is at odds with you. But we can't have that. Not in our organization! You know what they say about the squeaky wheel. Kill it! You hereby have my authority to murder anyone you suspect might be a threat to you, your family, or especially myself."

The drones were becoming restless.

"Hey, no, it's okay! Now that all the bad news is out of the way, we can get back to the good stuff. First, I'd like Greg Fitzgerald to stand up, please."

Greg looked around at his co-workers and slowly rose from his hard-plastic folding chair. Immediately, Greg was shot in the neck with a tranquilizer dart and collapsed back into his seat.

"*Free mandatory naps!*"

The cannon fodder grew well beyond restless. Frenzied might even be the word.

"Calm down, everyone!" screamed Claire. "Y'all are overreacting. You can opt-out. It's cool. We're cool. I'm your friend, remember. Your family. Your Goddess. Your supreme being of love, understanding, and bloody vengeance."

Chairs started flying as people fled for their lives.

"*Don't make me release the gas!*" bellowed Claire, holding up an ominous red button. "*I'll do it, you little fu—*"

There was a knock at the door.

"Time for your medicine, Dr. Reed," said Nurse Miller, shaking a small cup of pills.

Untamed
Jennifer Lee Rossman

FOOTSTEPS ECHOED DOWN the clinically bright corridor, preceding the arrival of the scientists for their regular administration of inhumanities. Three sets of ominous footsteps, with three hushed voices to match.

Kate tilted her head, listening as the two men she recognized gave a brief account of the experiment thus far and their numerous failed attempts at controlling her.

"—nor electrical shocks had any positive effect on her disposition."

"She's wild, dangerous. Attacks seemingly for the enjoyment of it."

"I would almost say for spite, were she capable of such complex emotions and thought processes."

"Indeed. You must remember, she is nothing like Bianca."

The third man, the stranger, chuckled. A soft sound, but one tinged with something dark that sent instinctual warnings through Kate's body. Her arms prickled with the sensation of her hairs standing on end, growing longer and more coarse, and she ground her teeth to allay the pain of her fangs pressing at the inside of her gums, threatening to erupt.

"I've yet to meet a creature, woman or animal, that I couldn't bend to my will," the stranger assured the others.

Curious.

There hadn't been a new behavioral specialist in over a week, not since that incident with the other experiment they called her sister. Kate's stark laboratory bedroom still smelled of the blood spilled pulling them apart; no amount of cleaning products could cover it.

Kate had assumed they'd given up on her, decided she wasn't worth the hush money and medical bills. Why the sudden interest in a failed experiment, she wondered, especially when their second attempt, the flawless and wonderful Bianca, turned out better than their twisted minds could ever have hoped?

A shadow appeared in the frosted window of her door. Kate crouched, snarling in preparation for an attack. Her already high heart rate quickened to the point that she could no longer hear individual beats, just a buzzing in her chest.

The door unlocked from the outside and where she had expected to see another white coat and superiority complex, there stood a man even more unkempt and hirsute than her.

He took one look at Kate, at her nails digging into the linoleum and her beady eyes lacking even a spark of humanity, and he laughed. Actually laughed.

"Is that all?" he asked with a grin, his hands in the pockets of his jeans. "They had me expecting a monster."

"I am a monster," Kate said between growls.

He shook his head dismissively. "Nah. From where I'm standing, all I see's a pretty young lady who can't control her anger."

At this, Kate stood up, silently crossing the room until she was face to face with the stranger. She pulled back her lips, enjoying his fascination as he watched her inch-long fangs pierce her gums and slide into place in front of her canine teeth.

"I was pretty once," she said, hoping he could smell the raw meat on her breath. "But they changed me into this, and they've sent you to torture me until I learn to control it, or until you learn to control me."

The man didn't flinch. In fact, he seemed rather unimpressed with Kate's threat display.

"Well," he said finally, "that's a shame then, isn't it?"

Kate narrowed her eyes. "The only shame is your fashion sense," she said, gesturing to his obnoxiously loud Hawaiian shirt. Didn't he know the only colors in the house of pain were stainless steel and bleach?

"Teeth aren't the only thing sharp about you, eh?" the man said with a smirk. He leaned against the doorway. "As I was saying, it's a shame, because if you weren't a monster, I could get you out of here."

It was a trick. It had to be.

But when he reached for her hand, she let him take it. For whatever reason, the scientists had brought him here; her choice in the matter was merely an illusion.

***

Peter wasn't like the others, the ones who tried to beat the animal out of her. The ones whose flesh Kate had continued to rip from the bone long after the screaming had stopped. He spoke *to* her, not at her, and without all the scientific jargon, as they took their daily walks around the uninhabited island.

"I'd forgotten it was an island," Kate said, sitting on the beach and letting her bare feet savor the warmth of the sand. The palm trees thrashed their enormous leaves in the wind, scattering the sunlight. She'd forgotten about natural light, too, light without that fluorescent buzzing.

"Been that long?" If he pitied her, he hid it well behind an ever-present smirk. "Well, maybe we ought to get you some proper island wear 'stead of your hospital robe, yeah? Matching outfits, you and me?"

Kate rolled her eyes. Peter's clothes—another flashy button-down paired with khakis today—matched his overall demeanor: casual, irritatingly friendly, and equal parts amusing and infuriating.

Nothing like those patronizing yet delicious specialists Kate was accustomed to.

But perhaps the most significant difference was that Peter saw her, despite her protests, despite the teeth and claws, as the woman she had been once upon another life, before the experiments.

It should have put her at ease, was likely his intention to put her at ease. She pulled her robe tighter around her neck to hide the wiry hairs prickling at her skin as they stood erect; it took all of her energy to keep her nails from growing in anticipation of an attack.

"Why—" Kate heard the growl in her voice, and disguised it by clearing her throat. "Why are we doing this?"

With a satisfied sigh, Peter sat next to her on the beach, lying flat and resting his head back on his forearms. He squinted up at her.

"Why are we doing what, Katie?"

She gestured to him, to herself, to the tiny island so far from civilization that no laws or ethics seemed to apply.

"You're supposed to be trying to fix me, but all we do is go for walks."

"Fix you. That would imply you're broken, and you've made it very clear that you are not."

"Then you're supposed to be—supposed to be trying to break me," Kate said, her attention momentarily drawn to the direction of the laboratory, to the sound of a door opening. She turned, pressing her back against the reassuring solidity of the tree, warily keeping both Peter and the small, ugly building in her line of sight.

"Closer," Peter admitted.

"Why?" It came out more as a command than a question, her tone uncomfortably similar to that of the others who had tried and failed to change her. "Before they brought you in, they were giving up. They were going to put me down."

"Sounds like a lot of people have put you down," Peter commented, unbothered by this information. "Any of them ever lift you up?"

Kate paused, eyeing him. Like a predator or like prey, she couldn't say at the moment.

"What changed?"

A shrug. Peter's version of covering a growl with a cough. "All's I know is, I'm here to break your spirit, make you bend to their whims like a trained dog—"

"Like Bianca," Kate said, and Peter raised his eyebrows in acknowledgment.

"—and I'm going to be the one to succeed, because I'm gonna try something no one else has: conspiring with you to fake the whole bloody thing." After a moment's thought, he grinned and added, "Maybe bloody ain't the best choice of words, your history considered. We'll figure out a better cuss tomorrow."

Kate stared at him. Fake it? Fake what, her total compliance? Pretend that screwing around with her genes had only resulted in positive changes and that she didn't turn into a hideous, hybrid beast sometimes? Pretend she didn't know what human flesh tasted like?

"I'll explain more tomorrow," Peter promised. He looked at the sun, still high in the sky. "Getting late," he said, standing up and wiping the sand off his pants. "Best get you back before nightfall, yeah?"

"It's not even noon," Kate protested.

A chuckle accompanied Peter's grin. "You really have been inside for too long, eh? Forgot what a sunset looks like?"

Kate didn't respond, just watched him carefully as they went back to the laboratory, the late afternoon sun shining bright.

✱✱✱

The scientists still needed Kate, as Peter explained, to impress the investors. Bianca, Little Miss 2.0, exemplified the success of the gene-splicing experiment, showing only the intended results. All without the unfortunate side effect of sometimes becoming a raging, highly-aggressive shrew-person.

"But they won't buy the proprietary technology that made Bianca," Peter said, "until they find out why your scientists ain't parading you around like they do her."

"So you want me to act like you broke me," Kate said slowly, watching the waves come in, "so they can say that we are both successes?"

He shrugged. "That's the gist of it, yep."

"But then what?"

"Then … whatever you want. Go back to the mainland. They won't need you after, they'll put you down regardless, but I'll get you out."

He said that with the same certainty with which he had told Kate the sun was setting, but what choice did she have?

And so began their twice daily sessions.

It was all for show, feigning meditation and psychological tests. In all honesty, Kate could have done it on her own months ago; aside from the more extremely emotional instances, she could control the beastly side rather easily. But they didn't want her to control herself, they wanted to control her. Punish her not just for transformation, but for showing any sign of anger or dissent.

That, Kate had long suspected, was the real purpose of the experiment: to create a method by which the less desirable behaviors of humanity could be wiped out by selective gene editing. Why they had ever decided to start with shrews, she had no idea, but they must have used something more easily domesticated for Bianca.

"She's different," Kate told Peter one day in the lab. "We came in together, I met her. She was loud and annoying, like your shirts—"

"You like my shirts," Peter teased.

In fact, she did, not that she would never admit it. The tropical colors and palm tree motifs reminded her of the world outside her stainless, fluorescent prison.

She couldn't remember the last time he had taken her out. She'd asked to go for a walk, once, but he ignored the question, getting visibly agitated, and she didn't dare ask anymore.

"Regardless, she had a personality," Kate said. "Not a great one, but it was hers and now she's just … withdrawn."

Peter tilted his head, looked at her curiously. "You didn't come in together."

"Yes, we did," Kate insisted. "The same day, the same boat, and we both have dark hair so they were joking that we were sisters—"

His curiosity turned to concern.

"Katie, love, I read your files. You came in months before Bianca. You've never even met her."

Every survival instinct kicked in, and Kate had to squeeze her hands into fists to stop the claws from emerging. That couldn't be right. She remembered it all so clearly.

"I've met her. We were tested together, we used to share this room—"

"And Bianca ain't no brunette," Peter continued as Kate shook her head. "Golden blonde. Which you would know if you'd ever met her."

Kate's heartbeat buzzed louder than the fluorescent lights, her breaths coming hard and fast. "She stole my food. We fought. I bit her arm—"

Peter stood up, looking at her with pity. "Shrew's memory, eh? Shame. Thought we were getting somewhere." He headed for the door. "See you tonight, not that it'll do any good."

Tears threatened to spill from Kate's beady eyes. "I'm sorry," she said, though she couldn't say quite why. "Could you, um, could you let them know I'm ready for breakfast?"

"You just had breakfast," he said without turning around.

"No, that can't be right. I'm starving."

Peter sighed. "Maybe if you controlled your metabolism a little better, you wouldn't be."

***

When Kate broke, it was not the way the scientists wanted.

Her anger, her frustration, her hunger, it all finally boiled over in a fury of claws and teeth and blood. So much blood.

After weeks of doubting herself, of starvation and punishments for things she couldn't remember doing wrong, she stopped pretending to be something she wasn't. She stopped pretending to trust anyone but herself to know what she wanted.

The investors were delicious. So were the scientists.

She let Bianca go, told her to run. She hoped that the brunette with the bite marks on her arm would find peace somewhere, somehow.

"See there, Katie?" Peter asked, his smile slipping and his voice trembling. "You let her go, you're not a monster. Not completely."

"There's only one monster in this room," Kate informed him, licking the blood from her fangs. "There were more, but they're dead now."

She took a step closer; he stepped back, pressing himself against the wall. He'd worn a proper shirt today, clean and white and stainless like the lab, because in the end he was no different than all the rest.

"You know," Kate said with a grin, "I think you were right. I do like your other shirts. This one ..." She crouched briefly to dip her palms in the bloody carnage before holding them up to him. "I think this one could use a little more color."

"Katie, please," he begged. "You're better than this, ain't ya?"

"I don't know, you tell me. You've gotten so good at telling me about everything wrong with me, even if it isn't true."

"I can still take you to the mainland."

Just like the first time they met, he held out his hand. And Kate took his hand.

Took it right off the arm.

✳✳✳

Kate sat on the beach alone that night, watching a sunset that was not a lie. The rancid taste of Peter still lingered in her mouth. A little ways down the coast, Bianca stood on the deck of the investors' boat, waiting.

Maybe Kate would go with her, try to find some semblance of a normal life. Maybe she would stay on the island, live in the seclusion she wanted and probably deserved. She hadn't decided yet.

She only knew that, for the first time in far too long, her decision, whatever it ended up being, would be hers alone.

The Sum of Our Parts
Nicole M. Wolverton

SOMEONE ONCE LIVED IN THIS COTTAGE. The front door hangs crooked, small porch barely more than splinters. Spindly flowers grow dark and wild over the broken windows, in through the open door. They used to be tame, well-behaved—just like us. We step crookedly into the house. The hem of our gown catches on broken boards. It can barely be called a dress anymore, what with the long, rending tears. We remember escape from the laboratory. We remember abandonment. We do not know the truth. Perhaps the man who made us ran away. Perhaps we'd had enough. Whatever the case, we woke alone, the laboratory in cinders and shreds.

Through a split in the fabric of the dress, our arm is visible. The black stitches that sew our parts together form the whole. The seams itch, but in the dark of this cottage, I can pretend this body is not an amalgam of unlucky girls and women, but mine alone— just like my brain, my soul. I feel my way through the gloom with my sisters' hands. A ruined cabinet with the remnants of a bowl. A rough-hewn wall. There, the solid heft of a chair.

It was the smell of lightning that drove us out into the rain, over the rocky field. Our body doesn't move the way it should— or the way I remember my own body moving. I force a word to our lips: *Rose*. That was who I was. Perhaps I am still. The doctor, when he unearthed me along with the others, said we have no name now. We would have no need of it. Yet when I think of us, that's the name I give. We are Rose because I was Rose.

We perch in the chair—and in that quiet moment, the deaths

of the women who carry me reveal themselves. Taken by the pox. A farm accident. The owner of the torso drowned in a pond beyond a town to the south. Accidents and purposeful deaths.

In the distance, out the ruined window, the stars glisten.

The doctor chose me for the reputation of my fine mind. That's what he said as he worked over us. He didn't care how we died. My father was always so proud that I could count figures well enough to keep stock in his store—and the doctor overheard him say so in the town. Perhaps there were smarter women buried in the kirk, but I was the freshest. The doctor dragged me from my grave, ropes under my armpits.

"You will be my great accomplishment."

Accomplishment. Our lips sneered just as though they were really mine. As though I'd had no accomplishments of my own. As if *we* could have no accomplishments on our own. There is a purpose in us. It glows like firelight under our skin. Outrage coalesces behind our eyes.

As dawn breaks, we creep out of the ruined cabin. The rain from the night before has given way to fog, thick as a forest. We can smell and feel and see, but the doctor has done things to us— we no longer hunger. I wonder how we function without the beat of a heart and blood in our veins. We can still feel pain, though. He made sure of that.

This body haltingly takes to the meadow, attempting to compensate for one leg shorter than the other. We fashion a walking stick out of a branch. When we come to the first row of homes on the outskirts of town, I realize I recognize this place— my father and I have come here for market before. No one would recognize me now, though. No one would recognize any of us, not puzzled together as we are.

At the backdoor of one house, a pile of clothes removed from a drying line yields a dark blue homespun dress, just large enough to fit our shoulders. The long sleeves and high neck cover our scars and seams. The fabric is rough over our palms. At the end of a dirt lane, a torn bonnet floats in rainwater—it is enough to hide our face. We have felt the contours of our cheeks, our nose, our eyes with clumsy fingers. Fine stitches traverse the curve of our forehead, grafting on a head of wild hair. The hair—ink black—blows across our neck, even with the bonnet tied.

We stagger from one end of town to the other. It has only been two weeks since Mother and Father found my body in the woods, two towns to the east. It seems a lifetime.

"Good morning to you, mistress." The voice comes from the doorway—a man with a sack of flour. The baker. Fog swirls at his feet.

We nod, the girls and I, head down, and continue on our way. Pebbles scatter in our wake. My instincts and memories are what urge us onto a side street to rest, only then catching our reflection in a dark window. Our face is a cracked moon, the mouth slightly off-kilter and the eyes pale and dry. The bonnet is a help. It will do us no good to draw attention; we pull the bonnet lower. When the town wakes, that is when we will find Jacob. Jacob and his treachery.

This is the justice left for us. *My* justice.

The sun burns the last of the fog to nothing within hours. We hide in the shadows cast along the squat buildings as the streets grow loud with the chatter of villagers coming and going, selling their wares, scolding their children. We swear it is Jacob's voice in a cluster of fishermen joggling toward the river, but his face is not amongst them.

Jacob. I have not thought of his name in days. Anger and helplessness compete with the rage. It may be *my* rage, but my sisters take to it as though it is their own.

Perhaps it is just as well that Jacob is not here—our body needs to practice maneuvering. Just as our legs do not quite work in tandem yet, our fingers make only the crudest of movements. We are ungainly and gawkish.

We practice and, after hours of limping along the edges of crowds, there he is. We are still graceless. The sky has gone the color of dirty ice, and orange light emanates from the window of the tavern. Smoke pumps from the chimney. The chill of the air encourages us to warm by the fire in its stone hearth. No one bothers us inside, even in our wrongness.

"I tell you, it was the Devil's work."

It comes from a table to our right. We turn just enough to see who speaks—it is an older man, gray hair peeking out from beneath a black cap. A plate of turnips rests before him. His companion is someone I have seen before at the market. He is tall with a nose like a rodent.

"And the Devil's work is over, I say."

"Murder, is it?" the older man says. Something in the way he speaks fills our ears.

"Think of it how you like. There will be no more monsters in our midst. We destroyed it all—the doctor, too. We saw to it."

They recount their activities the night before as we quietly wait.

At least now we know what happened to our maker—but these men should not fool themselves. There have been monsters in their midst for longer than they believe. Being sewn together from scraps and set back to life isn't the only thing that makes one a monster, nor is having the knowledge of how it is done. More mundane beasts reside in the village.

The door to the tavern opens, and Jacob sweeps in on the sour wind. He smiles at the barmaid—the same smile he offered to me. Flame from the hearth warms our hands, and we are suddenly strong. This body—this abruptly graceful and adroit body, with dexterous fingers that can ball into a fist with ease—nearly glows with incandescent rage. The feet, the hips, the breasts, the shoulders. We are powerful. We understand one very important thing: no girls will die tonight. Only *real* monsters.

We will see to it.

We cross the room to Jacob, the skirt of our blue homespun swinging like the bell in the tower of the church. His attention is properly drawn—not to our face, of course, for he is not interested in our face. His eyes chew over our bosom, our waist. Gauges what he perceives as our weaknesses.

"Aren't you a pretty thing," he says in a low, amused growl that I once found charming. Now, our lips curl into a humorless smile but say nothing.

Jacob tilts his head. "What's your name, girl? I am Jacob."

"Rose." Perfectly spoken. Our voices are melodious. We tug the brim of the bonnet lower over our face.

"Shy, are you? Come join me for a pint."

"Shall we take it in a room upstairs?" we say, giving our voices an alluring lilt.

He brightens. "Now there's a good idea."

We wait as he makes arrangements with the tavern keeper. Neither one can keep their eyes off us. The fire from the hearth has lit us through. Perhaps the sight of my murderer struck a spark of the miraculous within us — or perhaps we unknowingly carry with us the doctor's secrets. He made us, but we can make ourselves stronger with purpose.

The tavern keeper turns from Jacob when their transaction is complete, politely ignoring our presence — coin makes men forget if offered in enough quantity.

We can see Jacob fully now with our sudden new power: I was not the first. I was not even the first in the village. My sisters and I grow angrier, stronger with each step up the rickety wooden staircase. Jacob climbs behind us, a pint of beer in each hand. We make sure our skirt swishes as we go.

The room is small and stifled. It contains a small sleigh bed, the wood frame nicked and abused over time. Beside it, a thin stand topped with a basin of opaque water. A plain chair stands adjacent to the bed. A single window is the only source of air, and it is cracked open only enough to admit the smell of the stale, smoky street. The walls are stained yellow, completely bare of decoration, save a mirror hung next to the door.

Jacob hands us a pint and takes a long pull from his own glass. He wipes his mouth on his sleeve. We have no urge to drink — and, to be fair, I'm not sure what will happen if we do. The doctor left us no organs but my brain. He said I was the only necessary piece to bring life to the body; otherwise, we are no more than a shell of skin. He should have never underestimated us.

Neither should Jacob.

He pulls us close, and we do our part—we pull away. He tries again. His hands clamp hard on our shoulders. His lips mash against ours, and we wriggle from his grasp.

"What do you think you're doing?" he says. "You wanted to come here. You wanted this." He fumbles with the strings of our bonnet, and we allow it. We want him to see. To see us in all our glory. He snatches the bonnet from us.

The window bangs open. He startles backward. Our black hair is free on the wind now. It streams away from our head like wires, and he sees us. Our seams and our stitches. His face pales. Oh, he sees us.

"What is this?"

"Your Rose," we say. "We are your Rose." We hear him, see the others that he hurt—those who were not joined with us. We say their names. "We are your Emma. We are your Margaret."

The air buzzes. Jacob's eyes widen. He fumbles for his pocket, for his knife.

We laugh and take it from him. He stumbles backward, falls onto the bed. He stares as we unfasten our dress. Our now deft and clever fingers make quick work of it, and we peel our arms out of the blue homespun sleeves, push the fabric over our hips. The dress falls to the ground as though each thread is a weight. We stand, proud of our disparate parts. Proud to stand together, dangerous. Deadly. Joyous.

Jacob makes a noise like a rabbit caught in a trap.

We trace the lines of our stitches with the tip of his knife, undoing ourselves as we go. We unsew our seams, but we remain whole. The loss of our bindings cannot rip us apart now. The fire shines within us, through the cracks in our skin, bright enough to distract Jacob from what he must know will come next. He squeaks when we lay our naked self over him, loose of limb, perhaps, but still unified. He doesn't know what noise to make when our nimble little fingers unbutton his shirt—nor does he know what to make of it when our lips touch his skin. And by then it is too late for him: we bite down on his tongue.

The slick-slide blood soaks into the bedding, but the tavern keeper has been paid not to notice such things. Later, he will burn the bedding and scrub the floors himself.

Jacob thrashes and grunts. I remember—and now my sisters do as well.

"Shush." We smile gently and draw the knife's edge down Jacob's chest. Bloody rivulets run the topography of his ribs. The rivulets turn to torrents when we begin sawing through the muscle and sinew and bone. "We are grateful you keep your knife so sharp." But his knife could be dull, and it would not matter. Our strength is our blade.

His mouth is a red and gaping hole as I was once a red and gaping hole.

"You held me down," we say. "Ruined me. Threw me away. We remember. We reclaim ourselves."

Jacob burbles out a string of gibberish, but we can see in his eyes that he knows me—*me*—even within the skin of my sisters. He reaches his hand toward our face. We lightly push his arm aside.

It is time, my sisters sing. The air smells hot and coppery.

We plunge both hands into his chest and snap through ribs to grasp his heart. He pants just as we twist it out and away from the bits that anchor it to him. Our hands are as bloody as his soul. We set the heart in the water of the basin.

We carve him into pieces not unlike our own parts. But we will not see him put back together. We will not see him seamed and stitched. A word comes, and I command that it be whispered aloud into the blowing storm in the room: "Vengeance." Our lips can perfectly form the syllables.

We pack Jacob's heart in a bit of torn bedding and wash ourselves in the pink water. There is time to leisurely pull on our blue homespun, time to see ourselves—our unsewn seams now puckering as we cling to one another—in the tiny mirror next to the door, before placing the bonnet over our wild black hair and tying it beneath our chin.

The fire in us dims, but we can still manage the stairs. No one notices us leave, a small parcel tucked beneath our arm. Not in the dark. Not in the gloom. Not when money has been exchanged. Our seams loosen enough that we begin to stumble as we leave the village. There is enough strength in us to crawl back to our cottage. For the last time, we swipe at the bonnet strings and manage to free our hair. We unwrap Jacob's heart and set it in the ruined fireplace. Our fingers tremble for a moment when we start the fire. The heart blackens and crackles.

We stand together and watch, holding ourselves together.

The flames reach our blue homespun, and we bid each other farewell. My sisters, you were brilliant. We are powerful and true, and we understand one very important thing: only *real* monsters die tonight.

We have seen to it.

This Strange Machine
Josh Hanson

JENNY SAW IT HAPPEN. The car was moving so quickly—seventy-five in a residential zone—that it was almost instantaneous, almost too quick to see at all. But in Jenny's mind it played out impossibly slow, the images trapped in the sludge of her terror, her body straining forward toward the street, reaching out for Rae, her twin, her mirror image warped by not knowing. Rae's face was happy and open, slightly breathless. She'd chased the basketball into the road from the driveway where they were playing one-on-one, radiant in the early spring afternoon. Not quite hot, but the sun actually warming their skin, the tops of their heads. It was Jenny's shot, a three-pointer from the very edge of the driveway, where the grass met the sidewalk, and then it had gone in, all net, hit the bottom of the garage door, and shot back down the driveway at a wild angle.

Rae had called it, running with her loose, easy strides down into the street. The ball reached the far side of the road and bounced off the curb, and Rae met it somewhere in the middle. This was where the memory slowed, dragged, time gone syrupy, the light murky. Rae turned, ball at her chest, squeezed between her hands. At twelve, her hands were already large and long-fingered. Her face was radiant. Rae's second tooth on the right was crooked, the only sure way for the uninitiated to tell the two of them apart. Rae had fought the idea of braces. That tooth was a totem. Jenny saw her smile, and somehow she knew even before she heard the scream of tires. She felt herself clench with fear.

The car never slowed. There were no skid marks on the road to measure. The car just flashed by in a blue blur. There might have been a sound, but Jenny couldn't remember it. She just saw Rae thrown up into the air, and even as the car hit the curb and flipped, sliding upside-down across the Millers' front yard and striking their silver maple tree, Rae was coming down wrong on the blacktop, hitting with her shoulder first, her head already loose on her neck, and she seemed to fold backwards, her tennis shoes landing flat on the ground in a way that her spine should not have allowed—and then there *was* a sound. Jenny heard it even over the crushing glass and screeching metal of the car wrapping around the Millers' tree. A crunching sound like when you stepped on an old pinecone back behind the house. And then Rae was transformed into a pile of limbs, and as Jenny ran toward her, still caught up in the thick, viscous air of nightmares, the blood began to spread out in a pool beneath the crumpled body.

Ten seconds at the most.

Ten seconds for Rae's life to end, and for Jenny's to change forever.

It was early May when Jenny returned to school. The middle school was a concrete patch of ground ringed with portable trailers, with a low, brick building at one edge. The whole campus behind a cow field ten miles outside of town. Jenny and Rae had joked that the town wanted to hide the middle schoolers out of shame, but the truth was that this once-abandoned campus was a holding place while a new building was being constructed in town. Still, it was depressing and flat, and there were nothing but fields on three sides and the interstate humming by on the fourth.

Jenny made it most of the way through first period before it happened. It was pre-algebra, and they were all working quietly on their problems. One through fifty, even numbers only. Mindless and tedious and exactly what Jenny needed to stop her brain from working over the images that ran and ran on a loop.

Rae's body in the air. Rae's body collapsing into itself as it hit the pavement. Rae's blood spreading out from her shattered skull.

And then Andy Madsen had gotten up to sharpen his pencil, taking too long at the sharpener, whittling the pencil down to a stub. Just wasting time. Andy Madsen couldn't sit still for long. He'd been that way since kindergarten. And when he finally moved back toward his seat, he passed directly by Jenny's seat, and he leaned down, just a bit, and spoke one sentence, low, under his breath.

"Hear there's a new speed bump in front of your house."

He continued on, dropping into his seat, and then looked back over his shoulder, showing all of his yellow teeth in a wide grin.

Jenny didn't feel any kind of shock. She didn't feel wounded. Andy Madsen was a toad. He didn't have the power to wound her. But she was angry, and it was a cold anger. Calm.

Closing her textbook, she stood up. She'd covered it at the beginning of the year with a grocery bag, and the corners of the cover were worn through. She'd written "Math" in big, block letters on the front. She carried the book down the aisle and as she came up to Andy Madsen, she swung it away from him, brushing it against Francesca Sadler, who gave a little questioning gasp, and then swung it as hard as she could into Andy Madsen's upturned face. She felt more than heard his nose collapse, and when she pulled the book back, blood was already sheeting down the lower half of his face. His eyes—while open—didn't seem to be focused on anything, his head tipped back, as if he were examining the ceiling.

Jenny lifted the book up over her head with both hands and brought it down flat against his face. Teeth crunched and cut through his lips, and she was raising the book again to continue her attack on Andy Madsen's face, when Mrs. Lewis grabbed her arms roughly and pulled her away.

The room seemed to go silent. Jenny was floating in warm water. And she knew, even as she was being dragged toward the door, that this would mean big trouble, that she might be expelled even, but she didn't care, because she'd seen it twice. Two sudden flashes, as if the image had been spliced into reality for just a single frame at a time. Each time the book had connected with Andy Madsen's face, she'd seen Rae, standing, smiling, with the basketball clutched between her hands and the sun on her face. That's why she would have beaten Andy Madsen to death: just to see Rae one more time.

✱✱✱

The vice principal had been as kind as he could be while still suspending Jenny for two weeks. He'd explained to her mother that Andy's family were within their rights to pursue assault charges.

Before her mother had arrived, he had spoken to Jenny in hushed tones, about grief and about loss, and about anger. He said he understood. And he said this sentence that kept circling through her mind like some kind of riddle.

Hurt people hurt people.

It was too stupid to even think about, and its construction was almost insulting, but it caught on some jagged part of her mind and wouldn't let go.

Hurt people hurt people.

Jenny's mother had said very little at the school and even less on the way home, the car humming the ten miles along the interstate back to town. Her mother said little these days. She went to mass three nights a week and once on Sunday mornings. She read books she checked out from the library in big stacks: mysteries, thrillers, romances. It didn't seem to matter, and she didn't seem to get any real enjoyment out of them. They were just something to distract her from the real world, the world where one of her daughters had been snatched away from her in the most meaningless way. So she prayed and she read and she said little to Jenny, and less to Jenny's father.

Her father had started staying out later and later, coming home slurring and friendly in a way that was alien to him. Jenny had heard her mother shout one night about him driving home drunk, about how dangerous it was, how he could kill Rae. It

129

made no sense, was an accusation built out of sorrow and rage and recrimination. Rae was already dead. But in the new logic of the household, it made perfect sense, and her father had stormed out of the house, tires squealing out of the driveway, and he hadn't come back until the next day.

At home, Jenny sat in her room. She'd been instructed to think about what she'd done, and that's just what she was doing. She'd seen Rae. Twice. Once for each blow she'd delivered to Andy Madsen's face. She'd been real. Just as she'd been in that moment before.

She had to find out how to bring her back again.

She thought it must be her rage. The vice principal had said her rage wouldn't help, would only hurt, but she had her doubts about that. She thought now that her rage might bridge the narrow gap between her and Rae, might pull her back across the almost transparent barrier between their two worlds.

Nothing to do but try it out.

She left her room, slipping down the hall, through the dining area where they no longer ate, and the kitchen, spotlessly clean. There was no sign of her mother in the living room, so she slipped out to the garage. The light above the workbench flickered and finally came on, bathing the area in antiseptic blue light. Tools were scattered across the bench, on the pegboard along the back wall. Jenny picked up the hammer. She let it bounce in her hand a bit, testing the weight, and then she turned. There was her mother's car, and beyond that, the big, ugly motorcycle her dad took out maybe three weekends a summer. It had a tall windscreen, a padded backrest, and bulky compartments along the back, all of it in a sparkly plum color that made Jenny think of carnival rides.

If rage would bring Rae back, even for a moment, Jenny could provide a never-ending supply.

She took out the headlight first. It popped with a brittle sound that was disappointingly slight. So she attacked the front fender, using both hands, swinging sideways, sometimes over her head. It was all fiberglass and cracked and slewed but didn't really shatter in a way she found satisfying, so she moved around and started on the dials and displays. On the handlebars. Glass and metal smashed and crumpled; Jenny felt a joy mixing with the rage as she began to cave in the rounded gas tank. The noise was terrific, and her arms burned in a way that told her this was right and proper.

But Rae didn't appear, and the joy turned malignant.

Her mother had to almost tackle her to get the hammer out of her hands, wrestling her to the cold pavement of the garage floor, Jenny weeping, tears and snot running down her face, hands trembling.

Her mother held her tight. It was less an embrace than a constraint, a way of keeping her from doing any more damage, but it was enough in that moment. She buried her face in her mother's shirt and wept. She wasn't weeping for Rae's loss. She'd finished with that. She was weeping at her failure.

Rage wasn't enough.

Maybe it wasn't her anger that had called to Rae.

Hurt people hurt people.

Maybe it was pain.

✳✳✳

Jenny tried it on herself first. Nothing happened. She pushed a bent-open safety pin into the meat of her thigh, and when nothing happened, she did it again. And again. She stood in the bathroom, staring at herself in the mirror and pinched the skin on the inside of her upper arm as hard as she could, twisting it until tears sprang from her eyes.

Rae stayed away.

The problem, she thought, was that she couldn't call up the same giddy rage as she'd felt when she'd crushed Andy Madsen's nose in. To give herself up to that kind of release while slashing at her own inner thighs with a box cutter would lead to nothing but a hospital stay.

And her own pain wasn't what Rae wanted. She sensed that now. Rae wanted vengeance. Rae wanted all of the life denied to her, even the pain and rage. *Especially* the pain and rage.

Three days into her suspension, while her mother was still at work, Jenny parked herself on the front steps and watched as the kids came home from school. The buses stopped two blocks up, so a whole variety of school kids passed by her front door. Kindergarteners in big colorful backpacks, older kids, too, though fewer of those. When a trio of middle school boys passed by, she sat up straighter, looking not at them, but the way they had come.

And soon she saw what she'd been waiting for.

Carrie Donovan came up the sidewalk with her bag slung over one shoulder, her hair pulled back into a tight ponytail, eyes down. Carrie Donovan had made Rae's life miserable since the second grade. She operated an intricate whisper network of mean girl information. It was the usual lesbian jokes and cracks about her clothes. She was a terror. Always had been. And now, at twelve years old, she was a terror bottled up inside a perfectly-styled body, encased in the perfect clothes.

Jenny called Carrie's name.

Carrie looked up, shaken out of whatever dream of petty cruelties she'd been lost to.

"Hey," Jenny said. She put on a smile.

Carrie stopped and looked at her without responding, one hip out.

"We've been going through some of Rae's stuff. Getting rid of it. If you'd like something, you can take it."

Carrie looked suspicious. She was evil, but not stupid. She should be suspicious. Jenny had once knocked one of Carrie's back teeth loose in the locker room.

"It's not much. We took the stuff we wanted to save. But it's just going to go to Goodwill."

Carrie shifted to her other foot, clutching the strap of her backpack with both hands.

"Okay, sure," she said, and she had the decency to look down, to avert her eyes, to look shamed.

Jenny led her through the quiet house, down the hall and into Rae's room, right beside her own. She'd lied, of course. No one had gone through anything. The room was just as Rae had left it. Even her bath towel was pooled on the floor beside her bed, probably sprouting green mold. Carrie turned around, taking it all in. Soccer posters on the wall. Clothes stacked in multicolored plastic crates. Rae's desk, with the old cast-off family computer, its plastic yellowed with age and heat. The twin bed, its blankets still thrown back from the morning Rae had woken up and never returned.

"All of this?" Carrie said, but Jenny knew that in "all of this" there was nothing Carrie Donovan could want. She was sneering inside, but wise enough to hide it. Only curiosity had brought her here, and now she didn't know what to do.

"This is everything, yeah," Jenny said.

And then she hit her with the hammer.

✳✳✳

Rae was there. Jenny cried and laughed to see her. She hovered just at the corner of the room, near the ceiling, smiling down on her. She flickered in and out, like a bad bulb, but when the signal started to falter, Jenny would simply place her shoe on top of Carrie Donovan's broken fingers, and the shrieks would bring Rae's image back into startling focus.

Carrie was sitting on the floor, her back against Rae's bed. After the second blow to the head, she'd been unable to control much of her body. She'd pissed herself, the smell acidic and sharp in the room, mixed with the hot tang of blood. She'd passed out twice, Rae flickering out of existence completely, and it was then that Jenny understood the need for patience. Luckily, it really did seem to be pain and not rage that brought Rae back from wherever she'd been, because if Jenny gave way to her rage, Carrie Donovan would have been dead in minutes.

Rae looked down approvingly at Jenny.

"I miss you," Jenny said, and Rae just smiled sadly.

133

"I'll bring you back for good," she said, but Rae just twisted her face up into a frown.

"No, I can. Maybe I have to finish her?" Standing over Carrie's broken body, bloody hammer in her fist, she couldn't bring herself to say "kill." There was still a line, even if it was growing fuzzier with every hammer blow.

The truth was, she didn't want to kill Carrie. It wasn't out of some moral concern. It wasn't fear of punishment. The truth was that Carrie's pain was the engine driving this strange machine, and Jenny worried that if she died, her sister's image would blink out and she'd never get it back.

So she grew methodical, working on the small bones of her feet, first breaking them with the hammer and then pressing them with her thumb, just hard enough to make Rae's image come fully into focus but not enough to make Carrie pass out.

She could do this for days. There were so many bones. And so many soft parts, too. She decided she would leave the teeth for last, thinking how poking a bent paperclip into the exposed nerves of a broken tooth would turbo-charge the machine.

But then she heard the garage door rising on its mechanical track.

She shoved one of Rae's dirty socks into Carrie's mouth, left the hammer sitting on top of Rae's dresser, and slipped out of the room. In the bathroom, she washed up, scrubbing the dried blood from her forearms, checking her face and hair.

Her mother greeted her numbly and started making dinner. There was no danger of her going into Rae's room. She wouldn't. Maybe ever. Jenny knew of people who kept lost children's rooms like monuments. This wasn't that. This was absolute denial. They'd keep the door shut and pretend nothing lay beyond it.

And that was smart, because pain now lived in that room.

That night, after her parents were in bed, Jenny crept into Rae's room. Carrie was sleeping, or maybe unconscious. Jenny had a brief moment where she was suddenly concerned about the effects of a concussion. She'd given Carrie two good cracks to the skull, the second one really knocking something loose, and she knew from soccer that you weren't supposed to go to sleep afterward.

But when Jenny pressed her thumb into the purple swollen mass that had once been Carrie Donovan's left foot, the girl sprang awake, screaming down in her throat, the sock absorbing most of the sound.

Good.

She pressed again, feeling the pieces of bone scrape against each other deep inside the swollen mass, and she kept her eye on the corner by the ceiling.

Rae didn't flicker but instead seemed to fade in. The image seemed stronger now, but maybe that was the darkness of the room. Rae still standing in the spring sunlight, awaiting the car that would pulverize her perfect body.

Looking back at Carrie, Jenny saw the girl's eyes, round, looking up and behind her. Carrie saw Rae, too. That was good. If it was all in Jenny's head, that would mean something was terribly wrong, but Carrie confirmed the truth of the whole enterprise. This engine was real.

Jenny cupped Carrie's face in her hand, pulling her gaze back to her.

"I'm sorry," she said. "It's not personal. But you can see how important this is. And I forgive you for all those years of being a grade-A bitch, too. I understand things better now. Now I know that hurt people hurt people."

And then she went to get the hammer.

✳✳✳

Jenny kept Carrie Donovan in Rae's room for three days, into the weekend, right through the television reports of the local girl gone missing on her way home from school, through her parents moving zombie-like through the house, not speaking. Her father vanishing for hours at a time, her mother cleaning and cleaning.

She never got to the teeth.

Sunday morning, Jenny had slipped into the room to find Carrie Donovan staring fixedly at the wall, head at an odd angle, and a foul stench in the room. She'd shit herself was part of it, but the other part was death, a smell written into Jenny's genetic memory. There was also the smell of rot, some of the wounds already starting to fester.

She stood against the closed door and stared. She was less concerned with the practicalities—the need to dispose of the body, to get past her mother, to cover up the smell—and more concerned with her sudden inability to contact Rae, to call her back from the space beyond the walls.

The machine had broken down.

She needed a new plan—but she never got a chance to make one.

Jenny's mother was at mass, not even bothering to try to get Jenny and her father to come along, and her father was sleeping off last night's bender. He'd come in during the small hours, slamming doors and bumping into things, and Jenny had heard the low rumbling of argument from her parents' room down the hall, and then silence.

Jenny was just opening the door to Rae's room, a fistful of black trash bags in her hand, when her father strode out of his own room, stopping suddenly when he saw where she was going.

"What are you doing in there?" he said. And then his eyes moved to the garbage bags. "What do you think you're doing?"

Jenny saw it all on his face. All his assumptions and suspicions, so childish and petty. That she was stealing from her dead sister, or—worse—that she had begun the work of cleaning out the room, emptying it, destroying the last vestiges of Rae, even as the memories of Rae ate away at his insides and made him weak with pain.

He stepped forward, looming over Jenny.

"I said, what are you doing?"

Jenny raised her arm up, the garbage bags rustling in her grip, in some vague gesture of self-defense, as if her father might suddenly strike her, something he had never done in her entire life. He flinched back, as if it were she who was attacking him, and reflexively grasped her wrist. As soon as his fingers clamped down on her, Jenny responded like a cornered animal. She was overcome with a sudden terror of her father, certain that he was going to harm her in some irreparable way, that he would take out all of his own rage and hurt—the rage and hurt he tried so hard to drink away—on her, the walking, talking reminder of her lost twin.

She struck him with her free hand, a glancing blow across his chin, not even hurting him, but startling him, causing him to pull back, twisting her arm in his grip as he did so. Jenny screamed, the twisting putting impossible pressure on her elbow, enough to make her sure that something would pop, and she was slapping and scratching at him. A scream filling the tight confines of the hallway, a scream she realized must be her own, though it seemed so alien, so animal, so terrified, that she could not claim it.

In the end, it was sheer size that determined the outcome. Giving a deep growl, her father stepped forward, thrusting her backward, her feet tangling over each other, and she fell back against the partly opened door, her father stumbling forward with her, his hand still clamped to her arm. The door swung inward, and Jenny went sprawling, her hand slipping from her father's grip as he worked to remain on his feet.

She fell flat on her back, her head coming to rest between Carrie Donovan's shattered knees.

Her father stood frozen. He didn't look surprised or confused; he looked blank, as if his eyes were not taking in any information at all. As if all the lines were down, his power cut. Two scratches ran down his right cheek, thin trickles of blood running down his jawline. Then he sucked in a breath and turned his eyes to Jenny.

"Wha—"

Two flies were buzzing around the ceiling, startled up from Carrie's corpse by the ruckus, eager to return to their feast, and their sound seemed very loud in the room.

"I had to," Jenny said, getting to her feet.

Her father pushed past her, kneeling down, reaching out a hand as if to check for a pulse and then pulling it back again, either in disgust or in deference to the obvious fact that the girl was dead.

He raised the hand to his mouth, pushing a knuckle between his lips. "How could …" He bit the knuckle, tried again. "Why?"

He turned to look up at her just in time to see the hammer coming down. It caught him at the temple, his vision exploding into fireballs of white light, pain shooting down his neck and through his left arm. He fell sideways, landing in Carrie Donovan's lap.

Jenny's father tried to get himself upright, trying not to touch the already-bloating body beneath him. He got himself raised on one hand, raising the other to his face. He felt his eyeball resting on his cheek. He screamed and ran his hand along the side of his face, feeling the place where the hammer had shattered the orbital bone and torn open the flesh around his eye socket, his fingers coming away bright with blood.

"Oh, god," he said. "Jenny."

And then the hammer came down on the top of his head, punching through the fissures at its crown, the steel head pushing down, pushing shards of razoring bone with it, down into the soft jelly of his brain.

He jerked. His left leg kicked out, knocking over a metal garbage can.

Jenny stepped back in horror, the hammer still protruding from the top on her father's skull, his body shaken by irregular pulses of electricity, his tongue pushing out of his mouth.

That's when she heard the humming buzz of the garage door opening.

***

Jenny couldn't even move. She had no energy to try to hide what she'd done, or to run away, and she refused to hurt her mother. Dad had been a mistake. Things had gotten out of hand. But she wouldn't hurt Mom.

She heard her mother's keys hit the dining room table and her mother speaking almost to herself.

"Christ, what's that smell?"

And then she heard her coming down the hall.

When her mother stepped into the doorway, Jenny was half-sitting on Rae's desk, the computer keyboard pressed back against the CPU, her arms hanging limp between her thighs. Her mother didn't scream, and Jenny was thankful for that. Her father had collapsed, lying across Carrie Donovan's legs, his body still jerking, his tongue still working.

Her mother raised a hand to her mouth as if to hold something terrible back, and then she looked to Jenny.

"What did he do?" she whispered.

It took a long beat for the question to register, for Jenny to piece it together, to understand her mother's misunderstanding.

"No, Mom," she said, her body still limp. "It was me."

"I understand. But what did he do?"

"It was me," she said. "I did it all. For Rae."

Her mother jerked back as if slapped.

"She was here," Jenny said, only recognizing that she was crying by the tightness in her own voice. "I just wanted her to stay."

"What? How?"

"I'll show you," she said, pushing herself forward off of the desk, dropping down beside her twitching father. White foam was now dropping from his open mouth, his tongue pushing it out.

She grasped the handle of the hammer and wrenched it upward. Her father's head jerked with the movement, and her mother gave a sharp intake of breath. Jenny stood, getting better leverage, and, putting her knee against his shoulder, she pulled the hammer free. It came loose with a sound like a spoon pushing into crème brûlée. She grabbed his face with her other hand, turning it toward her, making sure he was still with her. His eyes stared out at crazy angles, seeing nothing, his tongue still pushing in and out of his mouth.

"Look up there," Jenny said, pointing with the gore-clotted hammer.

Her mother obeyed, happy to look away from the carnage before her, her eyes going at once to the corner where the wall met the ceiling.

Jenny got down on her knees, pushing her father's hand down on the carpet and raising the hammer. She brought it down on the first and second knuckle, and there was a sound like gravel under car tires, and her father gave a muffled scream, seeming to be already choking on the foam that was dropping from his lips. Her mother gasped.

Jenny looked up, and there she was. Rae held the basketball between her hands, and the sun beat down upon her head and shoulders, and she was alive and beautiful and perfect. Her mother dropped to her knees, crossing herself and rapidly muttering an incomprehensible prayer. Jenny should have seen it before. Of course her mother would understand. What else had she learned from three nighttime masses a week and another on Sunday, if it wasn't the connection between pain and redemption.

Rae began to flutter out of sight, and her mother reached out toward her.

"It's okay," Jenny said, smiling. "I can bring her back."

She raised the hammer again and brought it down in the same place she'd hit before, her father's index finger now pointing off at a sickly angle, the flesh where it met the hand a pulp of blood and bone.

Rae's image surged into sight. It was as if she were being projected directly from her father's wounds.

"It's like a machine," Jenny said.

She didn't need to explain. Her mother didn't want explanations. Instead, she leaned forward and pressed her finger into the place where the hammer had split her husband's hand open. She hooked her finger, digging in, and he jerked, trying to pull his hand away, and Rae's image surged, bright against the wall.

"Oh, baby," she cried. "Oh, my baby."

Jenny was ecstatic. She hugged her mother, and the two of them looked up at the image of her dead sister smiling down on them.

✳✳✳

It was in that perfect moment that her father began not just to twitch but to jerk violently. His ruined hand flew up into the air, his legs kicking out, and then he was convulsing, chest rising up off of Carrie Donovan's legs and slamming back down, blood-flecked foam spraying from his mouth.

Jenny and her mother pulled away, horrified.

It went on for some time, and then it stopped.

His body seemed to deflate, and a rattling gurgle escaped from his throat, and then he was still, and Rae vanished from her place in the corner. Jenny's mother howled, clambering forward, pulling at the front of her husband's shirt, demanding that he return her daughter to her. Jenny had to pull her away.

"It's the pain," Jenny said, and her mother looked at her as if she were speaking a foreign language. "I didn't mean for them to die," she continued. "It doesn't work if they're dead. It's the pain that makes the machine work."

Her mother tilted her head, exactly like a dog listening.

"We need someone we can hurt. Just hurt. And Rae will come back."

Her mother looked down at the floor, up at the spot where her daughter had all-too-briefly hovered over them, and then she looked at Jenny.

A smile transformed her entire face.

✲✲✲

Within minutes they had Rae's desk chair in the center of the room, and Mom was seated in it, facing the corner, her hands grasping its curving arms. Jenny sat on the floor below her, her mother's left foot resting in her lap. She held her mother's leg tight against her chest, and in the other hand she held the needlenose pliers.

"Ready?" Jenny asked.

Her mother nodded, squeezing the arms of the chair, her expression beatific.

Jenny grasped the toenail of her mother's smallest toe with the tip of the pliers and then angled them up and back. The nail pulled up surprisingly easily, with very little sound, coming away entirely with only another small twist of Jenny's wrist. She clutched her mother's leg, which had tensed against her body. The flesh where the nail had been was bright pink, the toe looking uncanny, almost alien, and then the blood welled up in a thick bead, almost black.

Rae smiled down at them both.

Her mother laughed, tears rolling down her cheeks.

This was it. This was her great purpose. Some thought motherhood revolved around childbirth, but Jenny's mother knew better. Motherhood was a machine that ran on pain, its only purpose to keep her babies whole and safe.

Jenny and her mother watched Rae as she dribbled the ball and then returned it to its usual place, squeezed between her hands. And then, when the image began to fade, Jenny looked up at her mother again. She nodded down at her, happy beyond all hope. She was happy to have so much to give. Her whole body. Her whole life. Grist for the mill, for this grinding machine.

Jenny peeled back the next toenail, and her mother almost fainted, not with pain but with ecstasy. Ecstasy mixed up with pain. It was all one here, under the hood, down where things got done, inside this strange machine that was a mother's love.

Your Heart Stops
Tyler Battaglia

I TELL MYSELF THAT I CAN FIX YOU. That no matter how many times you die, I can *save* you. If your heart stops, I can start it again. If your lungs stop breathing, I can force the air back into them. If your liver fails to filter toxins, if it poisons its own host, I can extract the offending contaminants myself.

This has been going on for a long time now. You die, I bring you back. A piece of you breaks, I mend it. A part of you fails, I fix it. Your heart stops, I start it again. Your heart stops, I start it again. Your heart stops, I start it again.

I have begun to be more intimate with the inner workings of your body than with the inner workings of your mind; the inner workings of your soul, should such a thing exist. How is it possible that I have held your kidneys more than I have held your hand? How is it possible that I have mended your broken bones more than I have made you laugh?

I recognize in the most familiar detail your organs, your blood, your bones. I have memorized the patterns of your carotid arteries. The texture of your tendons speaks volumes to me. The pulsing of lifeblood through your veins is music to my ears. I hear the faint humming of your heart even in my dreams.

No matter how many times you die, I can save you. I cannot lose you. I maintain you. Piece by piece, I bring you back. I rebuild you. And I learn to believe in the soul after all—because if I replace all of you, what remains but that? Like the Ship of Theseus, you are renewed. But it is your soul and your history that remain. It keeps me sane if I accept the soul. If I accept the spirit. If I accept that something of you is genuinely irreplaceable. That you would remember. That you would still love.

I am not sure which part of you the soul is tied to. I pray it is not the heart.

I have never prayed before. Not for anyone, not even myself. But I pray for you. With you there, lying there on the autopsy table, skin of your chest stapled open to offer your viscera to me, I discover God. There is holiness in your innards, there is grace in your entrails.

I have robbed so many graves to replace the pieces of you, I no longer recognize some of the individual parts you have been built from. Still, I learn the patterns again. I connect bone to muscle to tissue to flesh. Link it all back to the heart. Your heart stops, I start it again.

You are awake so rarely these days, clinging to this facsimile of life that I have created for you. You drift in and out of consciousness so rapidly that I never have time to speak to you, to ask you what your heart wants.

I wonder if you see God while you are under my scalpel. I wonder if you were to wake for more than a moment, would you recognize yourself? Would you recognize me?

Would you still love?

Your heart stops, I start it again. Your heart stops, I start it again. Your heart stops.

Baby
Samantha H. Chung

THE GUY HAS TAKEN UP RESIDENCE IN HER KITCHEN. The kitchen counter, specifically. He's splayed out on the laminate like a placemat or a meal, bits of him always open and red-weeping depending on what part of him Percy is currently working on. Mary has been ordering takeout for the last several weeks.

It's not that she's disinterested in the guy. Quite the opposite, in fact. Mary is, as a rule, extremely interested in guys. But this guy is cold to the touch, and at any given moment he has at least one sharp thing sticking out of him, and he doesn't flirt. He's also a live wire, which Mary would find sexy if it wasn't so literal.

"Percy's been experimenting with electricity," she tells Polidori over the phone. "The theory of galvanism."

"So the creature's his Lazarus."

"It's not resurrection, it's ... reanimation. Bringing the body back to life after it's expired."

In the silence that follows she half-considers inviting Polidori to Geneva—maybe a surgeon can see where Percy is going wrong, can determine the rate-limiting step in the creation of artificial life. She speaks into the receiver again.

"I think he feels sorry for me."

She doesn't have to explain why. Polidori already knows about the teen pregnancy, the unofficial elopement (and official disownment), and the preemie that died before she could give it a name. Mary has always loathed being the object of someone's pity.

"What, you're not saying he thinks this thing can replace ..."

145

Baby

"It's a little misguided," she admits. "But it's romantic. Would you mind getting us a little something from the blood bank? I know you like to keep it for yourself, but if you could snag a few extra—"

Polidori hangs up. The guy remains at the corner of Mary's vision. She stares at the phone in her hand, chewing her lip, then dials the number for delivery.

***

After Percy has gone to his study, Mary turns the kitchen lights on. The guy is there, death-white under the LEDs. Eight-feet tall, probably, although she wants to lie down next to him to get an accurate reading.

Instead she settles for touching him. (When did she decide the guy was a he?) The fingers of her left hand skim over his coxal bone, the slack muscles of his abdomen. The angry stitches pulled taut against his chest. Percy sewed him up himself, but this guy needs a girl's touch.

In her right hand is a boning knife.

Percy has never understood her fascination with opening things up. His interests lie elsewhere, mostly in the realm of putting-back-together. So she does this at night, when he's bent over his books and will never know. She touches the tip of the blade to the guy's cheek and draws a crescent moon underneath his eye.

Percy has been feeding the guy bagged blood through IV, hoping that maybe getting the juices flowing would trigger some kind of awakening. Mary presses the pad of her index finger to the wet spot, then touches the finger to her lips.

She's never found it erotic, drinking blood, not in the way Polidori does. But she likes the idea of iron under her fingernails, armor on her tongue. She licks her lips and the taste bubbles up into her nose like bad champagne.

146

***

Here is the first ghost story: nine months after her baby dies, Mary sees the guy in a dream. In the dream, she goes to the kitchen for a juice (her dreams are usually uneventful) and there he is, sitting upright on the counter, stolen eyes glittering amber in their pale sockets.

He makes a sound, a raspy rumble coming from his throat. His voice is like a rusty hinge.

"Did I solicit thee from darkness to promote me?"

She blinks. "So you can speak."

"I've been listening." He flexes his fingers, then curls them into a fist. "Who made me?"

"Percy." Then she clarifies: "My boyfriend."

The guy leaps down from the counter. He's not awkward or clumsy like she expected he would be, having only been alive for hours. He moves like an animal—like a big cat. Soft on his feet.

"I've heard him talk," he says. "What is a galvanic man?"

"Galvani was a natural philosopher. He theorized that passing an electrical current through dead tissue could reanimate its cells. One day, he shocked the corpse of a death-row prisoner from the Tower of London, made him move his arms and legs around in front of a big crowd. It freaked a bunch of people out."

He takes a step closer, and she can feel his breath against her face. She thinks, in some translucent part of her consciousness, that she should be afraid. But her dream-logic pushes the feeling aside.

"But the one thing Galvani couldn't do was make that prisoner alive again. Sure, electricity can make a dead guy sit up and do some tricks. The guy wasn't thinking on his own. He wasn't making decisions. So that's what we're—what Percy is trying to do. To reanimate the brain, to construct a true galvanic man. That's you."

"And what makes your Percy believe he can accomplish this where the original scientist so miserably failed? Why can't he wake me up?"

"He's trying. He's trying really hard, I promise."

Baby

It turns violent. Dreams often do. He shoves her against the wall with his hands around her throat, in the goth-coquette way she used to think was attractive at sixteen. No one can really hurt her though, not here, not in the dream. It's a play that her mind puts on for her body every night, a cash-grab theatre investment with a one-way fourth wall. Damsel as a verb. She rolls her eyes and shoves him back.

✳✳✳

Two days later, the guy wakes up.

Mary awakes to Percy's exclamation. He's figured it out, he explains to her between breaths, he's made the creature alive, and he pulls her out of bed.

The guy is standing in the middle of the kitchen, illuminated by the single yellow ceiling light above the sink. Blue veins of electricity are crackling up and down his limbs—lightning runs through his veins. His eyes are black and empty. When Mary looks into them, she knows this is just a body, not the guy from her dream. Yes, Percy has made something, but he hasn't made a man.

And he is so, *so* ugly.

"He's a failure," she says to Polidori a day later. "He can't walk, he can't speak, he can barely keep down solid food—"

"Why do you expect him to?"

"Because he's a guy. He's a man."

"Well, he wasn't alive until yesterday. Speaking in those terms, he's a baby."

"He's *not* a baby." The sentence comes out harsher than she intended.

"He was your idea, wasn't he?" Polidori says. "That night we told ghost stories. Your story was about him."

Mary pauses. She has honestly never considered this before, that Percy's project might have been inspired by the little story she told in the dark, during that year without a summer. But she won't bring up the question with him, even to ask if the idea was … a collaboration, and not necessarily theft. He would take offense at any implication that he doesn't own the guy entirely, even though she would be glad to give up her small part of him if only Percy asked.

"I told a story about a galvanic man," she says carefully. "All I did was take apart a dead scientist's idea. Anyone could have come up with it. I'm sure someone already has."

She's not sure. She's read a lot, and she has never read a story like hers.

"Besides, my story was a fictional endeavor, an exercise of the mind," she goes on. "What Percy is doing is purely scientific. It's an exercise in … reversal. If we can have sex without reproduction, why can't we have it the other way around, too?"

Polidori doesn't have a satisfactory answer, and after he hangs up, Mary banishes the conversation from her mind. She lets her suspicions go unspoken over microwaved meals until they disappear from her memory completely, because Percy wouldn't steal from her, he wouldn't take anything from her without her consent.

Percy is a pinned-back grenade. He believes in veganism and no God and the liberation of asthmatics. His hair went gray at seventeen and he has never dyed it. He is mercurial and strange, which is what Mary loves so much about him. This is something he said on their first date: "Did you know I'm missing a lung?"

"If you think that's sexy," she replied, "it's not."

"I'm not trying to be sexy."

At this Mary laughed.

It's rarely been only the two of them as it is now, in the suburban Illinois house let to them by Polidori's patient-lover. Other people have always fit well in those spaces between them—Polidori, Byron, her sister Claire. The previous summer, when Mary was pregnant, was the last time they had all been together. That was a good season. Mary remembers it as the time when Percy's favorite topic was free love.

"Look at us, all gathered here together," he said one evening. "Untethered from the constraints of society, from the abomination of marriage. This is how we lived before the rich among us built cities, free as animals."

149

Baby

"But animals don't really practice free love, at least not in the way you're describing it," Claire said. "A pride of lions only has one male. And when a new male decides he wants a pride of his own, he takes over a group of lionesses by force and kills all the cubs he didn't sire. Only male animals have the privilege of free love. Females are coerced into serial monogamy."

"You're using the wrong phraseology," Mary replied. "Animals aren't rational creatures. A lion can't understand consent."

"That's what I'm saying. It's not free love—it's rape."

Mary considers herself monogamous by choice. She's been with Percy for two years and has never wanted another partner during that time. But the guy is different. On some days, she believes he *is* the two of them—a product of Mary's mind and Percy's hands, an intellectual exercise made flesh. On other days, Mary sees him on the kitchen counter and wants to swallow him, lightning and all.

✳✳✳

Here is another ghost story: the guy is alive. When Mary meets him in her dream, he now thrums with an electric glow, a comic-book hero with luminescent bones.

In her dream they're in an empty cinema, seventh row center. He's a beacon in the dark. She reaches into the bucket of popcorn between them and comes up with a handful of teeth.

Mary has seen this movie before. On the screen, Percy works at their kitchen counter, bending over a body. The flickering ceiling light paints the room yellow. The camera pans jerkily from his hands to the scissors lying on the counter.

She can tell he hasn't slept in days. His face fills the screen with a close-up on the dark circles under his eyes, the sweat glistening on his forehead. He wets the tip of a polypropene thread between his lips.

"Who made me?" the guy asks again.

In the nights between that first dream and his awakening they've developed a dialogue, a kind of Socratic back-and-forth between them. Mary has settled into her new role well—her as instructor, him as student. The camera zooms on Percy's knuckles.

"You were made through a combination of scientific inquiry and its application."

"What was the aim of my creation?"

"To build a galvanic man."

The guy takes a fistful of teeth from the bucket, crunches, and swallows. "And am I a man?"

"Well, I guess that's up to you."

The needle flashes in and out. Percy's hands are marked with evidence of his past work, thin healed scars in all the places where he's pierced the wrong skin. He leans over the counter, nose to nose with the body underneath him as he finishes a suture across its forehead.

Beautiful, he says to himself. *Beautiful.*

Then he looks off into some unseen room, alerted by a sound that must have been muted in post. He takes off his apron and hangs it on a hook over the door, tugs at his shirt, and walks offscreen as the scene fades to black.

The guy stares at his dim reflection as the credits start to roll.

"Am I ugly?" he asks.

"Terrifically."

He makes a noise that sounds vaguely like disappointment.

"He tried to make you beautiful," she says.

"Is that a good thing? To be beautiful?"

"Yes. Evolutionarily. Beautiful birds attract mates."

"I think you're beautiful," he says.

He still hurts her, in the end. When the movie is finished, he leads her to a break room with her baby in it and wrings its neck like a chicken. She helps him dissect the body with her boning knife.

Matriphagy is what it's called when mothers eat their children. Mary has never felt that urge. She debones her baby neatly and cleanly. When she's done, she wipes her hands on her blouse. In the dream, her clothes are white.

Baby

✱✱✱

Polidori turns out to be right. With Mary and Percy's pseudo-parental help, the guy learns to crawl, and then walk. He learns to hold a spoon. Ten times faster than a human child, Percy says with awe. The guy still doesn't speak.

On his two-month birthday, he disappears. They can find no evidence of a breakout—all the doors remain locked—but he simply isn't there anymore. This disturbs them for several weeks, but as with most disturbing things, they eventually move on from it.

Percy's uncle dies, and from the inheritance combined with the meager proceeds from his chapbook sales, they scrape together enough money to buy the house from Byron outright. Percy carries her over the threshold as she shrieks in delight. They've finally made it, high school sweethearts who've beaten the odds. More than once, Mary thinks of asking him to marry her, but she knows he'll refuse on principle, so she keeps her mouth shut.

She decides to write a novel. Once she puts her mind to it—*I have decided to write a novel*—it becomes stupidly easy to do the thing itself. Percy approves of this project because science fiction is for girls now, apparently, and he says she'll be able to identity-politics herself onto a bestseller list. Mary thinks this is rather dismissive, but she appreciates the support.

At some point between the novel's genesis and its publication, Percy has decided to replicate his experiment. Several times. The house has, one by one, become infested with eight-foot-tall scavenger babies, shuffling wordlessly through its rooms. Mary grows tired of them quickly. They take up space on the couch and interrupt her in the bathroom. One time she walks in on two of them having sex.

"Where are you even getting the bodies?" she asks Percy one day. He declines to answer.

Percy wants a baby. Why, she demands, when the house is already so overrun with them. He snorts at this, and Mary is reminded of her conversation with Polidori two years ago. *He's not a baby.*

152

Despite this, Mary discovers that she isn't opposed to the idea. She remembers the first baby, the one who was lost, the one who never had a name. They didn't know what a baby meant back then; they were only children themselves. But they can get it right this time, they *will* get it right, and then maybe Mary will be absolved. Maybe she'll understand her novel.

The first baby is miscarried before she even knows it exists. Then the second baby, too, during the sixth week. She tells Percy they'll try IVF as soon as she receives her first advance payment. The third lasts long enough for them to name him Will. But then he, too, is gone.

It grieves her to no end — the pageantry of biopsies and genetic tests, the cult of U by Kotex. Why should she have to go through all this when it happened so easily, so *accidentally*, the first time? She tries to explain this to Polidori over coffee one afternoon, hoping for a second doctor's opinion.

"I just don't understand," she says. "I would accept it, and Percy would, too, if we could only understand. Am I deficient somehow?"

"Well, speaking broadly, there are two things that could be going wrong," he says gently. "It's either the body, or it's the baby."

When she arrives home, Mary goes to the bathroom and stands in front of the mirror for a long time. She mouths the two words over and over, silently and without feeling. *Baby. Body.*

Baby.

✳✳✳

Mary goes on a book tour. Her novel has been purchased at auction in a very nice deal, and now she will spend the next six weeks taking rideshares between bookstores, airports, and hotels of varying quality. Her days are a blur of interviews, podcasts, and signing lines. The reviews say her book may have invented a new genre. Her publicist suggests applying to the Forbes 30 Under 30.

But who was really the monster? is the question she hears more than any other. She scribbles her signature and says it's up to the readers' interpretation.

She doesn't dream of her baby anymore. Since he disappeared, she doesn't dream of the guy, either—she's dealt with enough of them in real life.

Instead, she dreams of Percy. He stands in the open front doorway of her house as she runs to him, dragging her suitcase behind her. She stumbles inside and they crash together, her arms thrown around his shoulders and his hands clutching at her hair. Her tongue in his mouth, him always inviting her in.

The morning after she finds Percy in her dream, she miscarries again. She's familiar with the feeling by now. She stumbles to the mini-fridge and presses a cold Coke can to herself. She leans her head against the side, letting the cold numb her cheek. She sits there for two hours as blood seeps into the hotel carpet. Then she calls her publicist and says she needs to go home.

On the red eye from Heathrow to O'Hare, she dreams that she's in an old-school operating theater. She is on a stage, looking out at a mezzanine of spectators in bright red velvet chairs. Some she recognizes, some are strangers to her. A few of them are holding copies of her book.

She looks down. She's standing at the feet of a corpse on a metal gurney, naked and gray. Her eyes travel upward past his navel (he is a he) and to his face. His eyes are closed beneath a mop of hair that has gone prematurely silver. He is Percy.

There's something stuck between her back teeth. She tries to push it out with her tongue, but it doesn't budge. So she turns her back to the audience and does something medically unsanitary: she reaches into her mouth with a gloved hand. The thing comes loose, and she spits it into her palm.

It's a molar, glistening with saliva and half-rotten in her hand.

She hurriedly closes her fingers around the tooth. She doesn't know what to do with it—she feels around her mouth with her tongue, where there's now a cavity in the back where her third molar should be—and the people are watching, the people are waiting.

Casually (she hopes), she rests her hand on top of Percy's mouth, letting the tooth fall between his slightly parted lips. Then she starts talking.

"When I was eighteen, I told a story about a galvanic man."

Mary doesn't look up at the audience as she speaks. Her gaze is trained on Percy, his corpse, his body, the postmortem grayness of him.

"Galvani was a natural philosopher. He theorized that passing an electrical current through dead tissue could reanimate its cells."

As she speaks the speech she knows so well, she walks around the gurney to Percy's side. She reaches for her boning knife, because all she knows how to do is to take things apart—to rip skin away at the seams, to unwind the things inside her. But the knife isn't there.

She pauses to recollect herself. Then she reaches for the pile of metal roach clips on the bedside table. She can work with this, she thinks dimly, but the thought hardly matters. Her body is being moved by something beyond her control, some instinct deep within her that her conscious mind has yet to touch.

She affixes a clip to each of the body's index fingers. Then to his toes.

"Galvani sought resurrection. He never achieved it. But he could have gone further. The true leap forward, the thing of which he never even conceived, was creation."

She reaches upward and grasps a lever attached to one of the gurney's poles. She closes her eyes. There is water and flesh in her mouth, muscle and spit and air.

She brings the lever down.

Sparks fly from the gurney, bouncing off its metal surface. The electric current travels up the body's arms and legs. They reach a glorious double climax in his chest and skull, a white-blue explosion of light beneath his skin. The theater goes dark.

The body, silhouetted, convulses. His eyes fly open, the irises rolling back into his head. His back arches and his knees curl upward. A low moan emits from deep within his throat. It's not coming from him. Inside his chest, something has come alive.

When Mary lands, she has twelve missed calls. None from Percy.

✻✻✻

Here is one last ghost story: they find Percy's body while Mary is waiting in baggage claim. Polidori sends her a terse text and she abandons her luggage to call an Uber.

A coroner is already at the lake shore when she arrives. She pushes him away and the throng of people around him parts like a wound. She throws herself over the body like a mourner in a Greek tragedy and they can't pull her off, not even Polidori. When anyone approaches her, she hisses at them and snaps at their hands with her teeth.

She carries him to the car and barks her address at the stunned driver—she'll leave him a fat tip after all this is over—and then she drags him up their driveway. She doesn't make it quite all the way, and she collapses on the concrete several feet from the front door.

Percy is bloated and pale. His eyes are swollen shut. They must have tried resuscitation already, tried to jolt his heart back into motion. She hopes they didn't—chest compressions could have hurt what was inside. Maybe he was in the water too long and there was no hope even before they hauled him out of the lake. Mary kisses his fingers, his knees, the soles of his feet, and she licks a combination of tears and lakewater grime from her lips.

Then, a sound. The front door has creaked open, unlocked from the inside. Visible in the darkened doorway is one of Percy's guys. *Her* guy. Mary chokes back a cry.

"I made you," she says. "Don't ask. I remember now. You are a creation of my mind."

The guy doesn't respond. He just stands there, half-visible and completely still. They behold each other. He's so different from the guy in her dream, the guy who walked like a cat, who spoke to her like an intellectual equal. She wants to scream.

156

"You can speak. I've *heard* you speak. Here you're constrained by this man-body, this baby-body …"

His eyes flicker to the body on the ground. Anger oozes into those amber eyes and she thinks that maybe he's going to hurt her again. Or maybe he'll place his hand on her clavicle—gentle, so gentle—and hold it there. You never know with guys.

"You were jealous. But I loved you. He was only the host. My body wasn't right for it. And you were jealous."

She puts a hand on Percy's chest, and he growls.

"Come on. You know what I have to do. You saw me put it there."

The guy lumbers down the front steps, closing the distance between him and Mary. When he's within arm's reach, he holds out a knife. Her boning knife. He's holding it handle out, and the blade has cut a deep rivet into his hand.

Mary takes the knife. Her hands are shaking. Her hands cannot shake, she tells herself. She was a surgeon in her dream. She lays the tip of the knife against Percy's chest, on the opposite side of his heart. Then she cuts a clean slice all the way down to his abdomen.

She spits into the palm of her free hand. No teeth come out this time, just a translucent glob of saliva. She rubs it between her fingers and palm. Then—gentle, so gentle—she traces her thumb across the incision's raw edges.

She pushes her index finger into the cut. The skin parts for her and she crooks her finger inside the body. She slides in a second finger and the skin tears, perfect little beads of scarlet blood forming where her fingers have pulled it apart.

A third finger. Her breaths are coming in short gasps now, the little exhales of a beached swimmer. The guy watches unblinkingly from his position over her, his eyes glimmering insistently. She pushes her whole hand in and, coated up to the wrist in Percy, she gulps for air.

Her fingers brush against something stiff—a rib, broken—and a voltaic shock jolts through her nervous system. She rummages around the cavity of his chest until she finds what she's looking for.

Baby

When she pulls out her arm, she's holding a lung. She pulls it free of the body with a weak tug. And then something inside the lung moves.

She makes a careful cut down the organ's side. It deflates and water gushes out from the opening. Mary crumples into the wetness pooling around her, the lakewater slick spreading out across the driveway.

She pulls the lung's two edges away from each other—*she's always been so good at pulling things apart*—and there's a creature inside, a little guy, a baby, blue in the face and quiet. Mary rips the filmy membrane from its face.

It opens its mouth and wails.

No wonder Percy drowned with this gestating inside his body, the baby conceived in her dream. She presses her lips to its small head and she does not want to eat this one, she just wants to be as close to it as she can possibly be.

Then she starts to feel a tingle around her ankles. It works its way up her legs, accompanied by little sharp bursts of pain. It's the water, she realizes—the water has been electrified. And she looks at the guy—looks down, looks at his bare feet. He's ankle-deep in water.

He has always been a live wire.

The electric feeling travels up to her arms, and the baby cries harder. It starts to glow—not the crackling, bottle-bright blue of the guy in her dream, but a soft shine that radiates from everywhere on its body. Luminous.

"Look." Mary laughs. She holds the baby out toward the guy. "Hold it."

The guy looks down at the electric baby. For a moment his eyes flash with something Mary has only seen in her dreams—a look of intelligence, of ambition, of paternal desire.

And then he backs away.

He keeps his glowing eyes trained on Mary and the baby in her arms, walking back over the threshold and into the house, into darkness and distance, and then he's gone.

The Sun in a Box
Brianna Nicole Frentzko

MOLLY SEARCHES FOR THE SUN. Except for the little blinking frog, she hasn't seen light for a very long time. The frog is a nightlight. His name is Kermit. He sits on the wall and makes her skin glow green. Kermit is the nicest thing Monster ever did for her.

No windows bring light into her room. In the place-she-was-before, there were big bay windows with curtains the color of sunrise. Sitting in the window seat, she could look out to the wooden path across the marshes to the sea. On bright days, her mama would braid her hair and take her and her sister to jump over green waves. They'd argue over who got to hold Mama's hand. They would laugh until Molly's tummy ached with the laughter.

Monster told her there was nothing before this room, but she knows Monster lies.

She never listens to Monster, but she does listen to Cynthia. Cynthia says the sun is in one of the boxes. Her home now is a forest of boxes. They are brown and white, as small as her head and so big she can fit her whole body inside them. In some places, the boxes reach all the way up to the ceiling. They form a maze around her, hills rolling up and down for her to climb, valleys to walk through, hidden corners to explore. She sits on boxes and sleeps on boxes. And, every day, she opens boxes searching for the sun.

She has been doing this a very long time.

Inside one box are newspapers, magazines, and three

159

cockroaches. She moves the newspapers over to the potty corner so she can wipe herself. The cockroaches she carries to Cynthia. She names them Charley, Bugs, and Gloria. Her favorite is Bugs because he is the smallest. Even though Cynthia does not approve, she kisses Bugs on the head. Her mama would not approve of kissing cockroaches either, but Bugs looks very sad without a mama to love him.

Lots of books are in the next box. She turns them into a tower as tall as her chin. She puts Cynthia, Charley, Bugs, and Gloria on top. Cynthia is frowning. She can't see because her eyes fell off. The cockroaches don't move at all as they sit atop their book tower. Cynthia says they are dead, but Molly doesn't believe her. Molly's mama told her that cockroaches could survive the end of the whole world.

In the next box, she finds a can of food. It is hard to make her fingers grip the knife she uses to open cans. Her fingers aren't right anymore. All six are rusty. She stares at them. They squeak when they go up and down. It was different before.

Peaches are inside the can. They were her sister's favorite fruit. She eats them slowly. Once, she stole all her sister's peaches when she wasn't looking and made her cry. Now, she wishes she could share them. The peaches don't taste like anything. They are supposed to be sweet, she thinks. Eating gets sticky juice all over her face. Spitting on her hands, she tries to give herself a bath, but it's hard to spit. She goes to the leaky pipe and lets the water drip-drop-drip on top of her. She still feels sticky, and she misses bath time with her sister when they would play with boats or pretend to fly spaceships like their father.

She doesn't remember her sister's name anymore. Monster told her that her sister is dead, but Monster lies.

Her tummy rumble-grumbles. Before, she ate rats, but they have all gone away. She used to stab rats with her knife and then eat them up. They weren't very tasty, but she liked the eyes because they would pop in her mouth. She would scoop out the eyes to eat as dessert. Rats were very crunchy, and their fur scratched her throat. The only rat she did not eat was Waldo because Waldo was her friend. Waldo died, and she buried him where-it-is-most-dark. The dirt still stains her fingers from Waldo's funeral because she has not had a real bath in so long.

She used to bathe with her sister and pretend to fly spaceships. She remembers. Her father flew spaceships, and she has been on many spaceships. She remembers.

Now, she walks to where-it-is-most-dark, very far from Kermit the nightlight. She tells Waldo about her day. She especially tells him about the tower of books and the peaches and her new cockroach friends Charley, Bugs, and Gloria. Because Waldo is dead, he is a good listener.

***

Molly wakes up and searches for the sun. She thinks there are more boxes then there were yesterday. The opened boxes from yesterday are gone.

This happens every day.

She remembers opening boxes yesterday, but she wonders if her memory is wrong. She knows she has been opening boxes for a long time. And yesterday she made a tower out of books. There it is: her tower. And yesterday she found Charley, Bugs, and Gloria. There they are: on top of her tower.

She remembers right, and this makes her happy. It is much easier not to listen to Monster when she has proof that her memories are true.

Cynthia asks where the boxes go after she opens them and why there are still so many boxes. Molly doesn't listen to her. Instead, she opens three boxes that have dolls inside of them. She puts them in the box where she sleeps so it will feel safer. When she lived with her parents and her sister, her room was filled with dolls and stuffed animals, but only Cynthia was allowed in her bed at night. Her bedspread was green with seashells, and she had a nightlight. Maybe it was Kermit. Monster could have brought Kermit from their house by the sea.

In her potty corner, she squats low and tries to pee but only a very little comes out and it is brown and smelly. She wipes herself with newspaper. Her father used to read the newspapers at breakfast time. Sometimes she would sit on her father's lap and pretend to read, too. There were always pictures of new planets and colonies in his newspaper.

She misses her father most of all. He used to hold her on the bridge of his spaceship and let her pretend to fly. He used to swim with her in the sea and tell her about space, floating in the great void filled with stars.

She sits in a big box with sweaters and cries because she misses her father.

Cynthia tells Molly it is her fault her father is gone. Cynthia tells Molly she will never see the sun again. Cynthia tells Molly that Monster is right, and she has been here always.

Molly goes to Cynthia and grabs her by the throat and she swings her around and around and around and around and throws Cynthia against the wall towards where-it-is-most-dark as hard as she can and she screams.

There is a thump.

She listens to the quiet. The quiet is loud. It will eat her if she lets it. She should hear something. There is something that even in the quiet she used to hear but it isn't there. Nothing is ever this quiet. But it is now. She thinks about this, and then she gets very scared. She misses Cynthia, so she runs over to where-it-is-most-dark and picks Cynthia up off the dirt that covers Waldo.

Cynthia's nose has fallen off!

Crying, she tries to put Cynthia's nose back on, but it won't stick. She puts the nose and Cynthia next to Kermit. Cynthia won't speak to her now.

She asks Charley, Bugs, and Gloria to talk to her. But they don't. The cockroaches are dead. She screams at them. They won't answer.

The quiet is coming again with the noises that should be there but aren't.

Molly eats the cockroaches to hear the crunching. She eats all of them. Even Bugs.

Then her tummy rumble-grumbles, and she goes and hides in the box with sweaters and cries, but her eyes can't make any water. She thinks that when she cried before her face got wet. Her nose got so snotty that it would leak down to her lips. Her eyes got puffy and sore. None of these things happen now, no matter how hard she cries.

***

Molly wakes up and searches for the sun. Cynthia is still not talking to her. There are lots of boxes around her, and none of them are opened.

Didn't she open boxes yesterday?

The first box she opens has a mirror wrapped up in newspaper. She thinks it is a magic mirror because it shows her a very scary monster whose face is peeling off. It looks like a doll but old and broken and made of metal. She wonders if it is a picture instead of a mirror even though it reflects everything else properly. Perhaps it is a portal to another dimension. She tries to talk to the monster in the mirror, but it only mocks her. She and her sister used to play a game where they would be captains and fly spaceships through dimensions. Her father used to say that someday humans would learn to go into wormholes.

She touches the dimension hopper disguised as a mirror. Nothing happens. Her father would tell her that she must keep experimenting with the dimension hopper to understand how it works. He always told her to keep trying and keep thinking. This is why she misses him so very much.

Her mama would say that she is holding a mirror. But it isn't a mirror.

After wrapping the dimension hopper back in newspaper, the quiet scares her again. Up above where the sun used to be before it was put in a box, she hears thump, thump, thumping.

It is Monster.

She wonders if Monster will come visit her today. She doesn't think anyone has been here for a very long time, but time is hard for her to remember properly. Every day she opens boxes. Maybe Monster was here yesterday. Maybe not. She built a tower yesterday. Or was that before?

In one box she finds a dead rat. It smells worse than the potty-corner. She eats it anyway, and her stomach rumble-grumbles. The rumble-grumble makes her tired. She decides to go to sleep in the big box with the sweaters. She doesn't take Cynthia with her because Cynthia is not talking to her.

When she dreams, Molly sees her mama and father and sister. She dreams of her house by the sea. She dreams of green waves crashing on the beach and running from the waves and giggling when the waves catch her. And her sister is feeding the waves sand. Molly holds her hands up to the sun. It is very warm, and she can feel the light all over her arms and legs.

Then she looks down in the water and she sees Monster. She turns for help, but her mama and father and sister do not have faces. Then Monster swallows up the sun.

And Molly is alone.

✳✳✳

"Molly, Molly, wake up, Molly."

She doesn't want to wake up. She wants to stay on the seashore with the sun.

Monster is looking down at her. She tells Monster good morning, then she rolls around in her box. She doesn't like looking at Monster because Monster has stolen things from her. Monster is so much louder than Molly. Blowing in and out and in and out. She doesn't blow in and out and in and out. She used to do it, but not anymore.

"Why do you call me Monster, Molly?"

Monster sits on a box and puts a hand on Molly's head. Monster's hand shouldn't look like that. Monster's hand is stolen. All of Monster's body is stolen. She does not look at Monster, but she does shake her head to make the hand go away. No one should touch her, especially not Monster.

"I am trying to help you, Molly. At least let me put your face right." Monster sounds sad. "Did you try to eat things again? You know you can't eat. It makes you sleepy. You don't need to eat."

Molly's tummy rumble-grumbles.

"That isn't hunger. It only happens after you eat."

Cynthia says Monster is heartless. Cynthia says Monster is cruel. Cynthia says Monster lies. Molly agrees.

"Cynthia can't think for herself. You know that, right?"

She hates Monster. She decides not to talk anymore.

"Can't you just come away from this place, Molly? We'd like it if you'd come out of here. All you have to do is wake up. Why stay here in the dark?"

She will not listen to Monster because Monster lies. Instead, she stays still until Monster sighs and goes away. Watching Monster's shadow on the wall, she hears thump-thump-thumping and then squeak, squeak and then dust falls from above. Thump, thump.

Monster is gone.

But now there's a talkie-walkie on the box next to her. It doesn't say anything to her, but she knows it must be a new present from Monster. Someone must want to talk to her. She and her sister had a talkie-walkie. When she went with her father to the special place where they took a picture of her head, she was allowed to have a talkie-walkie. The picture took hours and hours, but she was allowed to talk with her sister.

This talkie-walkie must be bad because it came from Monster and all of Monster's things are bad.

Cynthia thinks they should murder Monster, but Molly doesn't know how.

She decides to go back to opening boxes.

What will happen when there are no more boxes? Cynthia asks.

But there seem to be as many boxes as there were before. There will always be boxes.

Forever.

Cynthia says it has already been forever. When did Monster come? Was it just now or long ago? Molly throws Cynthia into where-it-is-most-dark and does not go back for her. Cynthia can keep Waldo company.

***

Molly wakes up and searches for the sun. Monster's talkie-walkie is saying things that do not make sense. She throws the talkie-walkie into a box with sweaters. This box looks familiar. She thinks it would be a good place to hide.

Inside the next box is a mirror but it is broken into many little pieces. She wonders who broke it. One of the glass pieces scratches her hand. This should hurt but it doesn't. She looks at her hand a long time. The scratch makes her afraid. Wrapping her hand in a handkerchief hides it from her.

She opens a box with books and decides to stack them to make a tower as big as she is! The books pile up and up and up. One book has a big A and a big I on it and a picture of a brain. She cannot read any of the other books except the one that has a D and an A and an R and a K. She knows these spell "dark." It has a picture of a man with a cowboy hat in the desert. Her favorite book has a picture of a man coming out from underground. He is covered in dirt and standing in the bright sun.

She decides to tell Waldo about her tower. She goes to where-it-is-most-dark. Cynthia is there. She is dead. Molly buries her next to Waldo. Then she tells Cynthia and Waldo about her tower. She tells them that she will find a friend to put on top of the tower.

They are good listeners because they are dead.

She remembers that she had a sister. She thinks her name was Sarah. Maybe her name was really Clara? Or Samantha? She can't remember Sarah's face. They used to play space captains together. That was a fun game. Her father told them one day they'd be space captains for real. When she went to have the picture taken of her brain, she and Sarah talked with talkie-walkies.

She hears talking and jumps. It is coming from a box. Maybe it is the sun!

She opens the box and sees the sweaters and Monster's talkie-walkie. The talkie-walkie is saying things that do not make sense again. She hears Monster's voice, and Monster is saying that "Molly still won't come out of it. What is it, the tenth time?"

And then someone says, "Fifteen. She's gone under fifteen times now."

"It's time we abandon the project."

"You've already hacked into her?"

"Twice."

"But still, the limitless possibilities of a child—"

"She's eating rats!"

Molly buries the talkie-walkie deeper in the sweaters so she can't hear them.

✳✳✳

Molly wakes up and searches for the sun. Cynthia, who is dead, told her the sun was in a box. There are a lot of boxes. She remembers opening some. But all the boxes are closed. She wonders if Cynthia ever told her the truth. If Cynthia lied, then the sun is not in a box, and she will never be able to find it.

She thinks about this for a long time.

Next to Kermit, there is a square of light. She does not know why she did not notice the square of light before. It is strange light, different from Kermit. Slowly, she walks over to sit by the square of light. She sniffs it and places her hands in the middle of it. The wall moves and makes a big gap. She puts her head into the gap. On the other side are stairs. The square of light is a door. She wonders how long the door has been there.

If the sun is not in a box, maybe it is up the stairs.

She thinks about this for a long time.

The talkie-walkie is speaking again. It is talking about "programming loops" and "horrific truths" and "studying Molly" and "just leave the computers running; we're going."

She feels tired and goes to sleep.

✳✳✳

Molly wakes up and searches for the sun. It is so dark she cannot see and finds boxes with her hands. She remembers seeing things in this place before. There was a green light before: Kermit. She called the green light Kermit. It is gone now. Now the only light is from the open door. She pretends it isn't there. She opens boxes until she is tired, and then she goes to sleep.

✳✳✳

Molly wakes up and searches for the sun. She is opening a box when she sees the stairs. When did she open the door? She opens a box filled with newspapers and brings some over to the potty-corner so she can wipe herself. She opens another box filled with sweaters. Under some of the sweaters is a talkie-walkie. It has been torn apart into little pieces, but she knows it is a talkie-walkie.

She feels afraid. Who could tear apart a talkie-walkie into pieces? It is very quiet.

Slowly, she walks to the open door. She looks at the stairs. They are very dusty. Her feet move towards the first step. There are no footprints in the dust, not even from the rats because the rats are all gone. She had a friend who was a rat once, but she cannot remember his name.

If the sun is up the stairs, she should go looking for it. She is searching for the sun. That is what she is doing. She has been doing it for a very long time. If the sun is not in the boxes, then the sun is up the stairs.

She puts her foot on the first step. She puts her foot on the second step. The dust should make her sneeze. It doesn't. The dust from the boxes doesn't make her sneeze either.

She goes up a third step, and she is afraid. Her footsteps sound very loud.

Everything starts shaking. Maybe she shakes, and everything else stands still.

She can see a door at the top of the stairs. It looks different from the other door at the bottom of the stairs. It is shiny.

She goes up five more stairs. For a while, she thinks about sleeping here. But then she goes up three more stairs and there are only two more to the shiny door. That is enough for the day. She will sleep.

✱✱✱

Molly dreams about being sick. Her mama comes and brushes her hair and makes her soup. She doesn't want to eat the soup, so her mama brings her peaches instead. She loves canned peaches almost as much as her sister. She eats them all up, and her face gets sticky. Her mama wipes the stickiness away. Mama says that if she is ever bad, she will have to eat rats. She laughs because her mama is joking. She will never eat rats. If she did, she wouldn't be Molly. She would be a monster. Afterall, she has a pet rat named Waldo, and eating him would be awful. Her mama crawls into bed and snuggles with her.

"You will always be my Molly."

But her hand in her mama's hand looks wrong. It is torn open in places and the insides are metal and shiny. It only has three fingers, and they are hard. Her hands are robot hands.

She screams and wakes up. She is on the stairs. She is searching for the sun. If she can find the sun, then maybe she can find her mama and her father and her sister.

There are two more steps, and she is so very tired and so very afraid, but she is searching for the sun. Molly closes her eyes and runs up the last two steps. She opens her eyes. Her hands are on the shiny door. Her hands look like they did in the dream.

She pushes the door open.

And her eyes open.

Molly didn't know her eyes were closed. She turns around and around but there are no doors or stairs. She is in a very clean place, and there is a lot of light. Everything in this place is shiny and made of metal. The lights are different colors and blinking. Some of the blinking lights are broken and there are places where the room looks like it was smashed to bits.

This is a spaceship that looks a lot like the one her father used to fly.

She stands up. She didn't know she was sitting down. When she stands, she hears clicking noises, and her body feels stiff.

The ship beeps. Then suddenly Monster appears in front of her. This Monster looks much older than she has ever seen her before.

"Hello, Molly," Monster says.

She says hello to Monster, but her voice sounds wrong.

"If you are seeing this, it means that you decided to wake up again. I would be here to welcome you, but I'm afraid you've missed me."

She asks how she missed Monster.

"This is a hologram, my memory banks are stored here."

She doesn't understand what Monster means.

"You are searching for the sun, aren't you, Molly?"

Behind her, there's a great crunching noise. She turns around and sees the whole wall opening. The ship is lowering its shielding. She looks out into the void, space, the bright stars. And there is the sun!

It looks very close because they are on a spaceship.

"Very good."

Molly tells Monster that she has been in the place with the boxes, but it must have been a dream.

Monster laughs. "You always do have the same story. You'd think, given your capacity, you'd come up with something different each time."

She tells Monster that she wants to take the sun and go home to her mama and her sister and especially her father. She misses her father very much. He flew spaceships like this one. He always promised one day she would fly a spaceship. He helped her build a robot once and held her out in the ocean. And her mama fed her peaches and told her she would eat rats if she was bad. She doesn't remember her sister's name, but her sister fed sand to the waves and played boats in the bathtub.

Monster looks sad.

Molly hates her.

"Why do you hate me, Molly?"

She turns away and looks at the sun.

"Is it because I look like you? I mean, I don't really, anymore. I grew up. You didn't."

She will not listen. She stares at the sun. It is too close. This is a dream. She wants to go back home to Cynthia and Waldo. She can tell them about the sun in her dream.

"It isn't a dream, Molly."

She will not will not will not will not listen to Monster.

The window showing the sun starts to close. She tells Monster to stop it.

"I will stop if you look in the mirror."

Molly turns around, closes her eyes, and walks to the spot next to Monster and the beeping lights where there is a lot of cracked glass.

"Open your eyes, Molly."

She looks into the mirror.

That is not Molly in the glass. It is something else. It is horrible. It is a robot wearing Molly's skin, but the skin is falling off. The hair is gone. The hands are all metal and shiny. And it has eyes that are red and glowing. It is a scary thing, a very scary thing.

It is a monster.

She tells Monster to make the mirror go away. She turns back to the sun. Monster is still saying things, but Molly isn't really listening. This is a dream, after all.

The sun is so bright and big, staring at her, making her metal hands glow, laughing at her. The sun is laughing at her. She hates the sun. She hates Monster. She will not will not will not—

"Molly, don't you see? You can keep going. You can go and explore the whole universe. Become a captain. You can do anything. You can't die, can't grow old. You don't need to eat or breathe. You could float out there in space forever and survive it. You are the greatest thing I ever made. You are me as I was when I was most happy."

Molly looks at Monster and looks at the sun. She looks at Monster again. She sees her own eyes staring back at her, but they are old and tired. They look wet. They are green like Kermit and they are filled with light. Molly is looking at herself. Monster is Molly. And Molly is Monster. And —

No.

She screams at Monster. She runs at the beeping lights and slams her metal fists down on the controls. She slams them again and again. She finds the places from where she slammed her metal fists before.

How many times has she done this?

"Molly."

But the hologram turns off. Something breaks. The doors showing the sun crunch shut.

She closes her eyes.

And there is the dusty staircase through the metal door. She runs back down the staircase and slams the door shut. There is Kermit with his green light. She runs to a box. She opens it. There are sweaters inside. Hiding inside the box filled with sweaters, she cuddles Cynthia tightly in her arms. Cynthia still has her eyes and her nose.

Molly is safe.

✱✱✱

Molly searches for the sun. She hasn't seen light for a very long time except for the little blinking frog. The frog is a nightlight. His name is Kermit. He sits on the wall and makes her skin glow green.

There are no windows here. In the place she was before, there were windows. She remembers her mama and father and sister running down the path to the beach as she sat watching from the window seat, dreaming of flying up in the stars. She would be a pilot and explore all of space forever.

She will find it all again, but first she must find the sun. Cynthia says that the sun is in one of the boxes, and so, every day, she opens boxes.

She has been doing this a very long time.

Monster says she has been doing it forever, but Molly knows Monster lies.

Untethered
Eirik Gumeny

A HAND, A SQUEEZE, ON HIS SHOULDER, AND THEN SHE'S GONE. Up and across the room, welcoming another guest, an older Native American man in a banded cowboy hat, a satchel full of wires and electrode caps over his shoulder. Hugs and hellos and they're sitting on another couch, in another conversation with another scientist. The fabled Southwest Invention Exchange in action, an informal conference for everyone's off-book projects, the studies too wild, too dangerous, to get proper funding. A dozen great minds already, at least, scattered across a handful of rooms; half the Los Alamos scene's expected by the end of the night. Everyone who's anyone, everyone who's not, milling, chatting, drinking, smoking, sharing ideas to fix this, get rid of that, that could change *everything*, if only.

But he can't take his eyes from her.

Noah studies—remembers—her every movement. The way Van positions her boots, half-crouched on the couch, one foot on, one foot off. The angle of her wrist as she talks. The strands of dark hair falling across her forehead.

And suddenly it's him and Van on his old orange sofa, the one he'd dragged up from the curb, the two of them in his college apartment, barefoot and tangled up in one another. Her toes, her feet, are so tiny. He holds one in his palm, all but disappears it beneath his fingers. Her laugh, as carefree as a carnival ride. And then her hand is on his chest, and then she's leaning in, her breath on his—

Noah puffs out his cheeks and exhales.

That's never happened before, not without the machine.

He leans forward, elbows on knees, and runs his hands through his shaggy hair. The tachyon field absorbed into his blood, maybe, the half-life of chronons longer than he figured. But that's a problem for later. Instead, he sits, centering himself, tethering himself to the here and now. To his scuffed Chucks and his threadbare jeans, to his Oxford unbuttoned at the wrists. He sits, on the couch, on this couch, half of a matching set, fancy and leather and new.

He shouldn't have gone out tonight, he thinks.

He should have turned Vanessa down.

This was a mistake.

A cat brushes against Noah's leg. Winding and wending, purring between his calves. He scratches the orange tabby behind an ear, feeling the tactile surety, feeling his own exhaustion simultaneously. And then he's closing his eyes and breathing in deep, praying away the fatigue, to whatever god might listen, whichever one they haven't yet killed. He's been awake too long, drank too much, smoked more weed in the last two hours than he has in the last ten years.

Than he has since he and Vanessa were together.

The cat mewls and darts away; Noah raises his head again. Vanessa's looking at him now, distracted, her conversation faltering as a smile inches across her face, wide and real.

The first time she smiled at him like that, he walked into a desk. He remembers that. Sitting on the steps outside the earth sciences building shortly after, he remembers that, too. Talking about *The Simpsons*, the way she flexed her fingers in imitation of Mr. Burns before laughing and falling back against him to stare at the sky. Splitting an order of chicken fingers from the grease truck. The dog-eared pages of her books, a full half of her copy of *The Selfish Gene* highlighted in yellow and orange. Passing notes, secreting scraps of paper back and forth like they were in grade school. Her hand on his knee at the independent theater on Broad. The clack of the commuter train as he paid for her coffee early one morning. A salvo of small and sporadic events, moments Noah wouldn't have thought could be frozen in time.

Moments he's revisited, dissected, a thousand times since.

Noah coughs, louder than he means to, the souls of spent cigarettes rising past his face. He moves the ashtray, examines the coffee table. Heavy and rustic and reclaimed, littered with stems and seeds, with mushrooms and a pointillistic puddle of Ritalin. Cluttered to the corner, immaculate roses explode from a distressed stone vase; magazines about wine and art are piled beneath.

Noah failed his way out of art school.

He knows even less about wine.

He's killed two cactuses in the month since he moved out here.

An elbow hits his and he's surrounded, he realizes that now, by Vanessa's friends and associates, by renowned doctors and disgraced professors, by disruptors and do-gooders, makers and hackers and burnouts from 'burque and ufologists from Roswell and more than a few folks he's seen around the lab. There's as much gray hair and clunky turquoise as there are inked arms and ocular implants.

How long have they been here?

How long has he?

There's a woman sitting next to Noah, speaking rapidly, fervently. She's bald on one side, a waterfall of faded pink on the other. Her ear nearly lost inside a bulbous freon scar. Older than she's pretending. There are faces trained on her, nodding in steadfast agreement with the words spilling out. Her oversized army jacket flails with her every gesture, punctuates every proclamation.

The world, she explains, is fucked.

The solutions, she says, are inaccessible, unpalatable. Obvious but unobtainable.

But, goddamn it, she continues, we've got to try.

We've got to try.

Right?

✳✳✳

Eirik Gumeny

There was no moon that last night, no clouds. Wind, though, Noah remembers, that uniquely Northeastern winter wind, heavy and humid and hard. The kind that foretells a storm, that tears through clothing and digs itself into bone. The kind that stays with a person long after.

Too long, maybe.

Noah and Van held each other close that night, that last night, swaying, slowly, gently, their feet crunching the frozen lawn. He was tall and too skinny, then. She was perfect—then, still, now. He towered over her, stooping to be near her, dragged down into her orbit. He had his hands on her waist; she rested her cheek against his chest.

They stood like that for hours, despite the cold, the wind. No one said anything.

No one wanted to be the one.

There were, he knows—he knew, even then—almost as many bad times as there were good. The two of them as likely to fight as fuck, to stand each other up as spend the night. She'd gone home with a bartender once, to prove a point. He'd put his fist through a wall to prove her wrong. His bony knuckles bruised and bleeding. Van had stayed to bandage them, to wrap them in paper towels and duct tape, to drive him to the pharmacy for ice and gauze and rubbing alcohol. To crawl into bed with him. To tell him it didn't prove a goddamn thing.

They were a catastrophe together, he knows—he knew, even then—but that didn't stop their hearts from racing at the sight of one another.

They were too in love, Van had said.

That was why it hurt.

Noah remembers her eyes that night, the way they seemed to shine in the starlight, the cold and the tears and the sky conspiring against him.

They both knew what needed to be done.

They both knew it would hurt more if they didn't.

But they were still kids, back then, and indestructible.

The kind of together that couldn't be broken.

No matter how many times he's tried since.

***

The living room, sunken and expansive, is crowded now, unpleasant with bodies, and more so by the moment. Noah can hear the wind picking up outside, rain and rose blooms bouncing against the windows. He looks for Vanessa through the sea of new faces, can't find her.

The sermon still raging beside him—a screed about off-planet solar harvesting with very little in the way of operable data—he sneaks away to an empty dining area tucked beside the kitchen. The room's on the smaller side, separate from the rest of the house, a later addition, the adobe darker. Exposed vigas frame the room. Noah ducks as he enters. Two large canvases, stylized landscapes of red and orange and brown, hang on the walls, a cut-metal Kokopelli between them.

Before Noah can even sit, a white guy with dreadlocks walks over, calls Noah "Stew" and hands him a beer, something craft-brewed and limited. He assumes the alias easily. Van excepted, no one here knows who he is, what he's done. Even in these circles, even with all these brains, all the talk of cross-breeding spiders with dogs and genetically engineering merpeople, casually dropping "I figured out time travel, sort of" causes more problems than it solves.

Dreadlocks taps his bottle against Stew's and asks if he's still running the chop-shop out near La Cienega. Noah grimaces and shakes his head, tells the man no, he sold it last week. There was a bad fire, he explains, copper thieves ripping out the wrong wires. Besides, he continues, there's just no money in repurposing aeronautics anymore. Private sector means private security, and the risks aren't worth the reward.

Drone mods, Noah tells him, are the way to go.

Dreadlocks nods, calls it a wise business decision and takes a pull. He points to his shoes. Hemp, he says. Noah smiles, nods, drinks. The last thing he needs right now is more alcohol, but after an evening of Rieslings and merlots, it feels good to swallow down something he can actually appreciate.

Grinning, Dreadlocks leans against the table, then launches into a lecture about the government's anti-extraterrestrial-environmentalist agenda.

✲✲✲

There was no moon that last night.

Noah wouldn't see it again for almost two years.

He didn't make it back to his apartment that night, started coughing up blood that night. The end-stage, the terminal stage, of cystic fibrosis catching up to him. He was admitted to the hospital by breakfast, medevacked to Columbia by dinner. A cross-country convoy to the UCLA Medical Center, the longshot, the last hope for the desperate and the damned, by the end of the month.

Van wasn't there, for any of it. She couldn't handle it, back then, didn't know how.

He'd been angry about that, blamed her for that, for all of it, back when young and stupid still looked good on him. Back when the loneliness felt bottomless, when the drugs stretched every bad idea, every hurt feeling, into an impenetrable fog. Back when the panic and terror were still raw, before they faded and calloused and blended in with the rest of his scars.

Noah had been close to unlocking the relativistic mechanics of fixed temporal relocation—the ability to visit one's own past, to become a passenger in one's own consciousness—before his lung transplant. He'd finished the research as soon as he was able, after.

The first time he went back, he tethered himself to a pick-up basketball game at age thirteen. Watched, felt, for the first time, the cough that seemed to come from somewhere impossible, from every part of him all at once, the phlegm that rose like vomit. The kids gathered round and standing back as he bent over at the edge of the pavement. The goal had been to follow his disease's progression, see what he could have done different. Collect evidence, cold and impartial, and find a way to save himself.

Change the past so *that night* never happened.

And then he met Vanessa all over again.

Even if Van had been there, he knows, now—even if she hadn't been a smoker, hadn't filled his lungs with poison, night after night—even if she'd stopped him, stopped both of them, from spending half their time drunk, out, not sleeping, not eating—even if—

The best she could have done was stall things.

The best she could have done was watch him waste away. Suffer alongside him. Uproot everything she knew and move across the country and spend eighteen months living off a hospital cot, crying over his comatose body every morning and every night until the day of the transplant, and then every morning and every night after, as he struggled to become whole again, fought and flailed to be a human again.

The best Van could have done, he knows, was exactly what she did.

***

Dreadlocks is louder now, all but shouting, at the woman in the army jacket, over her, with her, each feeding off the other's energy. Heads start turning, voices start murmuring, and then there's a pause.

Exoplanet salvage, they say. They're on the same side of things, they realize.

The man with the dreadlocks makes his way to the living room.

Noah heads to the kitchen, empty bottle in hand.

***

There was the transplant, and then there was before and after.

Van was the last relationship he'd had, before. The only one, really. That night, that last night, they'd chosen to be together and he—*they*—had immediately fallen apart. She wasn't there with him, couldn't be there with him. They were still kids, back then.

Noah spent six months sick, sicker, then eighteen unconscious. Twenty-four hours in surgery, his chest propped open like a car hood, his insides out. Another year recovering, learning to breathe again, to walk again, to dress himself and feed himself again. Three years lost in total. Three years of agony and anguish and doubt and fear and then—

He wasn't the same, after. Not much was. He was stronger, healthier, had gained fifty pounds in a matter of months, muscle and fat, until he couldn't recognize himself in the mirror. Habits changed, too. Tastes. Immutable facets of his life suddenly foreign, wrong. He'd never had family, and friendships were, by design, sporadic. But now, after, that solitude he'd pursued, that absolute autonomy, was a prison of isolation.

It was the loneliness that broke him. The emptiness—the phone without messages, the walls without cards—that pushed him. The nothing he had a stark reminder of how little imprint Noah had left on the world. Of how little space the world allowed people like him, a sick kid who saw beauty in the cogs of a clockwork.

So he turned to the past, searching for a future.

The only time he felt alive, the only time he felt vital and worthwhile, was with Van. She'd left a mark, a bruise, her fingerprints seared into his skin. He thought—hoped—he'd done the same damage.

Noah tried to reach out to her, after, tried to let her know he was okay.

But a lot changes in three years. Emails, addresses, phone numbers.

Vanessa Vazquez, Van, had disappeared into the world. Become nothing more than a memory, a ghost, one more part of the before that Noah would learn to live without, that Noah would try to forget.

That he would go to impossible lengths to remember.

***

The refrigerator is massive, covered with photos, with Polaroids and prints. Of a bubbly girl Noah met earlier, of the guy with glasses she shares the house with. Engineers, both of them, friends of Vanessa's. Magnets pin pictures of each of them, both of them together, pawing at one another and pulling stupid faces. At the beach, around a campfire, a dimly-lit bar, the living room squalling behind him. There are a few with the bubbly girl and her friends — some raucous, some pensive, candid shots of them working, covered in grease and laughing, oblivious to the camera.

The collage continues, wraps around the side of the appliance. The photos are fewer over here, sparse shots of just the friends: Dreadlocks on a mountain trail, the pink-haired woman planting a tree.

And then there's a photo of Vanessa, alone.

She's standing on a bluff, an overlook, her body turned slightly, her back, her shoulder, to the camera. A camping pack rises over her, hands gripping the straps, another one buckled across her waist. Her left foot rests on a small wall of rocks, the other beneath the camera frame. Her gaze fixed on the ocean. The water is surging, crashing, blue and green and white; the sky is bright, clear, incredible. A town, or maybe a small village, sits off in the distance on the right.

There's only a hint visible in the photo, but there's a smile on Van's face, a smile Noah remembers, a smile he hasn't seen, until this week, until tonight, in over a decade.

Santa Fe, of all places, that was where it happened.

He'd moved here, after, clean air and a fresh start — and a government incentive program to get more "qualified minds" into Los Alamos National Laboratory, almost-finished graduate degrees less of a problem than usual. He'd been at the bar for an hour or two, in a booth at the back with some friends from the lab, when she walked in.

Noah knew her before he saw her — before he sees her — felt — feels — the fault line rumbling through his chest. He turns. Spots her sidling up to the bar, peeling off her peacoat and pulling back her hair.

Her friend catches him staring. Vanessa rolls her eyes.

Fuck.

Noah can see the word, even if he can't hear it, can feel the impatience and irritation as she turns to meet his gaze.

Her face changes instantly.

This is something new.

Noah excuses himself from the table; Vanessa leaves her friends at the bar. The two of them meet halfway across the sawdust-covered floor, rushing, slowing, each step more deliberate than the last. The din of the bar dying away as they near. Colors fading around them, the world evaporating, evanescing, everything ending.

Everything but them.

Hi, she says.

Hey, he says.

Your hair got long.

And then Noah's back in the kitchen again, alone again, staring at a photo of an ex-girlfriend again. At some picture someone took, some fraction of a second someone stretched out forever, during some vacation in some Mediterranean country at some moment, any one of a million moments, during the last ten years.

Ten years.

A lifetime.

This is a mistake.

Things go fuzzy then, the beer and the weed and the sleep deprivation. The exhaustion of temporal displacement. Noah plugs in the coffee maker on the counter beside him, starts rummaging through cupboards and drawers—

—catching his thumb on the splintering wood of the dorm's kitchen cabinets—

—looking for coffee, for spoons—

—for condoms—

—his inhaler, he needs his—

—hand against the refrigerator, feeling the—

—thrum of the oxygen concentrator, the only noise in the apartment—

—her laugh, wild and free—

—the clack of the commuter train—

—the cars outside, starting and stopping, the world spinning without him—

—her eyes, shining starlight—

—the coffee maker starting to steam and stutter.

Dreadlocks, perched on the arm of a sofa in the other room, a joint in one hand, the remnants of his audience in the other, sees Noah and points a finger. That, he says, his voice booming, that is the type of man we should all aspire to be. That is a man who knows what this world is about and what his place is in it.

Noah smiles and nods, not sure if he's him or Stew or someone new, if it's earlier or later. He raises an empty coffee mug to the room all the same. Because, credit where credit is due, Dreadlocks is right. For the first time all night, Noah Zaleski knows *exactly* where he is.

In a house thick with nameless strangers, longing for a woman he hardly knows.

✳✳✳

He's outside when Van finds him. The rain's gone, the storms out here torrid but brief. The backyard is manicured, xeriscaped, rocks and wood and not much else. Noah's hunkered down in a corner, beside a stepped outcropping, sitting on slate and leaning against a retaining wall stacked together from railroad ties. The damp against his jeans all the tether he needs, nothing more grounding than ground.

He watches her nearing, a coffee mug in each hand, steam twisting in what's left of the wind. She slides down next to him.

"Hey," he says.

"Hi," she says, handing him a mug. "Still milk and sugar, right?"

"Always," he answers. "Thanks."

"You trying to leave?"

"Trying to."

"You're not very good at it," she teases.

"No," he says, "I'm not."

Her smile wavers. "You all right?"

"Fine," he says.

"Don't lie to me, Noah, not yet."

He pauses, smiles, small. "I'm lost."

"Who isn't?"

"No, I mean, like—"

"—temporally," she says. "I know."

"You know?'

"Well, *assumed*. You're not the only one who's been casting furtive glances across a crowded room."

"What's it like, when I—"

"You're there," she says, "but not. Not really. Physically, functionally, you're there, you're moving, existing, but—"

"But you could tell."

"I could tell," she says. "You weren't *you*."

"It's been ten years."

"I know," she says. "But I could tell."

"The first time I went back," he starts, "I thought I could change things, I *hoped* I could change things. Anything, everything. I hoped I could find a way to avoid all the pain, the trauma, the transplant, the sickness—I thought I could find a way to live another life. A better life. But the machine, the chronons and the tachyon field and the synaptic web of space-time, that's not how it works. You can't *change* anything. Not even the small things. Every hangnail and ugly shirt is just *there*, always, every time.

"But it was the coming back that was the real problem, the returning to an empty apartment. To bills and appointments. To a nurse a few hours a week, only caring for me as much as I could pay him. To the homunculus looking back at me in the mirror, the hollowed-out husk who went through all that trouble to cheat death, and for what?

"And so I went back, again and again and again, telling myself I was learning from my mistakes. That I could build that better life going forward, on the back of everything I used to be. Every mistake I ever made. But I think—I think the truth is that the past was a pain I knew how to handle. A pain I knew I could survive."

"You realize therapy would have been *a lot* easier."

"Well, now, sure," he says, laughing. "Where was that advice before I broke half the laws of physics?"

Van brings the mug higher, to her lips, pauses. Then: "I'm sorry," she says, "about back then."

"It wasn't your fault."

"I could've—" She shakes her head. "I *should* have—"

"I could've, too," he says. "Believe me, there are a lot of things I could've. Literally pages, I made a fucking spreadsheet." He places a hand on her knee. "But we were kids."

"That's not an excuse."

"I know," he says, his brow creasing, "but I'm sorry, too."

"Jesus," she says with a laugh.

"Christ," he says, joining her. "We never apologized for anything, even when we should have. Now look at us."

"Look at us."

Van laughs again. Noah, too. And then the silence falls again, the wind whispering past. She curls up into him, winding her arm through his, resting her head on his shoulder. Noah smiles. And then he doesn't.

He sips at his coffee—

—the clack of the commuter train—

"I still can't get over the stars out here," she says, "even in the city."

Her eyes, shining starlight.

—her eyes, shining starlight—

—bins of bloodied phlegm—

"What are we doing, Van?" he asks, quiet.

"Getting some air," she answers. "Taking a break from glad-handing and pretending atomic chicken feed isn't a terrible idea. Admiring the night, the wide-open skies of the West, like we always talked about."

"That's not what I meant."

"I know," she says. "We're different people now, Noah. You, literally."

"That's what I'm afraid of."

"No," she says, finding his hand, sliding her fingers through his, "it's not."

The Potential Man
Katharine Duckett

I.

"WE'LL WEAN YOU OFF SLOWLY."

Dr. Lanyon's tone was kind yet casual, as though she were describing the weather: rainfall, sunlight piercing cloudy skies. Not the storms that could soon wrack my body, the lightning that could ravage my brain. Nothing like the vortex of withdrawal.

Several thoughts crowded into my mind at once, a pile-up, from the wreckage of which I could only discern screaming. I grasped for a coherent one and came up with the word *wean*: "To train an animal or infant to forego suckling," from the Old English *wenian*. Like I was a barnyard calf, a babe at the breast. Wasn't the medical term *taper*? If I'd had my phone in hand, I would have pulled the definitions up and spent hours comparing etymologies. But I didn't have time for that now. I was a patient. I knew my lines.

"Fine," I said. "All right. And there's no other way to address the side effects? Nothing else we can try? Because there are times when it works, and when it's working, it's—" I ran out of steam, my precious definitions and hoarded synonyms eluding me. They say pain destroys language, but the chasm between the doctor's clipboard and the truth of my life was what swallowed mine, every time.

Yes, my daily dose of Raptroxal came with consequences. Fatigue, dizziness, mood swings, zombie-like insomnia. Sleep paralysis, a few times, complete with visions of a man in black coming to strangle me in my bed. The drug wreaked havoc on the bowels and might eventually destroy the kidneys. Yet when it worked—in the rare, shining minutes where those needling problems dropped away, and my body felt like a seamless machine, one productive, pain-free entity instead of a thousand broken parts that refused to properly integrate—it was glorious. It was *worth* it.

I lived in those moments, jumping between them, clinging as though they were lifeboats in a treacherous sea. Nothing had ever worked for me like this medication, and I had been subjected to so many. Now they wanted to revoke the remedy: to leave me adrift, prone to drowning, once more.

"We've been monitoring your bloodwork," Dr. Lanyon said. "Raptroxal isn't meant for long-term use. We want to alleviate your need for a daily med using other treatment methods. They may not give you instant relief, but they'll be easier on your body."

I scoffed before I could swallow the sound. *Easier on my body.* As though anyone cared what was "easier" for me. Look at the routine I had to perform for them to take me seriously. *Be reasonable. Don't ask for too much: no, we can't take your pain away. No, you won't be able to do your work consistently, and you'll fall farther and farther behind in your field. But if you're patient, perhaps we'll provide a soupçon of solace. A spoonful of sugar we can take away whenever we please, lest your wretched life become too sweet.*

Dr. Lanyon's eyes narrowed. "This is for your own good, Mr. Zelkin. I'm trying to ensure that you thrive, and not just get by with a drug that could do serious harm to you."

I saw her face as though through a fractured mirror: the lines carving out deep caverns around her gray eyes and thin, pink lips; the clean fingernails on those healing hands. Shards of white obscured these details as I took in her coat, her spotless ivory sneakers, the diploma on the wall that gave her authority over me.

We were different creatures: doctor, patient. Had she earned this right to tell me how to control my body, my pain—my soul, if it was somewhere there within me? Or had the world handed it to her because her physical vessel worked as the world said it should, like every other doctor I'd ever seen?

I knew, deep down, that they all regarded me as a separate species. Pathetic. Unfixable. Dr. Lanyon would send me away from here, my prescriptions cut off, and chalk me up as another lost cause. Someone whose situation could only be mitigated, never remedied. Someone unworthy of demanding the resources that would assist me in claiming the life I wanted.

Before, I might have begged. Made my supplications, reciting my medical history like a litany of sins. *Forgive me, Doctor, for the diagnoses I have accumulated. For not stopping at one or two small impairments but bringing you a dozen. Forgive me for my being, which is causing you such confusion, while I wait, patiently, for you to see me as something like whole.*

But now I only bent my head, acquiescing, because neither Dr. Lanyon nor any of those other dry-eyed gatekeepers of medicine I had dealt with before, the ones who ushered me out of their examination rooms before they brought in another woeful specimen to inspect, had any idea of the tricks I had up my sleeve.

✻✻✻

I walked home in a fury, ignoring the throbbing in my knee and the siren in my skull, warning of collapse if I pushed myself too far. How dare she. Doctors, those puppet-masters: they had no idea what it was to be in this skin. Or perhaps they did, and were sadists, delighting in demanding I expend my effort striving for a summit I could never surmount.

I had done it all: the physical and psychological therapy, the years of being virtuous and diligent, the vast sums of money just so I could show them that no, the pain, the myriad problems, had not gone away. But this was the United States of America. I was meant to keeping pulling myself up by my bootstraps, no matter how bitter the aching in my arms as I did so.

I stomped hard on a curb, pain shooting through my heel, and clutched at my thigh while a passerby ignored me. Same old story.

No one had time for my agony—America, all over again—and when they did intervene it was too forceful, nearly bullying. Manhandling me, pulling at my cane like I was a bundle of used goods. I tried not to draw attention, wearing black whenever I left the house, and accepted the indifference: well-meant engagement was often worse.

It took me twenty minutes to get home, when it might have taken others ten. Home was a slate-gray High Victorian structure on the South Side of Providence that had seen better days. When it rained, the attic leaked, the ceilings sagged, and the whole weary house sighed like a pensioner desperate for death. But it was beautiful in its way: it had once been a grand mansion, with touches of glamour in the chandeliers (the ones too high for unscrupulous roommates to make off with) and the velvet runners of the stairs.

I had landed here fifteen years ago after my dismissal from Yale and was the senior resident and leaseholder of the house. I'd seen dozens come and go, some staying a few nights and others hunkering down for years. They had their reasons for remaining here, as I did. Money, of course, but more than that, too. We were the fringe society had cut off, and we had found this was the best place to position ourselves: in a fortress that no sane person would willingly go near.

I came upon Marielle, the second-longest inhabitant of the house, as I entered through the basement.

"Oh, hey, Henry!" she exclaimed, with a delight that never failed to astonish me. Her dark curly hair was pulled back in a red bandana, and she'd rolled up the sleeves of her black Molchat Doma shirt, showing off her tattoos. "I'm starting dinner. Pasta okay? I know we had it Monday, but I found some basil in the garden so I'm adding it. Maybe Piero brought home some of his mom's good sauce, too."

I often wilted under a torrent of words, unable to process and identify the moments when I was meant to respond. With Marielle, however, it was never any problem: I knew that anything she needed me to know, she would say at least thrice, without blaming me for not catching the information.

Marielle—who I sometimes called "Marigold," for her favorite flower, found in bursting yellow bunches in our garden in summer and autumn—was my oldest friend, though I'd always known she deserved better than me and this dilapidated labyrinth of a house. Even with her own laundry list of conditions that sent her to specialists—spastic cerebral palsy, low vision, depression—she was destined for greater things, like the cookbook memoir based on family recipes from Havana she wanted to write. I'd kept her close this long, but I hoped soon she would meet someone better suited to helping her accomplish her dreams than I was.

"Pasta's fine." I clomped into the hallway, ignoring the smell of piss on the carpet: Peludo, Marigold's cat and the third-most senior resident of the house, had recently become incontinent. We did what we could to clean, to cook collectively, but there was always more to do than could ever be done, especially with a rotating cast of roommates.

Upstairs, a door slammed, and Valentina, our resident diva, announced herself.

"Honeys, I'm home!"

Valentina was a vast improvement over our last attention-seeking roommate, an arsonist who had us quite literally running around putting out fires for a while. I had invented a fire-extinguishing cane during that period, but there was little value to it on the open market, and no one had wanted to invest in Marigold's home evacuation system for pets, either. Our eccentric attempts at contributing to society never panned out, though we each did our part in smaller ways: I by volunteering at the neighborhood science club at a school nearby, and Marielle by distributing meals at the local shelter when her body allowed.

"We're having pasta!" Marielle yelled back up to Valentina, who was kicking off her shoes in the foyer. She was a gifted dancer, but migraines often shut her down for days. Marielle, a childhood friend, had her move in with us when she was priced out of New York. Valentina demanded the spotlight when we gathered, but it didn't matter, because we gravitated to her like moths to a flame anyway. And when skull-splitting pain laid her up, I made her remedies from the herbs Marigold collected in the garden, as I did for the others when they fell ill. It wasn't much, but it was what we could reliably do, and Valentina returned the favor with performance tickets.

Piero, though—our youngest roommate, in his mid-twenties, there for the cheap rent—lavished care on Valentina. He was clearly in love with her, though I wasn't sure Valentina knew it. In her view, it was only right that the entire world be enamored of her presence.

***

At dinner that night, their familiar faces moved around me in a blur. I sat in my usual throne of a chair, where I chopped vegetables for Marielle on the oaken dining table when my arthritic fingers were feeling up to it. I laughed at Valentina's tale of an audition gone disastrously wrong; I smiled, as warmly as I could manage, as I told Piero to thank his mother for the addition of her delicious amatriciana sauce to our meal. All the while, though, I itched to get away, the watch on my wrist ticking forward the time. Nearly eight, now. Then nine. Then ten.

It was quarter to midnight when the conversation ebbed, the candlesticks that Marigold had put out on the table burning down their wicks. I might have left earlier, but I didn't want to arouse suspicion, to have anyone inquiring about my mood, my needs. I knew how to address them, and the answer lay just out of reach in my quarters in the basement, in the lab I had made for myself beyond my bedroom.

I stretched, pushing myself up on the arm of my chair. "Good night, all. Don't fret if you hear groaning coming from the basement—I haven't been sleeping well of late."

Marielle shot me a sympathetic look. "Do you need chamomile? Lavender? Because there may be some in the garden. You never know what you'll find out there."

192

"I'll be fine," I replied. "I've got the finest drugs subsidized healthcare can buy. But I may not be able to get back to sleep if anyone wakes me, so do me a favor and ignore me, please."

There: the groundwork was set. My room in the basement was far enough away from the others that I didn't think they'd hear a thing, but I didn't want to chance it.

With a last goodbye and nods all around—Valentina's indicating she'd like to get back to the conversation, Piero's solemn and brief, and Marigold's with a frown, like she was still thinking about what remedies she could pull from the earth for me—I retired to my room. My refuge, quiet and dim, where I spent hours existing without demands. In my room, there was no standard I was failing to achieve, no prying eyes making up stories for themselves of how I had gotten to be the way I was. I simply breathed, alone with my books, and let myself be. It was an oasis, as this house was, in a world with a dearth of understanding for people like me and my friends.

Yet I couldn't remain here forever. Trying to conform to the norms of the world outside had only brought disaster, but what if I no longer tried? What if I became what they wanted me to be, wholly? Did away with the disconnect, the need to strive; with the elements that kept me from plugging into society?

Could it be done? Could I be remade?

I had known from childhood there was another self within me. Teachers and caretakers alike had praised my potential, telling me I could become a great man someday if I could only overcome my impairments. But my impairments became me, and the praise dropped away. No more talk of that other self I might be, in some misty future. The people around me seemed at times betrayed, as though I had tricked them. As though they had been robbed of a brother, a beloved sibling less burdensome than me. I was the changeling in the cradle, the carnivorous twin in the womb, taking from the world someone who should rightly be.

I moved though my bedroom, kicking away the detritus of scientific magazines, and nudged open the door to my lab with my cane. I would need to begin locking it if all went as planned tonight, though I didn't think Valentina and Piero knew about the space; Marigold only did because she had helped me move equipment in years ago.

Flipping on the low amber lights, I did my best not to look at the framed items on the wall. Yes, I had put them there, but they pained me. Diplomas. Recognitions of merit. Clippings from periodicals in New Haven, about an exciting scientific discovery.

The ensuing exposés—the ones that had led to my firing—I hadn't mounted on my walls. I remembered every word, however; a few months ago, I thought they would haunt me to my grave. But not now. Now I suspected they might read like prophecy.

On my worktable, next to the cheval-glass I had found in the attic, I had laid out the required ingredients and equipment. I had stolen away from Connecticut those many years ago with some essentials, and since then had spent every spare cent on acquiring everything else I needed. It had been painstaking, and my humble lab would never measure up to those of the Ivy League, but I had something they lacked: vision. Knowledge of which they could never conceive. Only I, cast out from their halls, could see the divide in human nature clearly. Only I could suture the wound.

Slowly, hands shaking, I brought the necessary pieces together. The mundane stabilizers, followed by the compounds I had been experimenting with for nearly twenty years. Next, the crucial factor, the long-missing catalyst: Raptroxal's active ingredient, undiluted. Obtained from various spots abroad, ferried by routes of the shadowy Web that no Yale professor would visit. The couriers who came to the basement entrance of the house knew they carried contraband, but not what sort. They were messengers for hire. No one knew what was in the brown paper-wrapped packages they handed over, and no one saw them but me.

I braced myself. The experiments before had been of smaller scale—I had confirmed that a minor dosage of my new serum could reshape me. Make my thinking sharp, like a blade; release my limbs from pain, letting me stand tall and move freely. I had discovered what had been withheld from me, from all of us: a chance to become our better selves. The ones we had been told existed, the mythic figures we might have been.

Here was my retort to Dr. Lanyon's assertion that no substance could be a permanent solution: this vial bubbling with life, shining green-gold beneath laboratory lights. Before, I had consumed only drops, measured in milliliters. But this was the day of transformation, the time to prove the changes I had observed in myself could persist. That, in fact, I could shapeshift into that man I had once seen looking back at me in the cheval-glass, the one who resembled me as a twin and yet looked nothing like me at once. The man whose eyes seemed to burn with potential, who squared his broad shoulders, ready to assume his mantle of leadership. I wanted a taste of being that man, and, in time —should the serum work as I'd designed it— I might remain that man forever.

I glanced at the glass, noting my sallow complexion, my hunched posture.

"Goodbye for now," I whispered, not wanting to draw any attention from the rest of the house, not even Peludo. I raised the vial to my lips, drinking deeply. For a moment, I thought the liquid tasted strangely like soot: and then I remembered nothing, and was nowhere, as oblivion rushed to swallow me.

II.

Marielle detested Ted Hill with every fiber of her being.

Blonde, tall, and amoral, he had appeared as if from nowhere a year-and-a-half before, making a name for himself in real-estate development and generally being a bastard to the city's impoverished and marginalized. Now—though Marielle could hardly believe it—he was a hair's breadth away from becoming mayor of Providence. That slimy, self-satisfied prick, who seemed to charm everyone but Marielle with his booming voice and fascist stances.

"Oh, sure, I hate his politics and I'll do whatever it takes to stop him winning," Valentina had said, right before Marielle had roped her into a performance for their upcoming protest, "but there's just something about him, you know? Like that campaign slogan—Ted Hill Will Provide. He's got it, like, together. Real daddy vibes."

Marielle didn't get it on any level. His voice made her skin crawl, and, from the blurry outline she could see of him in news reports, he seemed like any other besuited product of abled male privilege out there. She'd been sure, at least, that Henry would loathe him, but she'd received the shock of her life six months before, when she'd stumbled upon Hill, of all people, coming out of Henry's room. He had mowed down Peludo, crushing his tail beneath his heel as Peludo let out a yowl.

"*Hey!*" Marielle had screamed, grabbing for his arm, but he was gone—out the back entrance and into the night, vanishing as though he had never intruded into her home.

"What the fuck?" she had asked Henry when she finally saw him next. "Do you know *Ted Hill* was here? In your room? Was he threatening you, Henry?"

Henry didn't speak for a long minute, his lips pressed together. He was leaning on his cane, looking as though he might collapse at any minute.

"No," he said, with deliberate enunciation. "We are ... friends, despite appearances. We may come from different worlds, but there are places we align."

He was always cryptic, and usually Marielle was patient: she knew his brain worked in its own way, same as hers did. But she couldn't let it go. "He nearly killed Peludo, Henry. Came down the hallway like a goddamn Juggernaut and almost broke his back. Is that a 'friend' to you? Is that someone you want in our house?"

Henry's eyes went wide. He began to cough, spasms wracking his body, and for a moment Marielle felt bad. He clearly wasn't feeling well, and maybe she shouldn't be pushing him, but: *Ted Hill*. Pure evil, storming through her home. He was a menace, and she didn't understand how Henry didn't get it. How was Hill capable of tricking everyone with something as simple as a steady gait and a voice that didn't stutter?

She'd long known the world turned on the axis of the able: that people conflated her limp, which wasn't always visible, and Henry's, which was, with some kind of moral deficiency, the way they'd been conditioned to since they first heard fairy tales. That Henry's idiosyncratic manner put them off the same way the shifting conditions of Marielle's body did; that they distrusted what they didn't understand.

But Henry was a man who wanted a better world. Marielle knew it, because they had imagined it for years. A world where people like them could thrive. Where pity was replaced with real action, with politics that advanced their cause.

Ted Hill, on the other hand—a man made in the mold of the strong and sane, who seemed able to summon unwarranted power with the snap of his fingers—clearly didn't care about anything but himself. If Hill had his way, everything complex and inscrutable in this old city would be reduced to rubble, replaced by his shiny steel-and-glass buildings, featureless as mirrors.

"Is he all right?" Henry gasped out once he recovered. "Peludo—did Edward hurt him?"

Edward. Marielle's stomach turned at the use of Hill's given name, which sounded more intimate than the shortened version. Like it was Henry and Ted who were the lifelong friends, and not Henry and *Marielle* who had stuck by each other through thick and thin.

Other roommates had mistaken them for a couple, but it wasn't like that between them: Marielle wasn't interested in romance, and Henry wasn't interested in sex. Their bond, however, went deeper—they'd chosen each other when the rest of society wouldn't, and made sure to care for each other when no one else would.

"Peludo's okay," Marielle replied. He'd licked his wounds—a tweaked tail—and moved on, while Marielle listened for the hissing she knew would herald Hill's return. "But I don't want that man in our house. Ever, Henry."

Henry's forehead beaded with sweat. After a pause, he nodded. "I understand. You will not encounter him here again." With that, he retreated to his basement, and, true to his word, Ted Hill hadn't darkened their doorway since then.

***

Today Marielle stood outside of Henry's bedroom door, as she had so many times over the last months, knocking and knocking, receiving no answer. He had been around more after the encounter with Hill: she'd almost thought he was back to his old self. But he had become scarce in recent weeks, and these days she hardly saw Henry at all. Whenever she checked in by text, though, he told her he was fine. Sometimes in a very Henry way—"I've taken to my bed and do not wish to be disturbed"—and sometimes with a thumbs-up emoji or a winky face. She hadn't realized Henry knew emojis existed.

Maybe he was planning to meet her at the school. She was supposed to be volunteering with the science club he led today, running a workshop on urban gardening. They'd had it on the calendar for months, but the last time they'd texted about it she'd only received a smiling halo face emoji in reply.

If she didn't leave soon, she'd be late, so she sighed and went upstairs to feed Peludo lunch. It was a short walk to the school, and normally a pleasant one. As she neared the grounds, though, she heard the commotion of a crowd, and the crackle of a megaphone, amplifying a voice it chilled her bones to hear.

"Thank you for your support!" Ted Hill called out from the top of the stairs of the school. Marielle could tell with a scan that not everyone assembled was on his side; plentiful grumbles underlaid the cheers. That didn't matter to Hill, however. "Your trust means everything. You know I have your best interests—and the *city's* best interests—at heart. For too long we've been second-rate, blighted, in shambles. No more. We're going to clean this place up. Starting with projects like this." He gestured at the posterboard display beside him, on which Marielle could only make out the shape of beige blocks. "Bringing investment and more resourced residents to Providence will lift us all up, allowing us to reach our full potential—to become a place where perfection is possible."

A few celebratory whoops rang out. Marielle leaned over to her closest neighbor in the crowd, a young Black guy with a bike she knew lived a few streets over. "Is this legal?" she whispered. "Campaigning at a school?"

"It's not a school anymore," he told her. "They're selling it. He's tearing the whole thing down to make condos."

"*What?*" Marielle hissed, but Ted Hill's voice drowned her out.

"These children deserve better!" he declared, sweeping his arm out toward a group of students gathered at the foot of the stairs. Some were clutching small shovels and spades: it was Henry's science group, she realized. No one had warned them away from this scene, and Hill was using them as props. "Let's stop pretending places like this serve them and give them a chance at becoming productive citizens. Principal Enfield here agrees that privatized education is the way of the future, and I'm proud to have his endorsement."

Marielle pushed her way through the crowd, marching up the steps. Hill barely seemed to notice her, but the man at his side — the school's principal, whom Henry had pointed out and complained about on her previous visits to his club—reared back like she was contagious.

"Did you tell anyone about this?" she said, jabbing a finger into his chest. "Consult anyone? Because Henry didn't know, or he would have done everything he could have to fight it."

"Who, the crip?" the principal muttered, clearly closer to the megaphone Hill held than intended, and then cleared his throat, leaning farther away to address Marielle. "C'mon, be serious. We don't need the word of kooky volunteers. The school's failing, end of story. We're trying to get these kids somewhere they can learn to be useful, instead of futzing around with—" He waved his hands at the gardening tools the children held. "—*this.*"

Marielle turned to Hill, ready to slug him square in his veneers, but she could see dark lumps detaching themselves from the wall behind him and moving forward. Bodyguards. Part of her wanted to take on the fight, but she was shaking; she needed to get back home.

As she retreated, Marielle was already calling Valentina to tell her the protest planned for tomorrow had to be bigger and more bombastic than anything they'd done before. They had to stop Hill at all costs. They had to save this city, and then Marielle would pull Henry from whatever pit he'd fallen into. Henry—the Henry she knew, anyway—would have done the same for her.

***

The next night, after the protest, Marielle came home exhausted but triumphant. Everything had gone off without a hitch. They'd taken over Burnside Park; they'd had speakers from every relevant sector of the city, explaining why Ted Hill spelled disaster. Valentina had put together a performance piece about gentrification that had people weeping and Piero looking like he wanted to build a monument to her glory. And they'd reminded everyone to vote in two days' time. Marielle unfortunately didn't feel strongly about Hill's rival, but at least he wasn't promising to chop the city up for parts.

She'd left the protest after she'd seen Valentina leap into Piero's arms, taking their make-out session as her cue to leave. There was more to do the next day—every second they had to fight Hill counted.

Settling at the dining room table, she pulled the marigolds she had threaded into her curls out, scattering the petals across the table. She hadn't heard Henry call her "Marigold" in months. Hill seemed to have sucked out some vital part of him, though she still couldn't fathom how they'd become connected. The scuttlebutt at the event had been that Hill's takeover of the school hadn't been aboveboard—that bribes were involved, that it was a publicity stunt. But Marielle couldn't understand why he had targeted the school that housed Henry's club. Weren't they supposed to be friends?

"Some friend," she muttered, and for a moment she thought the walls were answering her. But no: the murmuring she heard was coming from far below, from the basement.

She stood and crept, quiet as a cat, toward the stairs beyond the kitchen. Peludo was nowhere around, for which she was grateful; at this hour he was usually curled on the blankets of her bed. Careful not to let it squeak, she opened the door to the stairs, descending into the gloom of the basement, her ears perking up at the sound of an argument at the back door.

"I'm telling you, it isn't the same," hissed Henry. "Go back and tell them. The formulation must have changed—"

Marielle peeked down and could just make out the shape of a man in a cap shaking his head.

"Bro, do you think I know who sent this? I don't even know what's in there. I just want my money, so—"

"I can give you money," Henry broke in. "More money, plenty of money, if you'll only find me a more reliable source. Try Dr. Janice Lanyon—I know her practice closed but she knows how the Raptroxal helped me, and perhaps she—"

"Hey, dude?" The other man's voice was even, but whatever he had pulled out of his coat pocket made Henry stiffen. "The money, now. And how about a tip for me being patient?"

Henry said something in reply, too low for Marielle to catch, and then she heard the snick of bills. Where was Henry getting money? Why was he willing to pay so much for a few errands?

After Henry handed over the cash and shut the door, Marielle sneaked up the steps. In different times, she would have simply barged into Henry's life, demanding to know what the hell was happening. She sensed, though, that her typical approach wouldn't work this time. Henry was in over his head, and if she jumped right in, she might drown along with him.

***

Peludo, as expected, was waiting for Marielle on the bed. She pulled him into her lap as she fired up her old laptop and began running searches with her screen reader. First there was Raptroxal, the drug she knew Henry had once been prescribed by Dr. Lanyon (whose name she pulled up next). Initially hailed as a miracle drug, Raptroxal was wildly effective for treating pain and with a number of off-label uses, but its side effects could be severe: supposedly it could result in personality changes and even physical alternations, though only at much higher levels than could be legally prescribed.

She clicked over to the tab about Dr. Lanyon, landing on the top news result: *Longtime Providence Practice to Close After Investigation*. Apparently, Dr. Lanyon had been slammed for prescribing Raptroxal too freely, which seemed strange to Marielle, because Henry had lamented that the doctor was too cautious, if anything. Stranger still was the quote appearing a third of the way down the page: "We need to scrub this city of addicts and those who aid them. These pushers, these quacks, must be severely punished."

It was Hill. Hill, who, in a linked lifestyle piece, talked about how he needed nothing but adequate nutrition and hydration to keep himself healthy. "A good cleanse," he was quoted as saying. "That's all anyone needs."

Marielle's fists clenched as she ran her final search: Henry Zelkin—Yale.

✳✳✳

My dear Marigold,

When you find this letter, I will be gone. I hope you can forgive me. I don't expect you to understand what I've done, but I feel compelled to explain, here, at the end of things. My confession seems meager in the dying light of my lab, but let this be my final record, and a testament to the hubris that brought me to ruin.

The truth, plain: I was tired of the grinding wheel, crushing me beneath its weight. I grew weary of existing in a world whose higher realms I could never access, because I was told I shouldn't be here at all.

That my body was a waste, my mind a mistake: that I ought to be struck from the earth like a pestilence. If I made an ideal vessel that could carry my soul forward, at least, in that perverse way, I could keep it.

I was wrong, however. The soul and the vessel cannot be at odds. They are one, and I split them. I opened the abyss, and I could not seal it.

✳✳✳

Marigold rose early the next morning. Piero made muffins; Valentina brewed coffee. After that they should have gone out to shout about the treachery of Ted Hill to anyone who would listen, but instead they gathered at the top of the stairs, peering into the basement.

"Run me through it again," Valentina said, trying to keep her voice in check. "Henry's been doing experiments, and you think that's made him rich? And you think Hill's tied up in all of this?"

"She thinks he's *funding* this," Piero said in hushed tones. "To try to make us all into, like, Stepford drones. Perfect little people, just like him."

That was indeed the gist of it, though there were parts of the theory that didn't fit for Marielle. But it was the best she could put together from the evidence: Henry's "friendship" with Hill; the changes to his demeanor; the disaster at Yale. She had never wanted to pry into that part of his life, yet those old headlines illuminated everything:

Young Yale Professor Believes Radical Treatment Can Transform Minds — and Bodies?

Henry Zelkin's Quest for a More Perfect Human

And then, only months later:

Zelkin's Unorthodox Methods Lead to University Dismissal

Disgraced Professor Tested Substances Only on Self, May Have Falsified Results

The New Milgram? Yale's Long History of Unethical Experimentation

Henry had barely carried out any work before he was let go, but the very idea of it had clearly been too much of a liability for the university. It seemed that Henry's goal was to change himself:

to become a different man. Marielle thought Henry had accepted who he was, but maybe not. Maybe that seed of self-loathing had persisted, growing large enough for Henry to let someone like Hill in.

"Do you want us to come with you?" Valentina asked. "Make sure Henry's okay?"

"Just keep a look out for Hill," Marielle said. "If I'm not back up in half-an-hour—yeah, come get me."

Peludo meowed from above her as Marielle descended the stairs. When, as expected, there was no answer to her knock at Henry's door, she turned the knob, finding it unlocked.

Inside, all was dark. Scant light came in from the high, narrow windows: Marielle strained to make out much detail, but she could tell something was wrong with the room. Chairs were upturned, and the bedsheets, when she got close enough to see them, looked like they had been mauled by an animal. The only normal item she could see was Henry's well-worn copy of *Frankenstein* on the nightstand, but when she opened it, she found someone had scrawled all over the pages in red ink, as though the text were dripping blood.

She slammed it shut, the hairs on her neck prickling. A sound came from the laboratory to her right: a groan, or something dragging across the floor.

"Henry?" she called. "Are you in there?"

Her ears strained for a reply. She glanced around and caught the glint of something poking out beneath the bed skirt: a bronze key, abandoned on the floor.

As she suspected, it unlocked the windowless room that Henry kept for his experiments. Her phone flashlight illuminated little as she shone it through the door. She couldn't remember where the light switches were from her single visit; as she took a step in to check, the door closed soundly behind her.

She spun around, her phone light bouncing off the walls. "Who's out there?"

"You mean who's in here," said a voice, close to her ear.

Hill.

***

I'm so sorry, Marigold. I only sought a way to live, believing this world would abide nothing less than the eradication of my weakness and doubt.
 I did not know the destruction that was possible in perfection.
 Perfection has no place for you and me.

***

Hill muffled Marielle's shriek with his hand.

"Come on now," he said, in the bland tone that had charmed so many others. "Let's be friends. Henry and I are friends, so why can't you and I be, Marigold?"

She wrenched away from him. "How do you know that name?"

"Oh, I know all about you," Hill said, his voice advancing closer. "And it's so sad, isn't it? You're in such ragged condition. You and your friends." He paused, and Marielle swore she could see his teeth gleam in the darkness. "But what if I told you I could change all that? Fix you. Make you whole."

She ignored him, shouting at the top of her lungs. "Valentino! Piero!"

"They can't hear you." The lights switched on. There he stood, in the horrible, conventionally attractive flesh: Ted Hill, never out of a fine suit, grinning. "Soundproofing. Henry never told you that, did he? For all he told me about you, you know so little about our friend. But maybe I can provide some insight, because I know him well."

Being this close to Hill unsettled Marielle for more than just the obvious reasons. She hated, above all, that something about him felt familiar.

"Where is he?" she spat out. "What have you done to him?"

Hill laughed. "It's what he's done to me." He stepped away from the wall, coughing into his fist before heading toward the workbench. "He made me, you know. Cooked me up right here in this lab. Took the best parts of himself and created a better man.

One more suited to the speed and toil of this world, who could find success beyond Henry's wildest dreams." He picked up a vial, closing it in his long fingers. "He thought he would move in two worlds, being a bit Henry, a bit Ted — but why be Henry when you could be *me*? He imagined he could control the change, but progress marches forward. His body knew which of us was the superior being. And so he stopped becoming Henry —" He smashed the vial in his fist, not flinching, as though he couldn't feel it. " — at all."

"What the fuck are you saying?" Marielle demanded. "That Henry's experiments, what — turned him into you? That *you're* Henry?"

"Was," Hill corrected. "I was Henry. But Henry is no more. Henry was fortunate enough to change. As *you* can change." He stalked forward; Marielle stepped back, pressing herself against the wall. "It can correct your vision, you know. Let you see clearly, for the first time. Seep into your muscles and remake them, too. Reprogram the niggling illnesses in your brain that make you want to fight the future. Turn you into the ideal vessel." His ghastly smile reappeared, though it seemed to waver. "And then we would make quite the couple, wouldn't we? You could become the perfect politician's wife. I could use a leg up on the Hispanic vote when I make my presidential run."

Marielle slapped him; he staggered. Either he'd never been as strong as he looked, or —

"Henry got someone to lock you up in here, didn't he?" She took in the details she'd missed in her fear, the ones she hadn't been able to catch when Hill stood farther away: the perspiration on his brow, the sickly sheen to his complexion. "He did something to you — because he was *done* with you."

Hill lunged with the grace of a drunken bear; Marielle side-stepped him easily. He seemed to have used up the energy he had on his speeches, and his heaving breath had a chemical tinge.

Poison, she thought. *Henry's poisoned him.*

Before he could charge again, she went for Henry's cane, discarded by his workbench. He only used this one in the house:

with its heft and its solid brass handle, it was too impractical to take out. But it was the perfect weight for Marielle to lift and swing, taking Hill out at the knees before delivering a swift smack to his skull.

"I'm sorry, Henry," she whispered as the politician tumbled. She prayed it hadn't killed him—only knocked him out long enough for her to lock the lab. Long enough for her to snatch up the envelope she saw on her final scan of Henry's room: a letter addressed to her, in Henry's frantic scrawl.

***

Hill and I are one, Marigold. I know you won't believe me, but please: let him rot. Burn the evidence. The world must never know what I've done, lest they attempt to replicate the hideous result.

***

"Fuck." Valentina held the letter, eyes going over it again. "Is this real? Henry—is Hill?"

Marielle paced, flexing her hands. "It's real. The serum he created turned him. He thinks he needs to restore himself, but something's changed about the formula. So he knew he'd be stuck with Hill—and that all of us would, too."

"He tried to kill himself," said Piero quietly. "And take Hill out in the process."

"It must not have been a large enough dose," said Marielle. "Hill was woozy, but he wasn't going down until I hit him."

Valentina waved the letter. "Shouldn't we call an ambulance? The authorities? Anybody?"

"And tell them what?" Marielle couldn't stop moving, despite the way it made her calves ache. "Hey, we've got mayoral candidate Ted Hill locked in our basement and, yeah, that was us on the news out there at those protests against him and, yeah, when he wakes up he'll probably tell you we kidnapped him, but deep down he's our good friend Henry Zelkin, who did a bunch of experiments no one understands to make himself like this, so could you figure out how to turn him back, please?"

"Shit." Valentina leaned back in her chair. "When you put it that way ..."

"Is he still in there, do you think?" Piero asked Marielle. "Is there some way to pull Henry out?"

"I don't know," she replied. "Henry makes it sound like he's giving up, but this was recent." She took the paper up again, studying it as though it would yield more clues. "Henry was fully there—*here*—when he wrote it, which makes me think we just have to bring him to the surface."

"How?" Valentina pressed. "We don't understand anything about this serum he made, and if it took Henry years to get this far—how are we supposed to reverse what he did in a day?"

Marielle let her eyes linger on the letter. She couldn't make every word out—she'd had Piero read some of it aloud—but certain elements were becoming clearer.

"We don't need to reverse it," she said, voice subdued. "Hill, Henry—they're both parts of one person. It's not about eliminating one or the other. It's about making them whole."

Valentina was shaking her head. "Look, Henry may be a lot sometimes, but he's nothing like *Hill*."

"He is, though. Or he could have been." Marielle glanced at her. "Think of that part of yourself that voices the worst things about you. That wants to tear you down, tells you that you can't survive unless you change. It might have come from somewhere else, at first, or maybe it was always there, but either way it's part of you. You have to deal with it." Her fingers curled around the letter. "Henry couldn't shut that part of him down, and he couldn't live with it. But we're getting him back. Now."

"Marielle, what—" Valentina started. But Marielle had already turned on her heel, heading for the garden.

"Come on. Follow me."

III.

Cripple. Wretch. Waste of a man, misshapen, malformed, mistake—
That scent.
My nostrils twitched. Acrid, bitter, but pleasing, too. An aroma laden with memories, some sweet, some bleaker. All contained in one bouquet. A single bloom.
My eyes flew open to a riot of yellows and reds.
Marigolds.

IV.

No one knows if Ted Hill is dead.
The investigations were extensive. They've come to the house, but there's nothing to find. His DNA was my own. My lab has been dismantled, and the courier who locked me into it that day—not, luckily, the one who stuck a gun in my face, who would probably blackmail me until my dying day if he thought he had information the police wanted—left no trace of his presence. Interest in the case would have persisted even longer if Hill had won the election, but even before his disappearance, he was losing. The efforts of Marielle and the others worked. They kept him away from that seat of power, though I know he would have sought another.
I do not know if Ted Hill is dead. I am not certain what to call him—absorbed, perhaps. No longer do I allow him to rule from below, undermining my every thought and action. His influence had grown larger within me than I knew. The others do not ask, but I know they fear his return. Marielle is wary around me, which I understand. She saw my worst and brought me back into the world anyway. I don't deserve a friend like her, and yet I am immensely grateful to have one.
I have set aside my experiments. I spend my days in contemplation, seeking peace. I fail, most days, falling into despair

or self-reproachment, but I must thank Hill for one thing. If not for him, I would never know who I could have been. He was the answer to a question I spent my life asking. My potential made manifest. A man without flaw; without a soul. A man who—I could feel it—wanted to pull the tendrils of tenderness from the earth and burn them to ash.

Absent the slow, creeping growth of myself, the shoots and roots that form the garden of all I love, Hill might have ended Henry Zelkin. Yet here I sit, in winter air, waiting for the flowers to come again. I can retain myself, if only I recall their scent. I may keep myself, if only I have Marigold and my dear friends beside me.

About the Authors

TYLER BATTAGLIA is a queer and disabled author of horror, dark fantasy, and other speculative fiction. He is especially interested in subjects that interrogate the connections between faith, monsters, love, queerness, and disability. He thinks mad science could be a form of romance. He has publications in, or upcoming with, Crow & Cross Keys, *Devout: An Anthology of Angels*, and *The Cozy Cosmic* anthology, among others. You can find him on social media at @WhosThisTyler and online at TylerBattaglia.com.

SAMANTHA H. CHUNG is an undergraduate studying English and East Asian Studies at Harvard. Her work has appeared or is forthcoming in *F&SF*, *Fusion Fragment*, and more. She is the winner of the Ecker Short Story Prize and the Edward Eager Memorial Fund Prize. She likes writing about monsters who eat people and people who eat monsters.

KATHARINE DUCKETT is the award-winning author of *Miranda in Milan*, the Shakespearean fantasy novella debut that NPR calls "intriguing, adept, inventive, and sexy." Her short fiction has appeared on *Tor.com* and in *Uncanny*, *Apex*, *PseudoPod*, and *Interzone*, as well as various anthologies, including *Disabled People Destroy Science Fiction*, *Wilde Stories 2015: The Year's Best Gay Speculative Fiction*, *Some of the Best from Tor.com 2020*, and *Rebuilding Tomorrow: Anthology of Life After the Apocalypse*, which won the 2020 Aurealis Award for Best Anthology.

She is the winner of the 2022 CRAFT Amelia Gray 2K Contest for her flash fiction story "Birds x Bees." She also served as the guest fiction editor for *Uncanny's Disabled People Destroy Fantasy* issue, and is an Advisory Board member for the Octavia Project in Brooklyn, New York.

JONATHAN FORTIN is a neurodivergent author and voice actor from Oakland, California. His debut novel *Lilitu: The Memoirs of a Succubus* was published in 2020 by Crystal Lake Publishing, and his short fiction has been published by such markets as Dark Recesses Press, Mocha Memoirs Press, and *Siren's Call* magazine. In 2017, he won the Next Great Horror Writer competition from HorrorAddicts.net. He is an affiliate member of the Horror Writers Association, a graduate of the Clarion Writing Workshop, and a *summa cum laude* graduate of San Francisco State University's Creative Writing program. When not writing, Jonathan enjoys wearing elegant gothic attire, growling along to black metal in his car, and enjoying all things odd and macabre in the San Francisco Bay Area.

BRIANNA NICOLE FRENTZKO received her MFA from the University of Alaska Fairbanks in 2019. Her work has appeared in *The Crucible, Life on the Rez: Science Fiction and Fantasy Inspired by Life on America's Indian Reservations, Bluestockings,* and elsewhere. She runs the blog *Cats of Furry Tales* and the podcast *Through the Vortex: A Companion to Doctor Who.* She currently lives with her three cats in York, England.

A.T. GREENBLATT is a Nebula Award-winning writer and mechanical engineer. She lives in New York City, where she's known to frequently subject her friends to various cooking and home brewing experiments. Her work has been nominated for a Hugo, Locus, and Sturgeon Award, has been in multiple Year's Best anthologies, and has appeared in *Tor.com, Beneath Ceaseless Skies, Lightspeed,* and *Clarkesworld,* as well as other fine publications. You can find her online at ATGreenblatt.com and on Bluesky at @ATGreenblatt.

EIRIK GUMENY is the editor of Atomic Carnival Books and author of *Beggars Would Ride, The Greatest Gatsby: an American Werewolf in West Egg,* and the *Exponential Apocalypse* series. His short fiction has appeared in, among others, *Impossible Worlds, Kaleidotrope, Soul Jar* (Forest Avenue Press) and *Escalators to Hell* (From Beyond Press). His nonfiction has been published by *Cracked, Wired,* and

The New York Times. In 2014, he received a double lung transplant and technically died a little. He got better. Find him at EGumeny.com or on Bluesky.

JOSH HANSON (he/him) is the author of the novel, *King's Hill* (Wicked House), *The Woodcutters* (Outpost19), and *Fortress* (forthcoming from Off Limits Press). He lives in northern Wyoming where he teaches, writes, and makes up little songs. He reviews horror novels at FanFiAddict.com, and his short fiction has appeared or is forthcoming in various anthologies as well as *The Deeps*, *The Horror Zine*, *Siren's Call*, *The Chamber*, *Black Petals*, and others.

WADE HUNTER is an author of dark fiction and horror. He grew up in a small town in Pennsylvania rich in local myths and ghost stories. He learned early on that small towns are small for a reason. His short stories have been published in multiple anthologies and collections. He also has several novels available from various vendors. Under the name Aaron Buterbaugh, he has a series of YA books published and a children's picture book. He currently lives in West Virginia with his wife, daughters, and golden retrievers.

M.W. IRVING is, according to people who know about such things, a person. He was born, in the usual way, to a mother on Canada's stolen West Coast. You can find his other published poems and stories and coded pleas for freedom, written under no duress at all, and certainly without any deep-brain programming, at MWIrving.ca.

POOJA JOSHI is an Indian-American writer from North Carolina. She is currently based in Boston, where she is pursuing an MBA/MPP at Harvard University. Previously, she has worked in health tech strategy and management consulting. Her work has been published in *The Bombay Review*, *The Ekphrastic Review*, *Hive Avenue*, *The William & Mary Review*, *The Ilanot Review*, and *Five Minutes*.

ANDREW KOZMA'S fiction has been published in *Escape Pod*, *ergot*, *The Dread Machine*, and *Analog*, while his poems have appeared in *Rogue Agent*, *Redactions*, and *Contemporary Verse 2*. His book of poems, *City of Regret* (Zone 3 Press, 2007), won the Zone 3 First Book Award, and his second poetry book, *Orphanotrophia*, was published in 2021 by Cobalt Press.

ALLY MALINENKO is the author of *Ghost Girl* and *This Appearing House* which was a Bram Stoker Award Finalist as well as a Junior Library Guild selection. Her next two books, *The Other March Sisters* and *Broken Dolls*, are publishing in 2025. She can be found at AllyMalinenko.com.

K.L. MILL'S Midwest roots are so strong, she lives in the house she grew up in that her father designed. She's also a voice actor (another vocation that revolves around words), and when she's not talking to herself in her padded room (home studio), she tries to get the voices out of her head and onto the page. She will read anything in the horror genre, but prefers to write fiction that's short and a little strange. Like herself. She's currently a bit obsessed with drabbles, some of which have found a home with Black Hare Press.

LENA NG lives in Toronto, Canada. Her short stories have appeared in eighty publications including *Amazing Stories* and Flame Tree's *Asian Ghost Stories* and *Weird Horror Stories*. Her stories have been performed for podcasts such as *Gallery of Curiosities*, *Creepy Pod*, *Utopia Science Fiction*, *Love Letters to Poe*, and *Horrifying Tales of Wonder*. *Under an Autumn Moon* is her short story collection.

ROBERT PEREZ sleeps at the bottom of the ocean. Urban legend whispers that the writer can be summoned into your dreams if you read his work to a jack-o-lantern. You can find his poems and stories in the Horror Writers Association Poetry Showcase Volumes II, III, IV (Special Mention), V, and X, *The Literary Hatchet* #13 and #14, *Deadlights Magazine* #1, *Five Minutes at Hotel Stormcove*, and *Community of Magic Pens*. With his master's coursework completed and internship underway, Robert now works as a psychological counselor providing therapy as he accrues experiential hours required for graduation. Follow @_TheLeader on Twitter to keep up with future projects.

ZACHARY ROSENBERG is a Jewish horror and SFF writer living in Florida. By night, he crafts frightening and fantastical tales. By day, he practices law, which is even scarier. His work has appeared or is forthcoming in various publications, including *Dark Matter Magazine*, *The Deadlands*, and *The Magazine of Fantasy & Science Fiction*. His first book, *Hungers as Old as This Land*, was released by Brigids Gate Press, and his second, *The Long Shalom*, is out from Off Limits Press.

JENNIFER LEE ROSSMAN (they/them) is a queer, disabled, and autistic author and editor from the land of carousels and Rod Serling. Their work has been featured in dozens of anthologies, and they have been nominated for Pushcart and Utopia Awards. Find more of their work on their website, JenniferLeeRossman.blogspot.com, and follow them on Twitter @JenLRossman.

Demonic shape-shifter VIOLET SCHWEGLER has been writing absurd stories for over ten years, but from behind the eyes of a decoy for just about all of them. Her time withering in the void is over.

NICOLE M. WOLVERTON is a Pushcart-nominated writer in the Philadelphia, Pennsylvania, area. Her debut YA horror novel *A Misfortune of Lake Monsters* is forthcoming in 2024 (CamCat Books); she is also the author of *The Trajectory of Dreams* (Bitingduck Press, 2013) and editor of *Bodies Full of Burning* (Sliced Up Press, 2021). Her short stories and creative nonfiction have appeared in dozens of publications, as well.

Special Thanks to Our
Kickstarter Backers

Akis Linardos

Al Rodriguez

Ally Malinenko

Amber Bennett-Groves

Anne M. Gibson

Brandi Martinez

Buzz

Catherine W!

Chris Sandoval

Colleen Feeney

Dominick Cancilla

Eileen Gettle

Erik M. Johnson

Eron Wyngarde

Janet B.

Jay Gironimi

Jenny Ortiz

John Fanelli

Jonathan Gensler

Joseph Jerome Connell III

Kath

Kerry Goode

Laura Garrison

L.S. Johnson

Matt Brandenburg

Quin Boyce

Used Gravitrons

Vi and Sar

Victoria Nations

Yesenia Pelaez

Printed in the USA
CPSIA information can be obtained
at www.ICGtesting.com
LVHW051423061223
765524LV00077B/2301

9 798988 452003